LOVE

LIKE

HATE

LOVE

LIKE

HATE

a novel

Linh Dinh

Seven Stories Press
New York

A Seven Stories Press First Edition

Seven Stories Press
140 Watts Street
New York, NY 10013
www.sevenstories.com

In Canada: Publishers Group Canada, 559 College Street, Suite 402, Toronto, ON M6G 1A9

In the UK: Turnaround Publisher Services Ltd., Unit 3, Olympia Trading Estate, Coburg Road, Wood Green, London N22 6TZ

In Australia: Palgrave Macmillan, 15-19 Claremont Street, South Yarra, VIC 3141

College professors may order examination copies of Seven Stories Press titles for a free six-month trial period. To order, visit www.sevenstories.com/textbook or send a fax on school letterhead to (212) 226-1411.

Book design by Jon Gilbert

Library of Congress Cataloging-in-Publication Data

Dinh, Linh, 1963-
   Love like hate : a novel / Linh Dinh.
      p. cm.
   ISBN 978-1-58322-909-5 (pbk. : alk. paper)
   1. Vietnamese Americans--Vietnam--Fiction. 2. Losers--Fiction. 3. Vietnam--Fiction. I. Title.
PS3554.I494L68 2010
813'.54--dc22

                                   2010028878

Printed in the United States

9 8 7 6 5 4 3 2 1

ACKNOWLEDGMENTS

I'd like to thank my wife, Linky, and Hai-Dang, Matthew Sharpe, Leakthina Ollier, Noam Mor, Bob Malloy, Thuy Dinh and Phan Nhien Hao for enduring earlier versions of this novel. Their comments and suggestions were invaluable. I'd also like to thank the David K. Wong Fellowship, the University of East Anglia, the International Parliament of Writers, the Pew Foundation for their support, and my publisher and friend, Dan Simon.

Part I

1 ◆ REBIRTH

Dazzlingly mad, I died then came back to life gleaming.
—Bui Giang

S aigon lost its identity in 1975, but by the early nineties it had regained much of it back. A young metropolis with a raw energy, it is the least traditional of Vietnamese cities. Unlike Hanoi or Hue, it has never been the seat of an imperial court and therefore has no traditional monuments of any distinction. There are a handful of ornate Chinese temples on Nguyen Trai Street, but the city is still dominated by a French/Vietnamese hybrid architecture left over from colonial times. Now there's even a smattering of skyscrapers to give downtown a veneer of postmodernity. But Saigon is, in fact, thoroughly postmodern. A hodgepodge of incoherence, Saigon thrives on pastiche. Sly, crass and frankly infatuated with all things foreign, it caricatures everyone yet proclaims itself an original. On Vo Thi Sau Street, there are vendors selling *empty* liquor bottles: Talisker, Hennessy, Teacher's, Baileys . . . Picture a Saigonese sitting in a room gazing at an empty bottle of Johnnie Walker Black Label. When friends come by, he can boast, "I drank all that by myself!" Or picture him pouring moonshine into a fancy bottle. "This is imported from France!"

With economic reforms, Vietnam could more or less feed its own people by the early nineties. The worst thing about Communism is not that it stops you from thinking or writing poetry, the worst thing about it is that it can stop you from eating altogether. Now that hunger was no longer a threat for most of the population, people's taste buds were becoming more sophisticated. Many restaurants catering to the drinking crowd now advertised "a mouse with a pouch," kangaroo meat imported from Australia. (It tastes just like beef.) In the suburb of Thu Duc, there was a restaurant, Hoa Ca, specializing in alligator meat. (It tastes just like chicken.) Several featured the meat of a "water dragon," a cousin of the man–eating Komodo dragon of the Malay Archipelago. (It tastes just like dragon.) At Tri Ky on Nguyen Kiem Street, poisonous snakes were killed right at your table. Deep-fried crispy snakeskin was a popular dish, as was snake soup with lotus flowers. One of the owner's sons actually died from a snakebite in 1997.

Some people looked west to revive their gustatory spirit. Trendy cafés advertised Italian ice cream, while spaghetti was available at most markets. On Pasteur Street, there was a restaurant called the Nutrition Center. Its blue exterior was painted with white slogans: DIABETICS; NUTRITIOUS FOR CHILDREN; STRENGTHEN BONES; FIGHT FAT. Inside, more slogans: GOOD FOR THE BLOOD; GOOD FOR THE KIDNEY; SMOOTH THE SKIN; COOL THE LIVER. There was a scale for diners to weigh themselves after a meal. The menu, however, featured such fatty foods as pizzas, cheeseburgers, fried chicken and cheesecakes. Although few of these "occidental" items were prepared very authentically, the reasonable prices suited a Vietnamese clientele. By contrast, the fancier international joints downtown—Sapa, with its Swiss specialties; Ristorante Santa Lucia; and Tex-Mex, etc.—catered almost exclusively to foreigners.

In short, Saigon reverted to being a city where eating is the main pleasure. Discos also sprang up. It was becoming a happening place again and Vietnamese who had escaped at the end of the war started to return for visits in sizable numbers. They brought with them money and news from overseas. These overseas Vietnamese were called Viet Kieus. You could always spot a Viet Kieu by the way he dressed, by the size and shape of his body, and by his body language. A Viet Kieu always took up more room and he usually overtipped.

One afternoon in 1999, a Viet Kieu wearing a gray T-shirt and blue jeans walked into Paris by Night, accompanied by Huyen, a girl from the neighborhood. Pale and muscular, he smiled easily and seemed amused by everything he saw. He chuckled at a ceramic statuette of the Goddess of Mercy standing on the counter. Abetted by a hidden pump, she was pouring water into the mouth of a carp, to encourage the free flow of money. He saw a Christmas tree in a corner, complete with gold reindeer, red stockings, tin soldiers, cherubim and a Star of David. "Christmas in August!"

"I bought that for thirty bucks!" Kim Lan exclaimed. "It was the fanciest tree I could find!"

"That's Mrs. Kim Lan," Huyen said, "the owner."

The Viet Kieu shouted at Kim Lan, "You have a very cool place here!"

"You should come by in the evening," Kim Lan said. "It's much more lively."

"I have enough liveliness in the United States. I just want a nice place to sit and relax and drink a beer or two."

"Where in America do you live?"

"In Philadelphia. I'm in business. I run a restaurant."

A restaurant?! This young guy runs a restaurant in America?! He's probably lying. He's probably a waiter or a dishwasher or something. Kim Lan continued, "Restaurants in America must be much more classy than the ones we have here."

"Well, I don't know about that," the Viet Kieu said modestly, "but they are definitely cleaner!"

Kim Lan wanted to ask about the Viet Kieu's income, but she didn't want to be rude. Suddenly Huyen blurted out, "We're getting married in two weeks!"

What?! This plain girl is marrying a Viet Kieu?! "That's very nice," Kim Lan said, forcing a smile. "How did you two meet?"

"We met in an internet chat room."

Kim Lan had heard of the internet, but she didn't know what a chat room was. She didn't want to betray her ignorance, however. She turned her attention to the Viet Kieu. "Is this your first time back?"

"No, I came back for the first time two years ago. It was a real shock. I had left as a kid, you know. I was overwhelmed by a lot of things."

"Like what?"

"Well, you know, like the traffic, for example. All these motorbikes nearly running into each other all the time. It was weird. I thought I was going to die!"

"It must be very different in America."

"They stop at red lights, for one. Even at three in the morning, with no cops around, and no cross traffic, a car would stop at a red light."

"That's incredible! And everyone drives a car, right?"

"Just about everyone. And everyone stands in line for everything. You don't have to take an elbow in the ribs just to buy stuff."

"But we have supermarkets now," Kim Lan said brightly. "People stand in lines at the supermarkets. I never shop there, however. It's too expensive."

"But the regular markets are so dirty!"

"Yes, they are," Kim Lan agreed, frowning. "I hear that all the countries on earth are clean now. Except Vietnam. Have you been to many countries?"

"Not really. I've only been to Montreal, Toronto and Vancouver."

"That's three more countries than I've been to," Kim Lan remarked before changing the subject. "Has your mom met Huyen yet?"

"They'll meet for the first time at the wedding."

Kim Lan smiled a tight smile. *If I were this Viet Kieu's mom*, she thought, *I wouldn't settle for such a plain girl*. She still couldn't believe that Huyen was marrying a Viet Kieu. She looked at the couple as they leaned across the table to kiss each other, their tongues sticking out, their faces glowing. Kim Lan had never seen Huyen so happy. Wearing a pair of expensive jeans, she already looked like a Viet Kieu.

After they had left, Kim Lan kept thinking of the Viet Kieu. Although Vietnamese, he didn't resemble any of the men in her life. The Viet Kieu seemed purposeful, unlike Sen, who spent his days playing chess and going to the whorehouses. The Viet Kieu exuded a quiet confidence, unlike her husband, Hoang Long, who seethed with wounded anger. The Viet Kieu made himself completely at home in a strange environment, unlike her son, Cun, who could barely talk to a stranger. Although they were contemporaries, the differences between the Viet Kieu and Cun were outright shocking. *If only we would drink fresh milk and eat a piece of cheese occasionally,* Kim Lan reflected, *we wouldn't be a country full of stunted bodies and rotting teeth, living in vast malarial swamps where the streets are paved with oil slicks and dog shit.* The Viet Kieu's teeth were even and white, while Cun's were crooked and brown. The clincher, however, was that the Viet Kieu seemed totally happy, and he had made his girlfriend totally happy. After Hoa came home from school that day, Kim Lan gave her daughter a thorough appraisal and firmly concluded: *My beautiful girl deserves nothing less than a Viet Kieu.*

2 ◆ WHATTUP?

The Viet Kieu's name was Jaded Nguyen and he was a manager-trainee at a McDonald's on Passyunk Avenue, a street of sooty row houses cutting diagonally across South Philadelphia. Geno's and Pat's Steaks were on Passyunk, and so was Ray's Happy Birthday Bar, famous for a disused ankle-high pissing trough hugging the length of the L-shaped bar. Jaded's salary was $16,000 a year, before tax, which forced him to live in Grays Ferry, one of the dumpiest neighborhoods in Philadelphia. He rarely went out and when he did, he rarely allowed himself more than three beers, either Rolling Rock or Yuengling, the two cheapest brands available. Like all losers, he alternated between meekness and aggression, and could only relax when he was totally drunk. These traits did not endear him to many women—of any race or shape—and he could not hit on the girls at work, for fear of being laid off for sexual discrimination.

Jaded was also Asian, which meant that he was smaller. If he were Yao Ming or Dat Nguyen, it wouldn't have mattered, but he wasn't even Ichiro size, more like Apolo Ohno, except not that good-looking, and he didn't have Michael Chang's born-again faith to rock himself to sleep each night. (If there was one guy who annoyed Jaded more than Michael Chang, it was Jackie Chan and his stunted sexuality. The guy clowned and kicked ass, but never got laid. About the only Asian guys to get laid in Western movies were the ones conjured up by the feverish mind of Marguerite Duras.) Being boy-sized and without facial hair, Jaded was regarded by other people, if only sub-consciously, as an incomplete man or even a boy trying to act like a man. During a good year, when all the stars were lined up right, he could bed a woman maybe five or six times, but Jaded had also gone through many months without even a cheap feel, unless he went to a go-go bar. He endured these dry periods by ogling amateur blondes flashing on the streets of Prague at nakedinpublic.com. He also sub-scribed to nastycheerleaders.com, republicanbabeswithguns.com, sexykitchens.com, innermostdreams.com and even youngpee.com. Upskirt, downskirt, dominatrix, hog-tied, slaves, elderly nuns in combat boots, elementary schoolteachers made to kneel naked then spanked, infants, corpses—he sampled them all with his eyes. He couldn't help himself because they were always available. The coolest website, however, was nakedmcbabes.com. Thousands of real McDonald's workers worldwide posed on the Web with only parts of their uniforms on. Nothing gross or tacky, no ketchup or mustard smeared in unlikely places, no showers of pickles, just crew members disrobing into artistic poses. It was terribly exciting. Jaded could rec-ognize Lakeesha and Tina from his very own McDonald's. *Dang, you gurls are real fine, I'm loving it.* There were even gay and lesbian sections. It seemed like everyone and his grandmother were posing naked on the internet. Jaded envisioned a day, very soon, when one could google any name whatsoever and find nude photos of that person on the internet. Perhaps one should call it the idternet. Jaded never sneaked into stables or pens, however. He didn't go there. "That stuff's sick."

The only lasting solution to his dilemma, Jaded finally figured, was to cut his dick off, or go overseas. If he were French, he would have booked a flight to Bangkok. Italian, he would have gone to Romania or Cuba. Since he was a Vietnamese American, Jaded sud-denly discovered a deep love for his ancestral homeland. Logging in to Vietnamese chat rooms as <alonelyvietkieu99>—both <alone-lyvietkieu> and <alonesomevietkieu>, his first choices, had been taken; <ahornyvietkieu> he dismissed as too crude—he attracted many girls inside Vietnam. They promptly emailed him their photos. Each morning, he opened his inbox to find it overloaded with girls posing in *ao dais*, prom dresses, pajamas and bikinis. Smiling, grinning and puckering their lips, they swiveled, bent over and arched their backs, to feature good sides and hide defects. They peekabooed behind beaded curtains, palm trees and potted cacti, then reemerged glistening from oceans and swimming pools. They sat cross-legged on swings and moon slivers in photo studios, stood shivering in front of Swiss chalets and Norwegian fjords. Some posed with musical instruments, most often a guitar or a koto. One girl in horn-rimmed glasses sat stiffly at a piano; an extra-gifted one blew into a flute, a clarinet, an oboe and a saxophone. Taking his time, he chose a dozen semifinalists and invited them to video chat with him. Five girls had to forfeit since they didn't have a computer or a webcam at home. That didn't bother Jaded since he didn't want to marry a poor one—her family would be too grabby, he figured. Three girls soon eliminated themselves by allowing their moms to pop onscreen to say hello. One mom even had her hair streaked blonde, as if she herself was auditioning. Among the finalists, only Huyen had a computer in a private bedroom, which allowed them to chat late into the night without interference. Neither was shy—whatever Jaded did, she matched—and that's why he finally picked her. They were both naked when he proposed. It went without saying that Huyen was also good-looking. Like most mothers, Kim Lan devalued other people's daughters, overvalued her own. Landing at Tan Son Nhat Airport, Jaded felt like a winner at last. He was the rich and ugly American come home to conquer.

For Huyen to be chosen by Jaded was like winning a beauty contest. To score this trip to paradise, and not for a two-week vacation but a lifetime, she had to compete with as many girls as Jaded had the stamina to weed out. Though she had outclassed the competition, Huyen was not enamored with her own beauty. She considered it a useful tool, of course, but not to be taken too seriously. It was a physical thing after all, something easily soiled and degradable. She was actually well educated. A third-year architecture student, she had to interrupt her study because she didn't dare make Jaded wait. If he changed his mind, she would lose the chance of a lifetime.

Before coming to America, Huyen's only knowledge of the country was through the movies. She had seen hundreds of American films in which smiling, beautiful people lived in vast houses with slick, space-age appliances. Even the dogs and cats appeared gorgeous. American gangsters dressed better and were better looking than Vietnamese ones. The rare American bums also had a sense of style. They were all professional actors, after all. The American films that made it to Vietnam were wet dreams of glamour concocted by Hollywood. These, more than anything else, were the root cause of America's immigration problems. John Cassavetes and David Lynch were not on the rental list.

The day Huyen left Vietnam was the happiest of her life. Feeling like an astronaut before liftoff, chosen and feted, she waved at her family standing outside the terminal, blurry through the smudgy plate glass, and thought, *This is too good to be true, they will stop me from leaving.* Going through the exit formalities at Tan Son Nhat Airport, she was frightened into stuttering by a grim-faced customs officer. As an instrument of escape, the plane itself felt forbidden. Boarding behind a wide-shouldered tourist, she entered the Boeing 727, her first airplane ever, looked around at the cozy cabin and knew she was already in an improved universe. Sitting snugly beneath her private spotlight, she felt like an undeserving extra in a Hollywood movie.

Fifteen minutes after takeoff, Huyen noticed food carts being wheeled out. "Do white people get to eat first?" she asked Jaded.

"What are you talking about?"

"See those people? They're eating before us."

"They're vegetarians!" Jaded shook his head and sighed. "You must stop thinking of yourself as inferior. We're equal to everyone here."

But she did feel inferior. The trained courtesy of the Singapore Airlines stewardesses moved and embarrassed her. She felt undeserving of their gentle attention. How different they were from the surly Vietnamese nurse who had forced her and five others to stand naked together at the medical exam, a process she had to endure before being allowed to emigrate. She was also embarrassed that there was a whole world out there she knew nothing about. *So this is how people really live.* During a layover, she went into downtown Singapore for a quick look and was stunned that any city could be so clean and orderly, with so many nice cars on perfectly paved roads, and everyone dressed so well. A public bathroom she entered felt positively luxurious, with no trace of mess, smells or mildew—no biology, in short. An uplifting experience, it was a sharp contrast to the dispiriting ordeal of Vietnamese shithouses. Arriving in Philadelphia, she was impressed by the airport, freeways and skyscrapers, but as the taxi dropped them off in Grays Ferry, she suddenly found herself on the set of *Eraserhead*. *We live here?!*

Unless you're living in the best neighborhoods, Philadelphia is indeed everything David Lynch claims it is: a very sick, twisted, violent, fear-ridden, decadent and decaying place. Huyen was so shocked, she wanted to go back to Vietnam immediately. Only pride prevented her from doing so. Grays Ferry was sullen and desolate and everyone seemed paranoid. Saigon is often squalid but it is never desolate. Vietnam is a disaster, agreed, but it is a socialized disaster, whereas America is—for many people, natives or not—a solitary nightmare. If Americans weren't so stoic and alienated, if they weren't so cool, they wouldn't be so quiet about their desperation.

Huyen could handle poverty, but she had no aptitude for paranoia, the one skill you needed to survive in Philadelphia. In Saigon you dreaded being cheated or robbed; in Philadelphia you feared getting raped and killed. In the end, Philadelphia was even worse than *Eraserhead,* because it didn't last for 108 minutes but went on forever. As in Vietnam, Huyen sought comfort in American movies to escape from the real America she could see just outside her window. Every American home was its own inviolable domain, a fortress with the door never left open. The rest of the world could go to hell as long as there was enough beer in the fridge and a good game on TV. And utopia was already on the internet, why go outside if you didn't have to? In the morning, Huyen kept the door locked, bolted and chained, and watched Jerry Springer—in his glasses and tweed suit the image of a college professor—to learn more about Americans and improve her colloquial English. In the afternoon, she took a bus to the YMCA to attend an ESL class. At night, the couple barely screwed in the land of bountiful screwing. His wife was so tense, Jaded went back to masturbating.

There was one girl on an amateur site, Cindy, who looked at Jaded—and Jaded alone—with such tender longing that he felt sure there had to be some mystical connection between them. Such openness, such generosity, such nice breasts. *Pornography is the mildest form of adultery,* he figured, *and nearly blameless.* Huyen almost caught him kneeling in front of the computer with his pants down a few times. Huyen herself was not above self-pleasure. She enjoyed seeing tall, muscular men run up and down a hardwood floor. Home alone, she liked to clog the lane as Allen Iverson wheeled to the rack for another monster jam.

Jaded said to her, "You have to be tough to survive here. It will get better. Things will definitely get better when I'm promoted to full manager." Working overtime, he always returned home exhausted. "Americans work for real," he explained. "How do you think they get so rich?"

"We're not rich, honey, and I don't see anyone rich in this neighborhood."

"There are plenty of rich people, believe me, and the country itself is rich."

"Well, I haven't seen a rich American yet."

"And you won't see them. They live out on the Main Line. We Vietnamese dress loud and wear gold jewelry to show that we're rich, but rich Americans just wear T-shirts and jeans like everybody else. About the only Americans who wear big gold jewelry are the drug dealers."

"I've seen these guys with gold chains sitting in big jeeps playing really loud music. Are they drug dealers?"

"If they're not, then they're trying to pose as drug dealers. It's cool to be a drug dealer in America. Do you like those cool trucks? I know a guy who owns a Jeep Cherokee. Maybe we can get one of those in the future. If we get the right financing, it won't cost much each month."

"Maybe you should just quit your job and start selling drugs."

Huyen thought about the young drug dealers with their gold jewelry. Although they acted tough and menacing, they appeared troubled and frightened in their Hummers, stuck in traffic with the ear-splitting music. The more insecure you were, the more simplistically your mind worked: I must flash gold in people's faces to show that I have money. Realizing this, she stopped wearing gold. She remembered how her mom used to wear pajamas in public, yet was never seen without her gold earrings, necklaces, bracelets, brooches, diadems, pins and anklets. Her mom had given her a jade bracelet for her eighteenth birthday. The more she stared at it now, the more it annoyed her. A status symbol, it was translucent green with a touch of red, and worth at least five hundred bucks. After spending half an hour trying to wrench it from her right wrist, yanking it against her carpal bones and bruising her skin, she finally banged on it with a butter knife, shattering it into pieces.

"Why do Americans say 'shit' all the time?" she asked Jaded.

"I don't know. Do they?"

"Yes, they do. It's always shit this, shit that."

"I guess you're right. If you're drunk here, they say you're shit-faced!"

Huyen thought about this and concluded that Americans said shit all the time because they lived in a *clean* country. In Vietnam, a filthy country where shit was often on display, where it was no mystery, people rarely conjured it up in a conversation, but in America, which was superclean, it was an inevitable verbal tic: "Holy shit," "That shit's wack," "She thinks she's hot shit but she ain't dogshit." She noticed the American penchant for personal slogans, as evident on bumper stickers and T-shirts: "Watch out for the idiot behind me," "I wasn't born a bitch, men like you made me this way," "Jesus loves you, everyone else thinks you're an asshole." She noticed that many Americans had volunteered to walk around town as advertisements for their favorite brands: Nike, Pepsi, Northrop Grumman, Raytheon, Halliburton.

She learned about American precision. Huyen became aware that America was a country of straight lines and geometric exactness where everything must be quantified: your breasts, your income, your batting average. Life must be constantly measured to show that profits and progress were being made. She noticed a parallel between capitalism and Communism: Both loved to count, since both were materialistic. More wealth equaled more happiness, hence the constant need to take stock of everything. But Vietnamese were poor counters, she reflected. Their traditional units of measurements were inexact. They liked to fudge, round off numbers, manipulate scales, ignore rulers. Before the French arrived, they didn't count the hours or tick off the seconds. Time was the angle of the sun and the shape of the moon. They went to bed with the hens and woke up with the roosters. Not knowing their birth year, many peasants couldn't count their own age. It's true they didn't have much to count to begin with. The only thing the peasants were adept at counting was their innumerable offspring. Instead of proper names, they referred to their kids as "fourth daughter," "tenth son," etc. People who couldn't count couldn't build very much. Vietnamese buildings, old and new, were often ill proportioned, lumpy, their lines inelegant. And there was nothing remotely like an Angkor Wat in all of Vietnam.

On his days off, Jaded took Huyen to the Franklin Mills Mall, the biggest shopping center in the Philadelphia area. There she could finally feel a sense of community. She loved all the smiling, attentive faces. "May I help you? May I help you?" Above all, she loved the luxuriously displayed merchandise. It pained Jaded to see his wife lust after so many things they could not afford. They ended each shopping expedition with only token purchases, such as cheap polyester underwear or junk from the Dollar Store. To his suggestion that they go to the zoo or a museum, she always answered, "No, I want to go to the mall, if only to look." The shopping mall was already a museum to her. Fingering blouses and skirts and sniffing leather coats, she appeared so enraptured he thought she might just steal something.

With so little money, Huyen always tried to buy the cheapest food available. When it came to meat, there was nothing cheaper than scrapple. A Pennsylvania delicacy, scrapple was made up of pig tendons, cartilage, feet, skin, ears, eyes, gums, snouts and rectums, all solidified with cornmeal and seasoned. The decidedly bitter eardrums were usually left out of the mix. Huyen read the ingredients and found everything agreeable but the cornmeal. She bought it anyway and boiled it with instant noodles. To her surprise, the scrapple dissolved into a gray slosh.

Later, Huyen would visit many other American cities besides Philadelphia. Some were beautiful, some not, but in all she would find the same remoteness and blankness. She tricked herself into thinking that her alienated state was only a result of being an alien. The natives must have a secret strategy to cope with it. She reminded herself that assimilation was a gradual process: You learned

English, met people, learned the country's history, its pastimes and perversions, then doors opened and you were allowed in. Only slowly did she realize that America was always a flat and transparent surface, with all desirable things just on the other side. To be disillusioned with paradise on earth was to be disillusioned with life itself. There were many other countries, however, 195 to be exact.

As the years passed, Huyen slowly changed. She got a job at McDonald's, did her job well and won many Employee of the Week awards. She even learned to talk shit with the best of them. When the other crew members greeted her with "Yo bitch!" she'd answer, "Whattup, assbucket?"

3 ◆ LET'S LEARN ENGLISH!

aving decided that Hoa would marry a Viet Kieu, that her future would be in America, Kim Lan wanted her daughter to study English immediately. There were dozens of English-language schools in Saigon. Any high-school dropout from San Diego to Sidney could get a teaching job there and be paid well for it, if he was white. The locals simply equated white skin with a mastery of the master language. Salman Rushdie or V. S. Naipaul would not have been hired. The less expensive schools used local teachers. There was the Lego Institute, which advertised: "Build your English skill block by block." There was the Gertrude Stein Academy: "To speak, on an endless shelf, there's English." Kim Lan enrolled Hoa at the most prestigious one: the New York School of English. Everyone on its staff was advertised as being a native of one of the boroughs. There was a mural of Manhattan in the school lobby and, standing on a cardboard box next to the registration desk, a foam Statue of Liberty. The school's bold slogan: "ANSWER ALL YOUR QUESTIONS IN ENGLISH WITHIN A YEAR."

Invigorated by her violent hope of acquiring a new language, Hoa threw herself into her studies. Kim Lan marveled at the sight of Hoa bent over her exercise book. She encouraged Hoa to practice her lessons out loud. Single words, phrases, anything. It was pure music to her ear when Hoa said things like, "I do. You do. He does." Or: "Skiing and skating are my favorite sports." Or: "I'm pregnant and I need to have an abortion." She asked Hoa, "How do you say 'mother' in English?"

"Mama!"

"From now on, I want you to call me mama!"

She bought Hoa a nice dictionary with a colorful illustration next to each word. *My First Dictionary*, it was called, "recommended ages: four to eight." Encouraging Hoa to use this dictionary, Kim Lan would say, "Remember Malcolm X!" Kim Lan had discovered Malcolm X in a magazine called *Today's Knowledge*. Although it had few pages and was no bigger than her palm, *Today's Knowledge* was chock-full of information. In the October 1999 issue, it asked: "Did you know that Malcolm X was a black leader against American capitalism? A pimp who rose to prominence while in prison, Malcolm X taught himself English by memorizing every word of a dictionary." Since *My First Dictionary* only had about two hundred words, Kim Lan figured Hoa could memorize the entire dictionary in about a year or so, and be fluent in English just like Malcolm X. In the same issue of *Today's Knowledge*, Kim Lan learned that Ho Chi Minh had taught himself French by scrawling ten new words on his arms each day. That's 3,650 words a year, she thought incredulously, on such spindly arms? Overlaid with a million words, blue-black with knowledge, Uncle Ho's arms lay dimly lit in a glass coffin. Kim Lan thought of Japanese *yakuzas* tattooed from head to toes. *Horimono*, is it?

Kim Lan also enrolled Hoa in an aerobic dance class so she could listen to American music as she learned how to dance like an American. To round out her daughter's education, Kim Lan took Hoa to Kentucky Fried Chicken. The first American fast-food joint in Saigon was a KFC that opened in 1997 near the airport. It had few customers. For the price of a two-piece meal you could feast on five courses at another restaurant. About the only people who ate there were tourists, expats, Viet Kieus and the nouveau riche. Kim Lan took Hoa to this KFC every weekend. It was a glamorous place where the floor was clean and the uniformed employees courteous. Staring at the brightly lit menu overhead, Kim Lan asked Hoa, "What does it say?"

Mustering up all her mental energy, Hoa slowly translated out loud, "Prepared the Colonel's way using the freshest select ingredients for a tangy, sweet, one-of-a-kind, satisfying taste."

"And what does that say?"

"The Colonel's famous freshly baked biscuits served up hot and flaky just like they've been for generations."

Finding the chicken greasy and the coleslaw inedible, they still pronounced everything delicious. Kim Lan ate the jive mashed potatoes with the little plastic fork/spoon while eyeing the Viet Kieus chowing down at adjacent tables. She loved the way their conversations were interlarded with odd bits of English, words such as "good," "you," and "boring." Annoyed by her stares, a Viet Kieu of Hoa's age glared at Kim Lan, shaking his head. "Good good!" she smiled at him, waving a drumstick. The other two English words she knew were "money" and "mama." She scrutinized the Viet Kieus' clothes for clues on how to dress her daughter. *You must look like them if you want to attract them*, she figured. She also took Hoa to the Baskin-Robbins downtown to sample all forty flavors of American ice cream. When Lotteria opened on Nguyen Dinh Chieu Street, Kim Lan and Hoa were among the first to enter. They quickly became fans of the hot squid, rye shrimp and bulgogi burgers. They never found out that Lotteria wasn't American, but Korean fast food.

Lotteria is actually a Japanese company. Why would a Japanese company peddle Korean versions of American fast food under an Italian name? Lotteria is a subsidiary of Lotte Co. Ltd. Its founder, Takeo Shigemitsu, named his baby after Charlotte in *The Sorrows of Young Werther*. He wanted his company's products to be as endearing as Charlotte, and as enduring as Charlotte. Lotte manufactures gum, chocolate and soft drinks. Besides fast-food joints, it owns hotels, department stores, a theme park and a baseball team, the Chiba Lotte Marines of Japan's Pacific League. Even with Goethe batting cleanup, it hasn't won a pennant in thirty years.

A new Saigon fad appeared in 1993. Street vendors started to sell used clothing known as AIDS clothes, not after the disease, but because they had been given by Western aid organizations. For fifty cents you could have an AIDS T-shirt donated the year before by some churchgoer from Toledo, Ohio. For two bucks you could own a frayed pair of AIDS jeans. AIDS belts, purses, shoes and underwear were also available. Kim Lan wouldn't let Hoa touch AIDS clothes. "Sooner or later you'll die from them. I'll buy you real American clothes."

4 ✦ THERE'S NO SUCH THING AS OHIO

n March 2001, Kim Lan had a phone installed in the house. It was a marvelous yellow thing that she placed in a custom-made box with a lock, to prevent the servants from dialing their home villages. Like the TV, the phone box was covered with a frilly piece of cloth to keep the dust away. She bought her first TV at twenty-five, her first fridge at twenty-eight, and now her first phone at fifty-four. She had been on a speeding train already so an airplane should be just around the corner. She would fly to America after Hoa had moved there. Who knows, she might be destined for hot water and a flush toilet yet. She had read in *Today's Knowledge* about a flying car they were developing. At this rate, she'd be rocketed to the moon on her deathbed.

Kim Lan marveled at the small machine connecting her to the rest of the world. At any moment—but cheaper on weekends, of course—she could dial Japan or Uganda, and talk to a real foreigner on the other side. With hardly anyone to call, however, she often picked up the phone just to hear its beeping pulse. As if heeding her wish to communicate with the beyond, a letter arrived for her from a Viet Kieu that same month. On a sunny afternoon, a young mailman stopped his motorbike in front of her café and shouted, "Mrs. Kim Lan. You have a letter!"

She walked to the curb to retrieve it from him. There was no name over the return address: 903 Stryker Street, Archbold, OH 43502, USA. Kim Lan had never received a letter from America so this was very exciting stuff. A letter from America also meant a tip was expected. She gave it to the mailman, went back inside, ripped the envelope open and read:

My Dear Kim Lan,

I'm writing to you from America. I've been here for eight years already. I have a good job and everything is OK. I've learned English and I'm working at a chicken packing plant. It's a very hard job and it doesn't pay very much, but I'm just happy to have a job. If I could endure fifteen years in prison, then of course I can handle this job in America. I have no hurt feelings about what happened between us and I still think about you every once in a while. I will never forget that pork stew you brought me while I was in prison. No one can make pork stew like you, not even my new wife. After I left you, I went to Cao Lanh and stayed for two years before I left for America in the Orderly Departure Program with a new wife. My new wife is from Cao Lanh and she also works in the chicken plant with me. I kill chickens, she packs them. Although she doesn't compare to you, I'm just grateful I'm not alone. I hope you are happy with Sen. Please tell him I do not hate him. And tell Cun I will send him $200 for Christmas.

Hoang Long

A photo came with the letter. In it, Hoang Long stood next to his new wife in front of a red Honda Civic, one arm around her waist, one pointing at his car. Wearing an AC/DC T-shirt, he flashed a bright smile, displaying his new teeth.

Seeing Hoang Long's dental work, Kim Lan unconsciously bared her own yellowing teeth and touched them with her fingers. Vietnamese toothpastes had really low standards. *Only $200 for Cun after eight years?* she sneered. *He complains that he isn't being paid very much, but of course he's making lots of money. Just look at that nice car. He only writes that because he doesn't want his son to hit him up. The address is probably fake: There is no Stryker Street, and no Archbold, Ohio. There's no Ohio, period. You can't even pronounce it, so how can it exist? He thinks* *he can just put down any combination of letters and I'll believe it. I've heard of California and Florida, but Ohio?*

She had already guessed that Hoang Long was in America. All ex-Army of the Republic of Vietnam (ARVN) soldiers who had spent at least four years in a reeducation camp were allowed to go to the US under the Orderly Departure Program. If she had dumped Sen, she could have gone to the US with Hoang Long, but no, she had her principles. And how had Sen responded to her incredible sacrifice? *By going to the whorehouses regularly*, she reflected with disgust. But the real reason she had not left with Hoang Long was because she did not want to abandon Hoa. Hoa was the most precious thing in her life, her very reason for living. Provoked by this letter, she wrote one of her own, not to Hoang Long but to Huyen, the neighborhood girl who had married the Viet Kieu:

Beloved Huyen!

How are you? I am so happy for you. You are very lucky.

How are things in Philadelphia? I think of you often and want to send you and your husband my deepest and most sincere wishes for your future happiness.

My mother is doing OK. I'm going to school to study English. Following your example, I'm very fashionably dressed now!

Perhaps you don't even remember me, but I remember you very well. You were always the best-looking and the best-dressed girl in the neighborhood. I model myself after you. In case you don't remember me, I'm the daughter of the lady who owns Paris by Night. I am seven years younger than you, so we didn't hang out much. In fact, we didn't hang out at all, but I still remember you very well, because you were my hero!

I was very reluctant to send you this letter. I was afraid you would mis-understand my intentions. Why am I writing to you out of the blue? What do I want exactly?

I've always wanted to stay in touch, my beloved Huyen, but I was only a kid before, distracted by school and play, and did not know a thing about writing letters. I also did not have your address. But your mother finally gave me your address recently and she encouraged me to write you a long letter. She said you love to receive letters from Vietnam.

In any case, I just want to congratulate you on being such a lucky girl! I love you very much. I'm not trying to suck up to you now that you have a rich husband. That's not how I live. But it's true that my family has fallen on hard times. The café is not doing so well. But a torn shirt need not stink. Just because you're poor doesn't mean you have to suck up to anyone.

If only I were as lucky as you, how happy I'd be. I have dreamed of going to America since I was ten, maybe earlier. I only want to go to America so I can help my mother out by sending money home each month.

To make a long story short: I'm just not a lucky girl. Not at all like you. But why am I boring you with my sad story? I better shut up before I put you to sleep! Seeing you so happy makes me a little happier.

With much love to you,
Hoa

Kim Lan rewrote this letter several times to make sure it sounded just like the heartfelt outpouring of a teenager. Favoring a felt tip over a ballpoint pen, she spent an hour practicing a loopy, left-leaning penmanship. She considered misspelling a word or two, but decided against it after much deliberation. Done with the final draft, she sent it away with several photos of Hoa—the latest, most improved version—including one in pajamas. Huyen and her husband must count among their acquaintances a lonely Viet Kieu or two, no?

5 ◆ ASSETS

On Hoa's fifteenth birthday, Kim Lan bought her a Wave motorbike. You were supposed to be sixteen to get a license but most people never bothered. If your legs could reach the ground from the seat, then you were good to go, and Hoa had extra-long legs. With sleek, large wheels to smoothly overcome the tribulations of a Vietnamese road, the Honda Wave was the hottest thing in Saigon in 2001. It could cruise up to fifty miles an hour. Zooming all over town on her motorbike, Hoa looked like an actress in a Hong Kong movie. She had learned how to put on lipstick, eye shadow, mascara, shimmer, blush, rouge, greasepaint, lip gloss, pomade and pancake.

When she opened her mouth, a dozen English phrases sputtered out, gleaned from Madonna and Britney Spears CDs. Every inch of her was brand named—CK, Revlon, Polo, Levi's, Adidas—albeit much of it was fake. She was rarely seen without a baseball cap from her huge collection. She bought them compulsively because they were so cool and so American. Each new cap made her feel like a new person, with her favorite featuring a shark biting a stick in half. Kim Lan fretted, "Your hair's so thick and shiny, Hoa, you shouldn't hide it all the time behind a baseball cap."

"You keep talking like this, Mama, and one of these days I'm going to shave all of my hair off!"

"You wouldn't dare!"

Kim Lan loved to take care of her daughter's hair. Braiding Hoa's hair one day, she said, "You know, Hoa, I see many girls dyeing their hair blonde or brown nowadays. I think you would look wonderful with blonde hair."

"Yeah, Mama. I'd look like a freak!"

"No, you wouldn't. I think you would look just like Elizabeth Monroe."

"I have no idea who you're talking about."

"It's before your time, Hoa. Elizabeth Monroe was one of Martin Luther King's lovers. She was also friends with Michael Jackson. You've heard of Michael Jackson?"

"Yes, of course, who hasn't? The thin nose, the moonwalk. He always grabs his dick when he dances."

Kim Lan tapped Hoa lightly on the head. "Watch your mouth!"

In general, Kim Lan was gratified by Hoa's progress, but she was becoming a little worried about her effect on men. Males of all ages were constantly eyeing her daughter. There was a weirdo of about nineteen who sat in the café all day just to catch a glimpse of Hoa walking in and out. He drank beer after beer until his face and eyes turned red. Once he pretended to lean down to tie his shoe just as Hoa walked by. As he brushed his head against her swishy skirt, redolent of detergent and fabric softener, his mouth coming close enough to kiss or bite her naked, marmoreal ankle, he felt a terrible jolt up his spine and let out a sad, preternatural moan that startled everyone present. That was as close as he ever got to Hoa. The weirdo knew he had no chance, knew that it would be at least a felony if someone of his constitution and smallness was to taint such an angelic apparition. Still, he thought that if he sat there in humble supplication long enough, God might feel so sorry for him, he'd be allowed to upset the natural order of things and be vindicated once and for all. At that age, it's easy to think one fuck could solve everything. Even the women were checking Hoa out, inflamed by jealousy or lust. *Hoa is becoming too popular for her own good*, Kim Lan thought.

Hoa was tall and well proportioned, but most important, she had very nice breasts, a trait she shared with her mother. Kim Lan was worried when Hoa's breasts started to bud at eleven, ahead of other girls'. She thought they might grow to melon size but, no, they ended up just about perfect. The only flaw was the dark coloration of the areolae. Instead of virgin pink, they were chocolate brown. A mother has to worry about so much. She has to pay attention to every detail of her daughter's development. "When you apply face cream," she advised Hoa, "you must rub upward, so your skin won't sag. If you rub downward, you will look like an old lady at age forty. And when you're in the shower, Hoa, you must rub upward when you soap your breasts. When it comes to your own body, never rub downward." Anticipating Hoa's first menstruation, Kim Lan advised, "The very first time it happens, you must dip your panties into a bucket of water three times."

"Why, Mother?"

"Just do what I say. If you dip them three times, you will bleed for only three days. If you don't, you'll bleed for seven days."

"I don't get it."

"And don't shampoo during your period or you will have bags under your eyes."

"Huh?"

"Just trust me, I know, I bled for forty years."

"Are you still bleeding?"

"No, of course not."

When it finally happened, Kim Lan said, "It's like this: You have to put *this* into *this*."

"But I can't walk that way, Mother, my legs are all splayed!"

"Stay home this morning if you have to."

"It feels funny, Mother, like there's a hand there!"

Kim Lan grimaced hearing that. Now that her daughter was fifteen, the danger of having a hand there was greater than ever. Kim Lan said, "I've had two husbands and two kids but my breasts are still firm. Many women my age have mushy breasts but touch these, see how firm they are? Your breasts are also nice, and that's good, but it means you must be extra careful. Every man wants to feel your breasts. Whatever you do, Hoa, don't let them touch you. If you let them touch you, it's all over."

"I understand, Mama."

"I will give you everything you want in this life, but you must not let a man touch you. Do you understand?"

"I understand, Mama. You always talk about this."

"Don't even let them touch your hand! If you let a man touch your hand, then he will grab your breasts the next time, then he will pull your pants down, then everything will be wasted, everything I've done for you will be wasted. Look at my ridiculous life: I've had two ridiculous men, two clowns! You must have a strategy, then everything will work out fine. You must be patient. Do not sleep with the first clown who grabs you."

"Don't worry, Mama. I won't let anyone grab me."

The best boobs deserve the best bras, Kim Lan firmly believed. They cannot be degraded and humiliated by cheap Vietnamese or Chinese products. After careful research, Kim Lan chose Arc de Triomphe bras for Hoa. Her daughter looked best in the Fragrant Mystic Flower Padded French Balconette model, the Lamborghini of bras. Combining full chalice styling with a plunging design, this underwire bra boasted central lattice detail and asymmetrical floral embroidery, ensuring an enticing look. Each one of these bras cost an average worker's monthly salary, so Kim Lan only bought two. It was worth it, she figured: An Arc de Triomphe bra would last a lifetime, maybe even several lifetimes. Hoa could use these in the afterlife, in heaven or hell, and when she was reincarnated, as long as she returned human. Not trusting the servant not to mangle them, Kim Lan washed them by hand herself, on alternate nights.

In the neighborhood there was a woman with no breasts at all. She lived with her sister, her aging mother and a male cousin. Neither sister had a husband, but the one with breasts took a lover occasionally. The woman with no breasts had only a lapdog for company. She took the dog everywhere, even to the shoe factory where she worked. As a teenager, she had massaged her chest constantly, hoping breasts would grow. She had assumed breasts were like muscles. Later she massaged her padded bra to make the cups less pointy. She finally stopped wearing this bra because it kept hitching up to her shoulders. Implanting themselves in her mind, her missing breasts tormented her night and day. She felt so much rage at times that tears would well up in her eyes. To add to her insult, her sister had huge, absolutely humongous breasts. All her mother's breast genes had been apportioned to her sister, apparently. The two of them walking down the street together constituted an unfortunate sight gag. She had read in *Today's Knowledge* that breasts were only a secondary sex characteristic. It was the only one she lacked. All the others—smooth skin, wide hips and fat deposits around the buttocks and thighs—she had plenty of. *Today's Knowledge* didn't mention pubic hair, but she also had a thick, luxurious bush that fanned out to her thighs even. *So it shouldn't matter*, she told herself, *that I have no breasts. I have everything else in good measure, and a pretty face besides.* But it did matter. Giving up on bras, she also stopped wearing panties except during her period. She never put on makeup and hardly combed her hair, but she always took a long time drying her body after a shower. At home, she liked to walk around in a nightshirt. It was comfortable but threadbare. She enjoyed standing in the doorway, so the sun could shine through her nightshirt, silhouetting her body. Every so often she would smile a very odd smile at her male cousin.

In the neighborhood there was a second woman with no breasts at all. This one was married to a sunken-chested man. Everything about him was sunken, with nothing jutting out to sniff or explore. Smooth and uniform, he resembled a well-encased sausage. Likewise, his wife. Lying together, they were like two synchronized hot dogs spinning in boiling water, barely touching. It was a mystery how they managed to produce three children. A skillful goldsmith, he had a steady, prosperous business. On her thirty-fifth birthday, he surprised his wife by taking her to a plastic surgeon. Three hours later, she came out with a new pair of breasts, curvy and pert, just like in the brochure. Her arms moved clumsily at first and her nipples were deadened permanently, but it was well worth it. For the first time, she could feel some resistance, some friction, when she hugged her husband. Standing naked in front of a mirror, she swooned with pride, cupping her bosom with both hands. But she was not satisfied. Stacked up front, she now felt disadvantaged out back. She returned to the same surgeon a month later for a buttocks augmentation. After her buns were well rounded, the doctor offered to tuck in her stomach and to peel her face at a discount. She readily agreed. With all these operations, her husband had to borrow money and to mix silver with gold to increase his profits. On the plus side, his wife was magically morphing into a goddess in front of his eyes. The next surgeries yielded more discreet results. Her strait was narrowed, its frilly fringe fluffed out. With a new body, her mood improved and her confidence shot up. She went out and got herself a handsome, well-muscled, twenty-two-year-old boyfriend, a stark contrast to her grimacing, coughing, sunken-chested husband, who was going steadily blind from overwork, then finally went to jail for cheating his customers.

Part II

I ◆ WEDDING AT A CHINESE RESTAURANT

Hoang Long, the groom, was a captain in the ARVN. He was a short, wiry twenty-four-year-old with a permanent smirk on his face, no facial hair, his skin the color and texture of beef jerky. As with many short men, his body language was a bit exaggerated. He sat (too) ramrod straight and stood with his feet (too) wide apart. When he walked, he swaggered, swinging his narrow shoulders from side to side. A first-strike guy, he was always ready to preempt you to a punch. Being small had sensitized him to the fact that there was conflict inherent in every human encounter. How one dealt with this determined the shape and tint of one's life—or even whether one would have a life. He never strayed into a shoe store unless he had to.

But he was in fact a tough cookie. As a leader, he had the respect of all the men in his company. Already that year he had survived the Tet and Mini-Tet offensives. That night, standing next to his prize catch, he felt particularly triumphant and invulnerable.

Kim Lan also appeared triumphant. As a twenty-two-year-old nurse, she had seen enough messed-up bodies to know that love did not come to everyone. Showing her nice teeth, her eyes gleaming, she felt saved and vindicated. Ditzy with joy, she could have died right after the wedding, or even during it, and been satisfied. She had never envisioned spawning children, weekly arguments, a pension plan, or widowhood. She had only dreamed of being feted at a

41

glorious wedding, and here she was. In spite of the red dress, she was still a virgin. No one had touched her. Hoang Long had never even pecked her on the cheek. They had sat on park benches to admire the Saigon River without incident, and he had never attempted to grope her inside a darkened movie theater. They always perched high on the balcony, away from the chatterers. Hoang Long loved Westerns. The dating couple saw *Hang 'Em High* and *The Good, the Bad and the Ugly*. Kim Lan enjoyed sitting through a foreign film just to hear an exotic language. Equally charmed by English, French and Italian, she thought they sounded exactly the same. Once she suggested *Born Free*, which left him dozing by the end, swathed in swooning music, his head resting on her soft, silky shoulder. Moved by the sight of the lioness being released into the wild, she secretly planted a light kiss on top of her boyfriend's head. His hair gel smelled nice but tasted bitter, forcing her to pucker and wipe her lips on the back of her hand. The only film they both hated was *The Poseidon Adventure*. It was resonant yet disturbing to see so many people, Americans, trapped inside a topsy-turvy world for three hours, trying to squabble their way into sunlight. They felt relieved when it ended, and even a little foolish leaving the theater.

At other times they had merely held hands on tense and romantic walks through the Saigon Zoo. They flung peanuts at lunging monkeys and extended sugarcane to shuffling, curtsying elephants. She was drawn to caged animals because she loved to feel pity for all living things.

In the end, it was Hoang Long's tact and composure that won her over. She saw him as her tender warrior. She was also touched and reassured by his patience, as proven by the fact that he could wait an hour or more whenever she showed up (deliberately) late for a date.

Just outside the circular entrance to the banquet room, the newlyweds stood next to a large photo of themselves, retouched, baroquely framed and placed on a frail easel. Slightly taller than the groom, theatrically made up and radiant in a red dress, the bride held a bouquet of red roses and wore a tiara over a bouffant, helmetlike hairdo in the photo, provoking mutters of "fake" from some of the female guests. A hairdresser had recommended that she balance and soften her sharp profile with a "Jackie Kennedy," poor woman. The groom looked spruce in his white tuxedo.

There would be 360 guests that night, seated at thirty round tables. Waiting for the first of nine courses—a lucky number—the men guzzled 333 beer as the women sipped Coke, the gas in the drink tickling their larynges, making some of them burp. A scowling, papyrus-skinned octogenarian, shivering from the air conditioner, thawed herself by compulsively gulping scalding tea. Having seen a thousand weddings, she no longer remembered any of them, not even her own. For the entire evening, she exchanged not a syllable with the drowsy old man parked next to her. 333 beer, 360 guests, 9 courses, on the 24th day of the 12th month: On this special night, nothing was left to chance.

Most weddings in Vietnam are occasions for ostentation and bankruptcy, with many families having to borrow beaucoup cash to stage appropriate feasts for their sons. Guests don't bring gifts, but legal tender in red envelopes. The ones who had arrived early were already getting bored with the lively music. Absentmindedly picking at dried squid and caramel peanuts, they joked about sex and soccer. Under a gathering haze, tin ashtrays fumed and filled. Playing tag, small children chased each other, shrieking. Some merged with potted plants or crawled beneath tables to mesh into a circle of darkened, anonymous legs, where they crouched in silent trepidation, hoping never to be found. In this sudden catacomb, seconds could stretch into minutes, into centuries, and all was peaceful, despite the cacophony just beyond the fluttering cloth. A middle-aged, mustachioed drunk draped his heavy arm across a neighbor's shoulders, confessing, "The only American song I like is 'Shake, Twist and Roll.'"

Hoang Long also had a sappy side. Courting Kim Lan, he had hand copied a dozen poems by the wretched poet Han Mac Tu, and given them to her under his own name. Using a ballpoint pen, he had written in purple ink on pink stationery, a bunch of pale roses ghosting the lower right corner of every page. "I have a new poem for you," he'd announce at the beginning of a date. "I wrote it just last night." He always insisted that she read each poem right away, to hear her gushing praise. He had also given her a handkerchief embroidered with two colorful birds kissing, and a gold necklace with two more birds dangling, their beaks welded together.

Later, after the champagne had been spilled and the cake eaten, after all the guests had gone home and they were alone at last, she would be shocked to discover how brutal a lover her husband was. He would make love to her with such force and haste, with such angry desperation, that it would scar her for decades. She did not suspect that everything he knew about sex he had learned from prostitutes. He would not kiss her, because the last thing a prostitute wants is to be kissed. A prostitute would sooner swallow you whole than kiss you on the lips. He would not caress her cheeks or stroke her hair, but only place a firm hand on top of her head to keep her stationary. He would not prolong the process but would try to get it over with as quickly as possible. He would fuck her as if he were paying by the second.

Done, he turned on the fluorescent light to look for his boxer shorts. "Did you like it?" he asked, chuckling, while examining his new wife lying there uncovered on the pink rayon sheet. Two pink pillows with embroidered swans were on the floor, kicked or tossed aside during the upheaval. Not hearing a response, he joked, "You were so cute. You lay there just like a piece of wood."

2 ◆ A FRENCHMAN AND PUBLIC NUDITY

Hoang Long was not Kim Lan's first love. Before him there was Dai Trieu, an army medic. A man of erect posture and firm principles, he was rather humorless but very gentle. Kim Lan became engaged to him in May of 1965. In June, he was killed at the Battle of Dong Xoai. Dai Trieu belonged to a very prominent family: His father had founded the Brimstone Tire Company of Vietnam. Everyone used Brimstone tires. Many people criticized Dai Trieu's father for allowing his son to enter the army in the first place. "What a heartless man," they cursed. "If I had that much money, I'd never let my son die as a soldier." After Dai Trieu's death, his mother told Kim Lan she still wanted her as a daughter-in-law. To prove her seriousness, she suggested that Kim Lan marry Dai Trieu's twin brother, Dai Truong, who resembled him in every way, down to the smallest habits and vices. "You won't know the difference," the old lady said. "Even I couldn't tell the difference sometimes. They dressed the same and had the same haircut. They even smoked the same cigarettes. I'll talk to Dai Truong tomorrow and tell him to break up with that slutty girlfriend of his. I never did like that girl anyway."

Kim Lan politely declined.

Hoang Long met Kim Lan at Dai Trieu's funeral and was smitten immediately. She looked striking in white, the color of mourning, an ethereal presence next to the garish coffin, which was decorated with dragons. Looking at her smudgy eyes, her powdered cheeks smeared by mascara, her open lips misshapen by sobs, he held her hands extra long, crushing, draining them of blood, and heard himself declare, "He was my best friend in life. We were inseparable. I was kneeling next to him when he died."

Teary, dizzy with grief, she could barely make out the dark, earnest face hovering just below eye level. His eyes were tearing up, too, from the incense smoke. Their pupils collided for a brief second. "What was his last word?"

"Your name, of course."

A week after the funeral, Kim Lan received the first of Hoang Long's endless stream of letters. Before long, their tone shifted imperceptibly from condolence to bonhomie to suave seduction. This disgusted her at first but, after six months, she agreed to go out with him. The turning point came after the insertion of an anguished, writhing poem by Han Mac Tu.

Kim Lan had always been a huge fan of the pathetic poet. As if spending one's life with line breaks and meters wasn't pitiful enough, the poet had also died, alone and unloved, of leprosy. *How pathetic,* Kim Lan thought. The celebrated poet had only pined after others, Mong Cam, Hoang Cuc, Mai Dinh, Thuong Thuong, Ngoc Suong, Thanh Huy, My Thien—the list was truly endless. But no one loved him back. *Who would want to?* The fact that Hoang Long also read Han Mac Tu indicated to her that their fates were somehow intertwined. She ignored the fact that everyone else in Vietnam also read Han Mac Tu. As for Hoang Long's signing his own name to someone else's poems, it did not bother her in the least. *He's doing all this to impress me,* she thought, smiling, tears gleaming on her long eyelashes. Since childhood, she had always felt like crying when extremely happy. She also loved to tear up at the movies. The oddest thing about Kim Lan's crying aptitude, however, was that she could always stop at will. One second, she could be crying, but the next, her face would be ice cold or she could even be laughing.

Thinking of childhood, most people can readily conjure up high-definition memories of riding a red tricycle or eating vanilla ice cream, sequences so cinematic they can replay them at will, complete with soundtrack, but not Kim Lan. Her mother had died when she was two and she was raised by a stepmother. Her father was a police captain who had patiently taken enough bribes by 1945 to buy a three-story house in the Cay Go district, a year before she was born. Kim Lan spent every day of her life in this house until she was nineteen. After she left, its pale green walls, smudged by dirty fingers, oversized boots, and gecko droppings, hundreds of charcoal black, slightly-less-than-rice-size grains, would haunt her dreams for as long as she lived. In these nightmares, the familiar rooms multiplied, stairs led to endless stairs, windows contracted into slits and slid toward the ceiling, allowing no view and only the faintest light. Chased, harassed, she could never find the front door.

Leaving home did allow Kim Lan to purge her father mostly from her consciousness. She eventually succeeded in scraping away most of his eyes, nose and mouth, sanding his face smooth, but his voice would always remain, though only faintly, as incoherent fragments devoid of authority.

Her father was a wannabe Frenchman, or, rather, an aspiring Corsican. He had studied at Lasan Taberd, a French school in Saigon, and supposedly spoke French, although no one had ever seen him talk to a Frenchman. His conversations were sprinkled with a dozen or so French words, such as *moi, toi, bon* and *écoutez*.

"*Écoutez*! Do *toi* want to drop by *moi* house this evening?"

The only book he had ever read was a biography of Napoleon, which he kept rereading until he knew all the details of Napoleon's life better than Napoleon himself. He was one of those people who simply assumed that whatever they happened to be thinking about had to be of *immediate* interest to everyone else. Looking up from his crumbling book, he would ask Kim Lan's mother, "Did you know that Napoleon was five foot six, only an inch taller than me?"

"Why are you always talking about that man? What has he ever done for you?"

"Did you know that Napoleon was killed by his wallpaper, which contained arsenic? Isn't that amazing? Did you know that Napoleon only had one testicle?"

"What's wallpaper?"

"It's something they do in France. You wouldn't know."

He kept a nearly full bottle of Napoleon on the highest shelf of a glass cabinet, flanked by upside-down snifters and brushed by cobwebs dangling from the ceiling. Even an adult standing on tiptoes could not reach it. He admired the liquor's amber glow and aroma, appreciated the bottle's elegant shape and brown-gold label, but had no stomach for cognac itself. He began each morning with a croissant and a *café au lait*, chain-smoked Gauloises, and snacked often on *pâté chaud*. Once a week he had to have a *steak au poivre* or a steak tartare, which he ate while scanning his wife's face for hints of amused disapproval. "What are you grinning at?" It also irritated him to no end that she could never tell cheese from butter. The only cheese she had ever tried was Laughing Cow, which she always enjoyed with a banana. The sight of his wife holding a banana in one hand, a wedge of Laughing Cow cheese in the other, chewing happily, always made him seethe. *I'm married to a monkey*, he'd think.

"Cheese stinks, but butter smells good," he would lecture her for the umpteenth time. "They are both yellow, agreed, but butter melts much faster than cheese. Laughing Cow cheese looks just like butter but it is still cheese. Camembert cheese smells worse than anything in the world, *ma femme*, but it is the champagne of cheese. Are *toi* listening to *moi*?"

"I heard you. I'll get you some more cheese tomorrow."

"*Écoutez!* Eating cheese, everyone grows tall and square shouldered. That's why we must learn how to eat cheese, starting right now. Turks and Arabs eat goat cheese...."

In 1948 Kim Lan's mother had a brain hemorrhage and died in

the hospital after an unsuccessful surgery. She was thirty-two. During the funeral, the house was bathed in brilliant sunshine, but was soon drenched by a cloudburst, an excellent omen. *Money is coming in,* Kim Lan's father thought with gratitude and relief, *and my wife has already forgiven me.* Wearing a sad face, he watched the coffin being lowered into the flooded pit. A month later, he formalized his relationship with the domestic servant—a fleshy girl from Phu Quoc Island. They had meshed a dozen times over the previous year, and he had never had the heart to fire her, as was customary. After each bout, he'd vow never to do it again, only to climb into her bed a few weeks later. She smelled very nice; her skin smelled just like butter. Parts of her smelled just like Camembert cheese. "Don't ever wash, Josephine," he'd mutter during sex. *She's already in the household,* he rationalized even before his wife had expired, *and will make a perfect replacement mother for my infant daughter.*

As the lady of the house, however, the stepmother was anything but nurturing. She yelled at Kim Lan constantly and gave her household chores inappropriate for her age. By nine, Kim Lan had to do the dishes, sweep, and wash the floor each day with a bucket and a rag. She had trouble handling the larger bowls, breaking many, and it was two more years before she reached the height of her broom. "The girl needs more discipline," the stepmother explained to her yielding father. "I learned to do housework when I was only seven. A girl needs to become familiar with all facets of running a household."

She scolded Kim Lan for taking too long to wash the floor, "You're using too much detergent. That's why it's taking you *forever* to wipe that floor. You're wasting detergent and water. A girl must learn to economize right from the beginning so she can save her husband money in the future. A frugal mother can buy nice things for her children; a wastrel will end up living on the streets. When you brush your teeth, for example, I notice that you use twice as much toothpaste as necessary. A ridiculously extravagant glob. That's why you have to gargle at least six times to get rid of it. You're wasting toothpaste and water. I never gargle more than twice. You're also brushing way too hard. I don't care if you destroy your gums in the process but why should I allow you to ruin the bristles, splaying them ahead of time? They're made of nylon, you know, not steel. It's in your blood to waste everything. You go through toothbrushes like there's no tomorrow. I've also noticed that you always use an extra toothpick after each meal. Now tell me: Do you have more teeth than other people?! Toothpicks don't grow on trees, you know. Just go ahead and jab at the gaps between your teeth until they bleed, why don't you?"

The root of the toothpaste problem, the stepmother figured, was probably a billboard Kim Lan strolled past every day on her way to school. Below a grinning black face, a twelve-foot-long toothbrush was crowned with a monster glob of Hynos. "SO FRESH YOU CAN ALMOST EAT IT!" They have to encourage a superfluous use of toothpaste, she reasoned, to sell their decadent product. Growing up in a village, she simply dipped her toothbrush in salt or ground-up charcoal and brushed away. Poorer kids even used their index fingers. It hadn't hurt her much: At twenty-six, most of her front teeth were still upright, though leaning slightly, some outward, some inward, in a subtle syncopation. All the ones in the back, however, in the hardest-to-reach regions, had long ago been uprooted.

At the dinner table, the stepmother even found fault with how Kim Lan held her chopsticks. "Look at that!" she snapped at the silent father. "If your daughter can't hold chopsticks properly, how is she going to hold a broom?!"

When Kim Lan was eleven, the stepmother caught her trying out some lipstick. "You're a damn whore!" she screamed while smearing lipstick violently onto Kim Lan's face. "I've always known you were a whore!"

As punishment, she forced Kim Lan to strip and kneel in the courtyard for all the neighbors to see. "Take your clothes off! Take them off! What are you waiting for?!"

To prevent her from covering herself, she also forced Kim Lan to stretch her arms out.

"Now do you see what it's like to be a real whore?" the stepmother sneered at a stone-faced Kim Lan as dozens of neighborhood boys, many of them her classmates, quickly gathered to gawk at their first naked girl. With scarlet lips and scarlet lipstick slashed across her face, Kim Lan looked like a bloodied clown. Someone pointed and laughed. Kim Lan could shut her own eyes but she could not shut the others'. Nor could she shut out their murmuring, snickering voices.

Kim Lan was still playing with a doll at that age. That night she held the doll by its feet and slammed it repeatedly against the floor until its head snapped off. "That's what you get for being a whore!" she hissed. She would have screamed, but she didn't want her stepmother to hear. Seeing the doll mutilated and in pain, Kim Lan quickly reattached its head, hugged it and apologized, and the two of them cried themselves to sleep. The doll's name was Hoa. In the morning, Kim Lan said, "Do you forgive me, Hoa?"

"Yes, I forgive you."

"You're the only one I have. But you know that already, don't you?"

"Why did you call me a whore last night?" Hoa seemed ready to cry. Much of the paint on her eyeballs had scraped off and all her eyelashes were missing. When she blinked, her eyes only closed halfway. Held together by a single button, her acrylic shirt hung from one shoulder. She wore neither skirt nor pants.

"You're not a whore, Hoa. I'm the whore!"

The word "whore" sounded so ridiculously funny that both of them laughed themselves silly.

Kim Lan's father was not around the house much to protect his suffering daughter. He was at work maintaining public order. One day his men brought to police headquarters the proprietress of an opium den. She was a woman of twenty-five, with large eyes, wild hair—a raw beauty. This was her first arrest ever and she was sobbing miserably. The police captain appraised the young prisoner and made a quick calculation. He released her within an hour and from that moment on, the only cop to raid her place would be the police captain himself. He grew so fond of her, he became an opium addict. Like an overgrown infant, he'd lie for hours next to his naked mistress as his sallow form wasted away. The opium cleansed him inside out, fumigated all his pretensions away, French or otherwise. It was soothing just to watch her roll an opium pellet before stuffing it into the little hole, smiling all the while. She had gotten him an exquisite pipe, with a green jade mouthpiece, a slender bamboo stem and a ceramic head shaped like a pubescent breast. An opium dream can last several days. Whenever he soiled himself, she cleaned him up. In his stupor he even babbled like a baby, "I'm not forty years old, Mama, I'm only four."

Kim Lan's only wish growing up was to leave the house as soon as possible, the promised freedoms of adult life pushing her forward. At seventeen, she asked her father for permission to enter nursing school. Two years later, she was a nurse in the war zone. Caring for victims in extreme pain, she always felt like crying, but was forbidden to do so. Her extreme self-control would be perfected during this period, to desert her only in the direst situations. Away from home, she heard praise for the first time. Her superiors praised her for her competence and composure. Men praised her for her looks.

Her first year away, she came home twice, obligated by a residual sense of duty, but since each visit was nothing more than a screaming rant by the stepmother, enraged as she was by the mere sight of Kim Lan's face, she stopped going. It was clear the step-mother wanted her out of the house permanently. In the old house, now as then, the rote ants continued to crisscross the pale green walls, lugging with their side-closing mandibles grains of rice, bread crumbs, salt, sugar and a young dead gecko, its sandy skin already slack and darkened in the wake of its premature end.

3 ◆ RICE BASKET OF THE SOUTH, A GHOST

Hoang Long was born in Can Tho, the chief city in the Mekong Delta. People in Can Tho considered their city the true heart of southern Vietnam. While they sneered at Saigon as a corruption of all things Vietnamese, they also envied it. People from Can Tho with ambition eventually moved to Saigon. Once there, they denied that they had ever lived in Can Tho.

As the rice basket of the South, Can Tho was a fairly prosperous place. Before 1975, the richest families owned vast tracts of land and lived in colonial-era villas built in a style that was a hybrid of East and West. Tucked in tropical gardens leafy with coconut, mango, plum, durian, jackfruit, guava, papaya, custard apple, banana, betel nut and lemon trees, each of these solid brick houses boasted a spacious porch with square columns. The high ceiling of the front room was often painted in pastel colors with bucolic scenes evoking somewhere in Europe. It was the rococo, Mekong style. On the floor were cool floral tiles, ideal for the hot weather. The furniture was made from teak, ebony or rosewood.

Hoang Long's father belonged to this landowning class. He was a legend in Can Tho. If you go there, ask the old folks about Mr. Mot. They'll tell you this story: Mr. Mot was not just a rich landowner, he was also the first in the city to own a gas station, which quickly multiplied into a bunch of gas stations. "Gas," he'd sigh, chuckling. "It's like blood!" A careful if unimaginative dresser, he was always seen in a white cotton suit, the pleats of his pants immaculately pressed. Wearing tennis shoes, he'd rush about town carrying an alligator-hide briefcase. Reputedly full of money, it was actually completely empty. On cool evenings, you'd find him relaxing by the river, leaning against the railing, gazing into the roiling waters. He had a good mind for numbers, but routinely forgot names and faces, even of people he had known for years, even of very important people. He'd wave at complete strangers on the street, thinking he knew them, and in conversation he often asked people to repeat themselves, leading many to assume he was slightly deaf. He had a beautiful wife whom he did not love, from a marriage arranged by his father. To escape his conjugal unhappiness, Mot took to going to the many whorehouses dotting Can Tho. At one of these, he became particularly fond of an uncommon beauty named Saigon Rose.

Saigon Rose was half Cambodian, a quarter Vietnamese and a quarter French, or maybe she was half Moroccan and half Chinese. In any case, she was by far the most popular whore in the Can Tho area, demanding twice the fee of any other prostitute. Provincial men fancied themselves world travelers when they lay with her. As Mot fell more in love with Saigon Rose, it made him retch to think that she was being fucked, practically simultaneously, by all the other male citizens of Can Tho. To rectify this deplorable situation, he decided to turn her into his private mistress. Unknown to his wife, he bought a house for Saigon Rose on the other side of town, where he could visit her four or five times a week, usually just before dinner.

At home, his mood improved. He told bawdy jokes at the table and complimented his wife on her cooking. Mrs. Mot was glad to see these changes in her husband. Their sex life also improved and before long she became pregnant with Hoang Long.

A year later, Saigon Rose also got pregnant. Mot was not pleased.

Grumbling, he had to sit up in bed to have sex with her. "You're going to kill the baby!" she whined, panting. At the hospital, the doctor and nurses were disgusted to deliver a grayish baby all gummy with dried love, his head covered with a billion dead siblings. Inside the womb, the boy could never figure out what it was that kept squirting on his head, his soft skull like a plastic tent in a thunderstorm. Even as an adult, he heard splattering sounds when it wasn't raining. People often saw him grimacing, cursing and rubbing his bald head while looking up at the sky.

Being with child forced Saigon Rose into thinking about the future and her own mortality. Gazing in the mirror, she saw wrinkles all over. One day Mot complained about her bad breath. "It's evil," he grimaced. "I'm not kidding." It turned out to be a cavity—all that chocolate he had given her—necessitating her first trip to the dentist. Everything was falling apart. Her prized body, gilded cage and carriage, was ignoring her daydreams for its own reality, careening creakily downhill from the glorious mesa of her youth. Fearing Mot would dump her eventually, she demanded much more money.

The woman had two distinct voices, a husky one for seducing and a reedy, girlish one she used to complain. "We've been together for three years now, and what have I gotten out of it? Next to nothing. You use me like a rag every day, keep me locked in this house like a prisoner, and don't even allow my friends to visit. Soon I'll be old and you won't come around anymore."

Mot looked at her pouting face. It was flanked by two enormous eighteen-karat-gold teardrop earrings he had given her for her last birthday. "How many times have I said it already? I'll never leave you."

"You must give me enough money to start a business, Mot. I'm thinking of becoming a hairdresser. And not just any hairdresser; I want to be a really classy one. I want to be a hairstylist, a beautician. I want to have a real boutique. And I'll need to have three or four girls working under me. You know I can't work every day, but I'll make a good manager. Think of the future of our son, Mot."

Though Mot never gave her the money to start a beauty salon, he kept reassuring Saigon Rose that she was indeed the love of his life and that he would never abandon her. He ended up keeping his word.

By now, Mot's wife had heard rumors about the other woman, but was too afraid of her husband to raise the issue. When Hoang Long was four, she became pregnant again. The day after she gave birth, Mot came to the hospital to see her.

Mot hated all hospitals for their odor of disinfectants and sad mixture of dread, absolute pain and hope, so this visit was indeed special. Some sadists might enjoy loitering in hospitals to feel better about themselves, but not Mot. The oddest thing, however, was that he did not come alone but accompanied by his mistress.

The Vietnamese word for a hospital is a "house of love." A nun led them to Mot's wife's private room at St. Judas, the best house of love in all of Can Tho, efficient, clean, with a ceiling fan in every room and never more than one patient to a bed. Excellent food also. Waddling down the endless veranda, her right shoulder dipping, the old nun tried to make small talk, but Mot paid her no attention. They finally turned in to a bright room. Mot's wife had just woken from a dream-racked sleep, her face pale, greenish, sweat beading her forehead. She had been tossed from one nightmare into another. In one, a bat jammed its cold, compact head into her mouth, forcing her to bite it off. In another, her head was dunked into a bowl of warm liquid swarming with tadpoles. In the last, the one that woke her up, she found herself lying on the sidewalk naked and bespattered with filth, under a sky blanching from a sun about to rise.

Still groggy, she heard the door open, saw her husband and smiled. Staring up at Mot's hovering face, she noticed that the thick hair in his nostrils needed an urgent clipping. *Poor man*, she thought, *I spend two days in the hospital and he's falling apart already*. Standing next to his wife's bed, with a smiling Saigon Rose beside him, Mot took a deep breath, then began, "We've been living a lie all these years and I cannot take it anymore. I've never loved you, not even one bit, and I'm sure you have no feelings for me either. We cannot deny that we are utterly indifferent to each other. We probably hate each other deep down inside, but neither one of us has the courage to admit it. Actually, I do not hate you, I respect you, but I do not love you. Seeing your face each day is pure hell for me. I also hate looking at your body and hearing your sweet talk in bed. None of this is your fault, of course, but that's just how I feel and I cannot deny it any longer. That's why we must stop it! As soon as you're out of the hospital, I want to start divorce proceedings."

Mot was so intent on finishing his speech that he did not notice that his wife had died. Her mouth was wide open in silent outrage and so were her eyes.

Overnight, Hoang Long had a new sister, a new half brother, and a new stepmother. The day after she moved in, Saigon Rose disinfected the house by removing all photos of Hoang Long's mother from picture frames, albums and envelopes, and burning them. She also burned every piece of paper that had her predecessor's name on it, including the birth, marriage and death certificates. Scattering the ashes into the river, she declared with a twinkle in her eyes, "Her soul will flow out to sea, and find peace and eternity there." Reduced to a grayish white powder, the dead woman's soul merged into the muck and flow of the Mekong River, a giant anaconda muscling its way toward the Pacific Ocean, overstuffed with half-digested cats, human beings, rats, toothless combs, toothpicks and rusted pull rings from exploded hand grenades. Saigon Rose also gave the dead woman's clothes away and told Mot she would never sleep in the other woman's bed, forcing him to buy a new, larger one with a fancier headboard.

Mot didn't like Hoang Long's sullen attitude toward his new stepmother. The boy refused to call her "mom" or even to look her in the face. Whipping him across the body with a bamboo rod, Mot screamed, "My wife is always your mom! Get it?!" Sprawled on the floor, cowering and covering his head, the boy did not cry, but, smirking, glared at his father, provoking even more blows. They finally arrived at a compromise. After two weeks of constant beatings, Hoang Long started to address Saigon Rose as "auntie," but always in an airless, mechanical voice that was almost inaudible.

Saigon Rose, for her part, had something else much more serious to worry about. Wherever she went inside the house, she could hear breathing noises and footsteps following her. She often felt an icy chill on the nape of her neck. Whenever she looked in a mirror, she could see a faint, disappearing face—it was always *that* face. She drew an *X* on all the mirrors, but could not get rid of the ghost. Even in bed, with Mot on top of her, she did not feel safe. It was always that face, a female face frozen in a silent scream, that she saw hovering over her as Mot worked up to yet another one of his endless climaxes.

4 ◆ RIFLES AS LIMBS

There's a song that goes, "This is a beautiful season to go to war!" Hoang Long couldn't wait to go to war. Any season was a beautiful season to go to war. At seventeen, using correction fluid and a borrowed typewriter, he changed the date on his birth certificate to join the ARVN. Apprehensive about their height and weight requirements, he was ecstatic to make it with the help of gel-thickened hair and a dishonest fishmonger's reckoning of an ounce. It was the summer of 1961 and the Vietcong were not causing too much trouble yet, at least not in the Mekong Delta, and the Americans hadn't yet arrived in massive numbers.

Hoang Long didn't join the army just to escape from his family, he also wanted to learn how to shoot his rifle accurately and repeatedly at a moving target. For a boy who had never experienced freedom, he now craved the ultimate, the freedom to kill. He wanted to eradicate all that he hated in his fellow men—the unthinking cruelty, the raw selfishness, the stupidity. Determined to flex his manhood on behalf of a righteous cause over a mound of fallen bodies, he was eager to wipe out a mess of people, even if he had to wipe himself out in the process. Joining the army was a win-win proposition. His premature death, should it come, would be another blow against his callous asshole of a father.

He had never seen a Vietcong, but he knew they were assassinating government officials in the outlying areas. Their aim was to abolish private property, or so he was told. Even with his limited experience, he interpreted this as a pipe dream if not a confidence trick. What they really wanted was to move into his father's house after killing the old man and his prostitute bitch—which he wouldn't mind at all; he'd probably help them—but why should they be allowed to steal someone's home? A house is sacred and should never be stolen, burned, bulldozed or bombed. A Vietnamese even refers to his or her spouse as "my house."

Hoang Long's first night away from home was the happiest of his life. Lying on his hard bunk, he breathed in deeply for the first time. He could feel each one of his muscles relax. In the months ahead, he would learn to love army discipline with a stoic pride. Ripped daily with insults and occasionally kicked in the ass, he gladly endured millions of push-ups, sit-ups and pull-ups. He ran until his balls dropped, skipping and plopping, into a ditch by the side of the road. Intimidated at first by the other recruits, he soon realized that he was superior to nearly all of them in strength, endurance and aggression. He learned how to strip and oil a rifle, to shoot standing up, kneeling, or lying on his stomach. He learned how to shoot straight, to spray, to effectively zap a limited-exposure target from multiple firing positions. Excelling on the range, he won many awards for his marksmanship. A skill to last a lifetime, in or out of the army. He loved the heft of his M14 and considered the rifle a continuation of his own body, an extra limb, his longest and most powerful, its reach extended by each flesh-seeking bullet. Later, when he had to switch to the M16, which was a little lighter, he felt as if a part of his body had been amputated.

Army food was plentiful yet bad. The grayish rice and fish sauce were of the lowest quality. Soup was a salty broth with scarce sprigs of water spinach and there was more fat than pork in the pork stew. Still, Hoang Long was grateful to eat without having to look at his father's and stepmother's faces, now banished to the back regions of his mind, living under a different sky, out of sight. In Can Tho, he sometimes ate with his eyes inadvertently closed, provoking the old man into angry outbursts. In the Army he regained his appetite. Everything tasted better, even a glass of water. He also loved marching in his uniform and despised the enemy for fighting in their underwear.

In January 1963, Hoang Long graduated from the Thu Duc Military Academy as a second lieutenant. Standing stiff in the bright sunshine, he heard a bracing speech by a highly decorated and much-amputated general: "How would you have turned out had you lacked the resolution to enlist? Just think about it. A stay-at-home draft dodger, you'd be a turd, a vermin, a piece of rag! Mark my words, soldiers: Everything hinges on the right decision made at the right time. A second here, an inch there, and you could be dead a hundred times over. Just think about it. If you had waited to be drafted, your being a soldier would be devoid of significance—you'd be cannon fodder and a slave—but, no, you acted of your own volition, flexed your will, and it has changed you. Just look at yourselves! Take my case, for example: Because I enlisted, just like you, my sacrifices have profound significance. For love of country, I chose to lose three of my limbs. Just think about it. And I didn't lose them all at once either. A single trauma is not worth talking about. Each time I lost an arm or a leg, I reenlisted."

Nineteen sixty-three was a pretty good year to be a lowly commissioned officer, perhaps, but not so great if you were president of a country. In February, Iraq's Abdul Karim Kassem was shot after a Baathist coup engineered by the Central Intelligence Agency (CIA). In November, South Vietnam's Ngo Dinh Diem, originally installed by the CIA, was shot in a military coup engineered by the CIA. Among the plotters were future strongmen Saddam Hussein and Nguyen Van Thieu. John F. Kennedy was also shot in November. In knocking off a leader, a killer becomes in effect paterfamilias to an entire population. Unwittingly, many of us have been orphaned, then adopted, by the CIA, the world's number-one deadbeat dad.

5 ✦ HUNCHES AND BELIEFS

After their marriage, it was decided that Kim Lan should quit tending wounds and stay at home. "You should not be around death all the time," Hoang Long said. She was more than ready to leave the blood buckets and maggots behind. She would not miss the incoming, and gurneys gliding on blood. She didn't want to hear words like "triage" or "trauma" ever again. Near death, a soldier, his face burned, his eyes useless, confused her with his wife. Another, clutching her hand, took her for his mother. Being a nurse had not persuaded Kim Lan that pain was a normal human condition. She still considered it an aberration, a freak occurrence afflicting only the most unfortunate.

The young couple bought a two-room house in the Thanh Da district on the edge of town. There you could hear the distant booms of outgoing artillery and occasionally, close by, incoming ones. To make up for her lost income, Kim Lan decided to open a café in their home. Saigon, then as now, was a city with a million cafés. You could not walk a few steps without running into one. They all had beach chairs facing the street, so patrons could laze under awnings to watch life go by as they imbibed caffeine, nicotine and nitrogen dioxide. Beggars and shoe-shine boys drifted in and out, while motorbikes, cyclos, tanks and ambulances paraded past. Every so often there would be an accident, a fight or an explosion to provide perspective and excitement. Kim Lan named her café Kim Long, which means Golden Dragon. "I like that!" Hoang Long said, chuckling.

Marrying her had indeed turned him into a golden dragon. Before, he was just another lonely short guy with an attitude, but now he had real confidence and class. She made him look and feel significant whenever they were seen together. Other men's stares embarrassed her, yet flattered him. Taller, better-looking men were constantly wondering how in hell such a short, ugly man had managed to attract such an attractive woman. They looked at the couple in envy and disgust and wondered if they had made a mistake with their own marriages. That evening they went home and picked a ridiculous argument with their wives.

Three years before he was married, Hoang Long had gone to a fortune-teller, Mrs. Cloudy—so-called because of her milky, pupilless eyes. Everyone consulted her, including high government officials, prominent businessmen and the station chief of the CIA. Her blindness only added to her reputation for clairvoyance. After making an appointment two weeks in advance, clients had to crowd into a waiting room like those at dentists' offices, with the overflow spilling onto the sidewalk. Many Vietnamese have never felt a dentist's probe, but they have seen half a dozen fortune-tellers. In the air-conditioned parlor, Mrs. Cloudy, a regal fifty-year-old dressed in white silk, sat in a rattan armchair, a black mutt dozing by her feet. A boy servant stood near, ready to pour tea. She stopped puffing on her Dunhill, traced the minute lines on Hoang Long's palms with her right thumb, then began, "Let's see, your face is slightly asymmetrical, but that's a distinction to be cherished. You are quite short also, but that's OK. You will find a smudgy facsimile of conjugal happiness, something akin to love, but not this year or the next. You will go far away and it will be a learning experience. Hold on: I can clearly see a wrinkled body, with all of its limbs intact and both eyes securely lodged in their sockets, lying in a state-of-the-art casket, complete with a drainage system. That's pretty good news, isn't it? That means you will live to old age and not suffer a violent death. Hold on: I can clearly see that you will be humiliated in Chapter

30. I'm sorry but you can't change this destiny, it's already published. After marriage, money will roll in." Mrs. Cloudy said many more things that night, but since we weren't there, we can't possibly know what they were.

Mrs. Cloudy's mind was a vast repository of other people's misfortunes: terminal diseases, gunshots, stab wounds, car crashes and bone-crunching, blood-splattering falls from ladders, cliffs and windows. Funeral after funeral coursed through her feverish head. They tailgated or collided into each other at busy intersections. Dozens of funerals merged into one, not to be disentangled except at the cemetery. Her eardrums vibrated continuously with the sounds of weeping, sniveling and howling. When it came to her own death, however, Mrs. Cloudy was clueless. "A fortune-teller cannot tell her own fortune," she'd say matter-of-factly. "And I'm too proud to go see another fortune-teller."

Knowing one's destiny, one became a slave to one's given plot, whether it was glorious then terrifying, or just continuously terrifying, an upside-down roller-coaster ride through the never-spoken-about and the unshowable. Knowing the arc of one's own life, one could only subvert it by means of annoying and desperate tangents, but Mrs. Cloudy preferred to fumble through each chapter, reading her novel as she wrote it. Remove the uncertainties and there would be no imagination, hope or frisson. That was why Mrs. Cloudy occasionally gave her cowardly clients wrong predictions, to make their lives more interesting down the road.

With great success came great jealousy, of course, and there was a rival who claimed that Mrs. Cloudy was not really blind, that she was only a masseuse masquerading as a fortune-teller. Then this other woman was run over by an M48 tank at a famous intersection. After that, no one dared to repeat the slander.

Regarding Hoang Long, Mrs. Cloudy was at least right about money rolling in after marriage. Stationed in Cao Lanh, one hundred miles from Saigon, he could come home every three months for a one-week stay. Each time he showed up, he took from his knapsack a nice stack of money. Soldiers under his command were bribing him to keep them out of harm's way. The ones who couldn't pay were assigned point-man duty or other dangerous tasks. Hoang Long himself was protected by a talisman Kim Lan had procured from a Cambodian monk. It was a cobra's fang he kept in a pouch strapped across his chest. She also got him a handkerchief blessed with a Cambodian phrase. Before each mission, he'd wipe his face with the handkerchief while mumbling some mumbo jumbo in mispronounced Cambodian. It had worked its magic, apparently, because he had not come close to being maimed since he got married.

Better safe than sorry. It can't hurt. The gods and demons must be placated, their ghostly pockets stuffed with hell dollars. Like the Chinese, Mexicans and southern Italians, Vietnamese are highly superstitious. They possess an unscientific mind set that allows them to believe just about anything . . . as long as there is enough poetry in it. To ward off an outbreak of thrush, a child's first excrement— an odorless yellow slime resembling egg yolk—is smeared into his mouth right after birth. At one month, a boy's scrotum is caressed upward with a warm hand, to prevent it from sagging. To tighten his nut sack, three pouches of uncooked rice are hung over a door, to be squeezed by those entering the room. For a girl, a heated betel leaf is rubbed on the vagina, to prevent it from flaring. A child with a drowned relative has to wear a brass anklet to ensure against being "dragged" to a similar death later in life. Children under ten are discouraged from looking into mirrors, lest their souls, embodied within the reflected image, should play tricks with them.

Innumerable superstitions guide you from the cradle to the grave. If you don't squash a snake's head after you've killed it, it will return to bite you three days later. A chunk of cactus, affixed to a door, prevents bad spirits from entering a house. Remove all buttons from a corpse's clothing or else the spirit won't be able to leave the coffin.

In the home of the recently dead, an *X* is drawn in chalk on all glass windows, to prevent the ghost from reentering. During the mourning period, strips of white cloth are tied to the legs of chairs and tables, and to plants, since a plant that does not grieve will surely die. When his sales are slow, a coffin maker will sleep inside a coffin to suggest death to the gods, to simulate/stimulate business.

Most interesting are brand-new beliefs, reflecting contemporary life. Some people believe that an X-ray would trim a year or two from your life span. Drinking milk would lighten your skin; ingesting soy sauce would darken it. Discussing a sensational murder, a woman told Kim Lan that if the corpse's eyes were wide open at the moment of death, the investigation was in the bag. "If they develop the frozen image in his eyes, they can see the murderer's face." Eyes were cameras, literally, in this woman's eyes.

Bay Dom was an ARVN general in charge of the Chau Doc area. It was said that he could not be shot with a bullet. Once he dared an American adviser to shoot him, point-blank, with a pistol. Feeling no special love for the cocky general, the American readily agreed. In front of the general's own troops, he aimed a .38 Special at Bay Dom's temple, the mouth of his six-inch barrel practically kissing the other man's exposed skin. He pulled the trigger twice and heard two loud bangs, but the general still stood there, smirking. On his third attempt, the American's pistol jammed. Suddenly everyone started to laugh uproariously, including the general and the American. They would later become drinking buddies. The only way to kill Bay Dom, it was said, was to shoot him in the eye or the asshole. Once Bay Dom pulled the pin on a grenade and placed it against his heart, but it would not explode.

6 ◆ CHECKMATE!

Where there are no seasons, each day feels pretty much the same. Winter doesn't come but neither does spring. The leaves don't change colors and there's no invigorating first snow. There's never a blighted sky at midday to lend mood and dignity to madness, only a steady glare to mock all neuroses and despair. In early March, there's no meek sun emerging to urge the timid seeds from the sullen soil, no trilling bird returning from up north to find its old tree still standing. There are no skeletal branches etched against a slate-colored sky, reindeers shaving roofs and chimneys, Groundhog Days, Oktoberfests, cherry blossoms, or March Madness. Each day there's the same heat, which can stultify one into thinking that the world is actually permanent and unchanging. Without a gust of arctic wind to chill the bone marrow, some people even forget that their personal winter is fast approaching. Kim Lan established a routine tending to her café and became very fond of many of her customers. Among them was Sen, a Chinese-Vietnamese man recently arrived from Vinh Chau. Cheerful, chatty and always in a brand-new shirt of an outdated fashion, he was an idler who had apparently bribed his way out of military service. His one passion was chess, and he brought a set to her café each day to play against all challengers. He was so good he always had to handicap himself by starting without a rook or a knight. Sen preferred Western chess to the more popular Chinese version. The differences between the two games are crucial. In Chinese chess, the king cannot leave his little area, a symbolic Forbidden City. There's also a river to cross and no queen. What is chess without the damn queen?! The most powerful piece in Western chess, a queen that can zap you in all directions, doesn't exist on a Chinese chessboard. Sen's favorite moment wasn't checkmate, but when he could finally bag his opponent's queen. He played quickly and distractedly, jabbering and hardly looking at the board, but the results were nearly always the same. He never competed for exorbitant stakes, lest he bankrupt his opponents, leading to hard feelings, retaliation, or suicide. Once he became a little too distracted and lost his queen early. Concentrating hard, he fought and fought and finally won, infuriating his opponent into cursing and overturning the chessboard. Everyone in the café anticipated an altercation, but Sen kept his composure. He simply sat and stared at his adversary with a peculiar smile on his face. Some interpreted this as amused contempt, others as fear. In any case, the sore loser quickly apologized, picked up all the pieces by himself, paid Sen, then left, never to be seen again. Sen made good money from chess, but Kim Lan had a hunch he already had lots of money. Carefree and leisurely, he seemed determined to sit out the entire war in her café. Months would go by, but he never seemed the least bit bored. She never suspected that he had a secret reason to stay put. Busy with the customers, she never noticed that his eyes were furtively surveying her every inch.

Sen's spoken Vietnamese was only passable but he was committed to improving it. Too self-conscious to buy a Vietnamese newspaper, he would from time to time peruse those left behind by the other patrons. He could string the lumpy roman letters together, forming sounds in his head, but many words remained opaque. In the *Tatler*, there was a section called "Car Ran over Dog, Dog Ran over Car." These brief accounts of accidents employed a limited vocabulary in simple constructions, such as: "An eighteen-wheeler struck a bicycle, killing a sixty-six-year-old coconut vendor." Knowing all the words except "eighteen-wheeler" and "struck," Sen could deduce that whatever an "eighteen-wheeler" was, it had killed a coconut vendor by "strucking" his or her bicycle. He also glanced at the battle reports. These were even easier to decipher: "Last night in Kontum, we killed twelve, captured three. Our side suffered three light injuries." Twelve to three, Sen concluded, *so we won!*, feeling more Vietnamese with the sentiment. Sen had noticed that many Vietnamese slowed their speech and raised their voices whenever they addressed him. Some even affected vaguely Chinese accents. He appreciated that Kim Lan never did that.

Though economically successful, the Chinese in Vietnam had no social standing. Children sang racist songs about them and their accents were mocked, even on television. In remote Vinh Chau, a tiny village by the coast, Sen's father had a business raising carp. He was one of the first to use fish feed with growth hormones and his profits were enormous. His carp often grew to the size of dolphins and could swim just as fast. He also had twenty acres of land on which he grew onions and other crops. A first-generation immigrant, he had arrived from Sichuan with nothing more than a straw hat, a shirt and a pair of shorts. He had neither shoes nor slippers. Even when he could afford quality footwear decades later, his splayed toes could not endure being jammed inside a stuffy pair of leather wingtips. Thank God, plastic flip-flops had finally been invented. Aiming for San Francisco, the old man had settled for Vietnam. He was satisfied with his life except that he had yearned for years, without success, to have a son. After the birth of his third daughter, he became so enraged with his wife that he threatened to give all of their daughters away. She had to kneel on the floor and beg him to hang on to their children. "Give me one more chance," she sobbed. "I promise I'll make you a son next year." True to her word, Sen was born a year later. Relieved, the rich man threw a month-long feast for all of his neighbors. He slaughtered cows, pigs, chickens and goats, and everyone drank the best rice and snake wines from sunset to sunrise for an entire month. The rich man grinned at his son's tapered sprout the size of a tabasco and rubbed his nose affectionately against his wife's face. Sen was breast-fed by his adoring mother until he was one, then he sucked on his grandmother's dry titties until he was six, then he nibbled on one pacifier after another until he finally went to school at nine—his father couldn't bear to let him out of the house any earlier. It took him three years to complete the first grade. If it rained or was too hot outside, Sen was kept at home. When he did go to school, he was always carried on the back of one of his three sisters. This arrangement lasted until he was fifteen and too chubby to be loaded onto anyone's back. Until ten, he was always bathed by his mother. Until twelve, his sisters had to spoon-feed him at mealtimes.

7 ♦ MOUSE CHILD

n late 1970 Kim Lan finally conceived. Hoang Long seemed delighted by the news, but she was apprehensive. All day long she stood sideways in front of the mirror, frowning and rubbing her belly. To help her out with household chores and the operation of her café, she hired a domestic servant, a dark girl from Cu Chi.

The war had displaced millions of people, forcing countless girls from the countryside to seek work in the city, but jobs were scarce. The Americans were withdrawing and most bars—the Golden Cock, Pink Pussycat, Magic Finger Lounge, Buffalo Tom, Bar Bar, etc.—had to shut down. James Brown ceased to holler, grunt and plead from the soulful joints of Khanh Hoi. No more roiling bass lines and gaggles of charming hostesses to offer full privileges nightly to the foreign-born, irrespective of age, weight, physical appearance, interpersonal skills or social class. No kidding! Sorry about that! Even the Royal on Nguyen Hue Street, open since 1962, the first eatery in Saigon to serve cheeseburgers with real buns instead of sliced bread, went under. Spanky, Cowboy, Slim, Pimp, Gladly, Killer, the Weasel were going back to their sweethearts and Chevies, leaving behind sons and daughters and half-empty glasses of Saigon Tea on the table. No more of the sweet-voiced, omniscient, if occasionally ungrammatical, Hanoi Hannah—"How are you, GI Joe?"—to needle them about race riots and cheating girlfriends back home, or encourage grunts to frag blowhard officers.

Many bar girls had to go back to the rice paddies or open small shops selling soft drinks and trinkets. Some shaved their heads, lit incense, chanting *namyo* or "Ave Maria." Some, with their very own Spankies and Weasels, even moved to America.

The locals never quite got the hang of sitting on high stools to drink liquor while contemplating their groggy faces in the mirror, a TV droning in the background. Perched on a bar stool, your feet removed from the ground and your head closer to the sky, you felt less a part of this earth. Hardly comfortable on chairs, much less bar stools, they preferred to squat on their haunches, like a woman piddling alfresco. That was another reason the bars had to shut down.

Meanwhile, Kim Lan continued to stand in front of the mirror, frowning and rubbing her belly. Visiting neighbors reminded her to look at the beautiful faces on calendars, so her baby would be just as beautiful. *Don't cut cloth with scissors,* they warned, *or your child will have a harelip. Don't use uneven chopsticks, or the baby's legs will be uneven.* At the sight of the deformed and the handicapped, they advised her to turn her gaze away. She was told never to squat inside a door frame, lest she have a difficult childbirth, requiring forceps, resulting in a pointy-headed baby. *Don't eat too much,* they also told her, *or the baby will be too big, and hard to get out.* She could barely eat anyway. At four months, she stayed in bed all day. Even in hundred-degree heat, she'd be under a mound of blankets, in complete darkness, shivering. She could not stomach anything the servant placed in front of her.

"What is this?"

"Crab soup with bamboo shoots, ma'am."

"You know I hate canned bamboo shoots!"

"You always liked it before, ma'am."

"And this crab stinks. Is it spoiled?"

"No, of course not. I can add some sesame oil, if you like."

"Please take it away and let me sleep."

The war kept up its intensity and Hoang Long had to skip his leave a few times. In 1971, he came home just twice and had to cut short his stay both times. "You must understand," he explained to his worried wife, "I cannot be away from my men at a time like this." In June 1971, as Hoang Long was fighting in Long Khanh, Kim Lan went to Hung Vuong Hospital to give birth to a boy weighing just four pounds. She named him Cun.

Cun resembled a naked mole rat at birth and would go on to resemble a naked mole rat for the rest of his life. When his teeth started to sprout, he even bit his mom several times a day. He also liked to bite other children and pinch them, especially on the inner thighs. He cried all day and night and rejected whatever his mom fed him—carrots, peas, pap or pabulum. Disagreeing with all baby formulas, he refuted both milk and soy, spat out Good Start and threw up the Dutch Girl. Exasperated, Kim Lan went to a medicine man and got a red string with a black bead to tie around Cun's neck. This was supposed to calm him down but she saw zero improvement in her son's mood or behavior. As Cun grew a little older, he never passed up an opportunity to yank an animal's tail or ear or squash anything that could be squashed. If he saw a live crab, he would immediately sever its antennae and wait impatiently for an eye to stick out so he could pinch it and roll it between his fingers.

When Hoang Long came home for Christmas of 1971, he saw Cun for the first time. He was so disappointed he could not even feign a smile. *This has to be the ugliest baby ever*, he shook his head. *Could this be someone else's child? Has she been screwing around with some of these losers loitering in the café? Look at how she banters with them, always laughing and giggling. A married woman shouldn't be giggling with strangers.* But as he looked more closely at the horrible mouse child, he noticed that the smirking mouth was unmistakably his own.

Kim Lan could clearly see her husband's discomfort toward Cun. More troubling to her, however, was the fact that he was not wearing his wedding ring. She had never seen him without his ring. Even odder, the skin where the ring should be didn't appear any lighter. His entire finger was uniformly brown. She was about to say something, but for some reason, unclear even to herself, she decided to let it pass. On his next leave, he was wearing his ring again.

Kim Lan also noticed that her husband seemed more tired yet more restless with each visit. He didn't take her out to restaurants like he used to. "I just want to stay home," he said. "It's so nice just to be home. I don't want to deal with the noise and the glares and looking at people stuffing their faces. It disgusts me to see people laughing and eating in a restaurant. People in Saigon act as if there's no war going on. All the restaurants and movie theaters are filled with hippie draft dodgers in bell-bottom pants!"

"Why don't we go to the zoo then? It'd give Cun a chance to see the animals."

"All he'll see there are the freaks! The zoo has been taken over by hippies!"

"How do you know? You haven't been there since before we got married. Remember how we used to take long romantic walks through the zoo?"

Hoang Long simply closed his eyes, scrunched up his face and sighed. The phrase "long romantic walks" had apparently upset some chemical balance in him. Kim Lan understood Hoang Long's irritation with hippies—she hated them, too—but her husband was hardly home when he was at home. He barely dealt with her at all. Instead of talking to his wife, he spent most of his time watching TV, either the American station showing *Bonanza*, *I Love Lucy*, or *Bewitched*, or folk opera, news, or sports on the Vietnamese channel. Instead of eating with a bowl and chopsticks at the table, he preferred his food on an individual plate, so he could eat and watch TV at the same time. He loved his sixteen-inch Fuji black and white, with its long, splaying legs and side-closing doors. It was the centerpiece of the house. He never played with his son. If Cun was making too much noise, he would snap, "Get this kid to shut up, will you?" Once, as he was watching soccer and Cun was crying, he even yelled, "Shut the fuck up or I'll smack your face!"

"Is that a way to talk to your son?" Kim Lan protested.

"Burma is ahead by a goal," Hoang Long replied, all tense, his body hunched up in front of the TV, five empty bottles of beer on the floor next to his chair. "Be quiet!"

At halftime, seeing that she was angry, he patted her on the butt and joked, "That kid is nothing but a screaming and shitting machine!"

Chopping onions, she had her head turned away from him, and did not respond.

"Chopping onions again, huh?" He sighed, suppressing a burp. "What are you making?"

Again she did not respond. They stood an inch apart, his hot breath fanning her upper arm. Seeing her knife starting to tremble, he shook his head, grabbed another beer and went back to the TV. Cun had passed out from crying. *Is it that time of the month?* he wondered. *There is plenty of time left. We can still come back. It's not over until it's over.*

Burma was ranked sixty-seventh in the world in 1973, South Vietnam eighty-second, and the match ended three to two in Burma's favor. All of Saigon groaned at the final whistle. Some bettors lost their houses that day. Crouching in their dark tunnels or lying on hammocks under triple-canopied jungles, the Vietcong also groaned, their ears glued to American-made radios. Away from home, from civilization, at war, horny and nostalgic, there was no better friend than your radio. There were rumors among them that the ARVN had a piss-seeking missile. This American military dream weapon could sniff out urea from the sky. To piss against tree or bush was to flirt with eternity, insist on nirvana. It was only safe to urinate into bodies of water. The guerrillas placed a bucket of piss out in the open as a decoy and, sure enough, it was immediately zapped by a piss-seeking missile.

The guerrillas had their own ingenious weapons. They fashioned booby traps out of bamboo, mud, beach chairs and beer cans. They smeared human shit onto punji stakes to cause deadly infection. They even catapulted beehives at their enemy. (The rumor about Americans shooting flash-frozen bees from air guns was absolutely not true. Hurled through the warm tropical air, the bees were supposed to revive to sting the enemy.)

Drunk and reeling from the loss to Burma, Hoang Long reflected that, short of war, nothing triggered more collective euphoria or despair than the final score of a game. Yet nothing was more meaningless or ephemeral, its dubious significance erased with the result of the very next match. The next day, Vietnam defeated Laos five to one, Sheffield United undressed and humiliated Arsenal five to zero, and the Red Sox edged the Orioles two to one. A defeat in sport was merely a symbolic death, just as death was merely symbolic so long as it happened to somebody else.

Hoang Long had never kissed Kim Lan before, but now he didn't even hug her. He had called call her "honey" and "sweetie," but now his endearment for her was "your mother," as in "Your mother take care, OK?" as he walked out the door.

8 ◆ THE TRUTH

n truth, it wasn't Kim Lan who had been screwing around, but Hoang Long. He had not shown up for some of his leaves because he wanted to spend time with his mistress in Cao Lanh. Though not as pretty as Kim Lan, she was also a nurse, younger and not pregnant. Clearly, Hoang Long had a thing for very young nurses. One benefit of the war was that it allowed a man to be in two places at the same time. If the war ended, Hoang Long would have to dump one of the two women.

This young nurse could screw like a pro. In fact, she was sort of a pro, a semipro. Though she never accepted cash for sex, men had to bring her expensive gifts. Hoang Long unwrapped a National rice cooker one time. Another time, a gold-plated Seiko watch with embossed leather band. For four nights of lovin', it wasn't cheap, but it was worth it. The young nurse had a drawerful of Citizens, Seikos and Bulovas, so many she couldn't sell them fast enough. She only stayed a nurse because she liked the white uniform and because she really cared about people—she had a gold-plated heart.

Hoang Long thought of the stiff, almost comical way his wife yielded to his sexual advances at home. While most people arrived at spousal sexual ennui two or three years into marriage, necessitating weird videos and training manuals, Hoang Long and Kim Lan had achieved it instantly. *My wife is still a sexual innocent after all these years,* he thought, *and she will always be a sexual innocent. My wife is unsuitable for sex.*

My mistress gives me something my wife can't . . . is not equipped to give me, is constitutionally incapable of giving me. She was made to be a good wife and she is certainly that, but I need something more. A soldier's existence is already abnormal, so I need abnormal solutions to go with it. When I'm with my mistress, I feel compensated, at last, for all the shit I go through. She makes love joyously. Screaming and laughing, she challenges me. I feel born again when I'm with my mistress. Lying next to her, I am no longer a bloodstained man but a freshly washed newborn. Her fragrant sweat cleans all that filthy blood from my body. Without her, my anger and hatred would turn me into a monster. I'd probably have killed my wife already if it wasn't for my mistress. I'd kill everybody if it wasn't for my mistress. Isn't it enough that I risk death every day to support my family? Don't I have a right to enjoy myself once in while? One week of pleasure for eleven weeks of hell is fair compensation, don't you think?

Hoang Long always took off his wedding ring before visiting his mistress. He took it off and on so often, he nearly lost it a few times. When he did wear it, it pinched his finger. *Either the damn ring has shrunk,* he thought, *or else my finger has gotten much fatter. Blocking my circulation, it's liable to give me gangrene. Soon I'll have to chop that god-damned finger off!*

9 ✦ NIXON IN CHINA

When Richard Nixon visited China in February 1972, he effectively ended the Vietnam War. With this rapprochement, Vietnam became a dispensable pawn. In January of 1974, Chinese warships sailed through the US Seventh Fleet to seize a handful of South Vietnamese islands. If China had waited until after the Fall of Saigon to grab them, it would have been stealing from its own allies, the North Vietnamese. In any case, the end of South Vietnam was near.

In 1974, Hoang Long came home only once, just for Tet. He spent his other three leaves intertwined with his mistress in Cao Lanh. His techniques had improved much over the years—he had a more diversified sexual portfolio now—but his wife was never the beneficiary. He brought a stack of money home as usual, which allowed them to buy a fridge, rebuild the kitchen and add a second floor to their house. It had become one of the better-looking homes in the neighborhood. Saigon has always been a city where the few building codes are routinely ignored. Houses grow haphazardly, ulcerously, according to their owners' fluctuating incomes and whims. Every Vietnamese is certainly not a poet, as is commonly claimed, but he's likely to be an architect—and a postmodern one at that. He will not hesitate to order a contractor to add Greek columns, Roman arches, or a Russian dome to his home. Few people moved to a better neighborhood simply because most neighborhoods were basically the same: a mishmash of fine homes, rising up to six stories, interspersed with shacks.

The inevitable finally happened in the spring of 1975. Hue and Da Nang fell to the North Vietnamese in March. On April 3, Nha Trang fell after a battle lasting just three hours. On April 8, the presidential palace in Saigon was bombed by a renegade ARVN pilot, twenty-six-year-old Nguyen Thanh Trung, whose name actually meant "loyal." He later claimed to have been a Vietcong mole from the beginning. If this was true, then he had dropped hundreds of bombs on his own comrades over his three years as a combat pilot. A mass murderer and, in some ways, a poet, he had sacrificed thousands of lives to make a single symbolic statement in the end. Of the four bombs he unloaded that day, two landed in the garden, two on the roof, causing one injury.

Also on April 8, the deputy commander of the Saigon area, General Nguyen Van Hieu, was found shot to death in his office, likely murdered by another ARVN officer. The bullet entered his left chin and exited the right top of his head, an impossible angle for a right-handed man to commit suicide. On April 9, the North Vietnamese attacked Xuan Loc, a town only thirty-seven miles northeast of Saigon. Outnumbered four to one, southern forces nevertheless held on for two weeks. Losing two thousand men, they destroyed thirty-seven North Vietnamese Army (NVA) tanks and killed over five thousand of the attackers. Their commander, General Le Minh Dao, would later spend seventeen years in a Communist reeducation camp. On April 21, President Thieu resigned on TV after a speech denouncing the US for abandoning South Vietnam. "The United States has not kept its promises. It is inhumane. It is untrustworthy. It is irresponsible." US aid to South Vietnam had fallen from a peak of thirty billion dollars a year to one billion by 1974. The humiliation of a minor country is that it is always at the mercy of a major one. A major power distorts everything in its path. A major power distorts the world. Thieu rose to prominence after a CIA-engineered coup that ousted Ngo Dinh Diem. Under Thieu, South Vietnam's military was compromised by his preference for loyal officers over competent ones. He was strangely paranoid about military coups engineered by the CIA. After his speech, Thieu fled to Taiwan, then flew to London a few months later. By 1990 he was living in Foxborough, Massachusetts. Kim Lan had always admired Nguyen Van Thieu, not for his policies, but because he had a high forehead, a sign of intelligence, and long ears, indicating longevity. He had a round face with a well-defined jaw—the face of a leader—unlike his main rival, Nguyen Cao Ky, who resembled a cricket with a mustache.

The North Vietnamese started shelling Tan Son Nhat Airport on April 28. On April 30, their tanks rolled into Saigon. It was a clear, bright day, with the temperature nearing one hundred. On many streets lay the hastily discarded uniforms, boots and weapons of the defeated army. In front of an ugly black statue in a public square, a white-uniformed cop lay dead, a jagged hole violating his right temple, his dark blood pooling, lumpy with bits of neurons, synapses and memories, a man's colorful life translated into gray matter, his capsized hat, rocked by the wind, lying beside him. A solitary ant rammed its head repeatedly against the spreading blood, trying to cross. Kim Lan hadn't heard from Hoang Long for nearly a month and had no idea where he was. She had prepared for the worst by stocking up on rice, sugar, cooking oil and instant noodles. The café had been closed for a week and the servant had gone home. Thousands of people with connections and/or luck had already left the country. With Cun on her lap, she sat next to a radio to follow the latest developments. Minutes after Duong Van Minh announced his unconditional surrender, shocking millions of people around the world, someone shook her steel gate. *Are the North Vietnamese at my door already?!* The rattling persisted even more violently, accompanied by a male voice yelling her name over and over, but it wasn't her husband's. She went to look and saw that it was Sen.

"Sen, what are you doing here?!"

"I came to get you!"

"What do you mean you came to get me?"

"I came to get you and your son. I have the means to leave the country. Listen, we don't have much time. I can drive us to Vinh Chau. From there we can take a boat to leave the country."

"What about my husband?"

"He's probably out already. Or maybe they've caught him. Listen, we don't have much time. If you stay here, they'll kill you. You should leave with me now, and meet up with your husband later."

"But I can't take off with you. I have a husband!"

"I'm just offering you the means to escape, Kim Lan. I have no other intentions. You should come with me for the sake of your son. Everybody else is escaping."

"I'm sorry, but I can't leave with you." And with that, she slammed the steel gate in Sen's face.

10 • A JAILED DEMOCRAT

The first week after the Fall of Saigon, Kim Lan stayed inside. She and Cun ate instant noodles and ignored whatever was happening outside. The usual sounds did not filter in—radio music, kids playing, the wooden clappers of soup-delivery boys. She took out old magazines and read them cover to cover, knowing the society depicted in them no longer existed. She stared at photos of famous singers—Hung Cuong, Thanh Thuy, Che Linh—and wondered if they were still inside the country. She read an article about Vo Van Bay, a tennis star who had won twenty Davis Cup matches before he retired. She read about an African king who returned to Saigon to look for a daughter he had fathered in 1953 while serving in the French Army. He found her working in a cement factory and took her to his kingdom of the Central African Republic. A photo showed a grim man, crowned, robed and holding a scepter, sitting on a huge throne in the shape of an eagle, its wings spreading, but there was no image of the fortunate daughter. Her real name was Martine, but she had to change it to Mai to blend in at the cement factory. Kim Lan had seen this factory many times, going to Bien Hoa, and never suspected an African princess was wasting away behind its gray cement walls. It was a colossal thing on the left just after you crossed the Newport Bridge, before you hit the National Cemetery. Everyone knew this cement factory. Lost in a particularly fascinating article, Kim Lan sometimes forgot, if only for a few seconds, that her world had been irrevocably changed. She often slowed the pace of her reading, as if by doing that, she was slowing the pace of time itself, making the night, her last refuge, last a little longer. But there would be no king or father to deliver her from her situation. She oscillated between apocalyptic foreboding and willful optimism. Each night, she stood at the altar to pray to the Goddess of Mercy to protect her missing husband. She was nearly certain he was dead, but somehow this prospect did not sadden or alarm her—she simply felt numb. Whatever his faults, Hoang Long had given her years of relative calm and happiness. As his wife, she had matured, and for that she was grateful. Lying in bed, she squeezed Cun tightly to her bosom, their bodies welded together, inseparable, and felt strangely secure, as if no danger could detect or devour them as long as they remained on the darkened bed, as if the glare of morning would never come. In the stillness of the night, the world felt safe and eternal and nothing seemed changed.

On May 8, she finally ventured out. Having not been outside for a week, she thought the familiar street looked extra bright, with everything—houses, pavement and trees—seemingly lit up from inside and saturated with colors. She felt exposed and nervous, yet strangely relieved. Maybe free was a better word. *But free of what?* She wondered. *I'm walking freely through this air. No one is stopping me. No one is waiting for me. I'm not bound by anything but air.* Her train of thoughts was interrupted by the sight of two North Vietnamese soldiers guarding a house several doors away. She had never seen the enemy up close before, only on TV or in the newspapers, and only when they were tied up, blindfolded, or dead.

The house belonged to Mr. Loc, a prominent critic of Nguyen Van Thieu. A Social Democrat, Mr. Loc was considered left-wing and accused by some of being a Communist sympathizer. An intellectual with an athlete's body, he was serious yet cheerful, with a distinctive booming laugh. He had translated the US Constitution, which he self-published in a pamphlet. He gave Kim Lan a copy several times, but she always threw it away as soon as he turned his head. *Why is he giving me political propaganda?* she wondered. He also had the annoying habit of leaving pamphlets all over her tables. For writing articles attacking corruption in Thieu's government, he was imprisoned five or six times, but each time he came out he was more aggressive than ever—he could not be cowed. He came to Kim Lan's café just about every morning for two cups of coffee with condensed milk. If he didn't show up for more than a week, she knew he was in jail. Mr. Loc only smoked American cigarettes, either Camels or Lucky Strikes. "You must go to the source," he explained to her once, smiling. In the evening he liked to kick a soccer ball against a wall with the neighborhood children. Everyone but Hoang Long seemed to like Mr. Loc, though the two hardly knew each other.

"I fight for real, defending the country, while that draft dodger fights I don't know what with his tongue!" Hoang Long would say.

"But Mr. Loc is not a draft dodger. He's nearsighted!" Kim Lan would reply.

"Nearsighted?! Everyone is nearsighted. What's nearsighted? If you're not blind, you should be fighting!"

Walking past the young soldiers that day, Kim Lan could only assume that they were keeping Mr. Loc under house arrest. They looked no more than seventeen. They were short, sturdy and dark, not unlike her husband, but in ill-fitting, faded uniforms, and yellow canvas instead of black leather shoes. One wore a pith helmet, the other a boonie hat. Their AK-47s, slung across their bodies, tilted downward. *We just lost to these people*, she thought, feeling oddly excited. She did not dare to engage them in conversation but quickly went back home.

When she went out the next day, the two soldiers were gone. Through the open gate of Mr. Loc's house, she saw three uniformed men talking to Mrs. Loc. Mrs. Loc seemed tiny that morning, her face drained of all color. Kim Lan would only find out later that what she was witnessing was the seizure of Mrs. Loc's home. Only one story out of four, the highest, was allotted to her and her four children. The rest became state property. Mr. Loc had already been taken to Chi Hoa Prison. He would return four years later, a sullen and broken man.

As Kim Lan walked around the neighborhood, people she knew greeted her as usual, but they seemed tense and unwilling to talk. There were many strange faces. Some shops were open. Hung Far Low, a Chinese restaurant on the corner, was actually filled with noisy customers, many of them North Vietnamese soldiers. Across the street was a propaganda billboard from the old regime with Thieu's famous admonition: DO NOT LISTEN TO THE COMMUNISTS BUT WATCH WHAT THEY DO. What the Communists were doing that day was eating fried rice and chow mien. Some of them were standing on the sidewalks, looking lost. Kim Lan remembered 1968, when there were so many reports out of Hue about civilians being shot by North Vietnamese troops or buried alive in mass graves.

That night, lying in bed next to her son, Kim Lan felt that she had made a serious mistake in not leaving with Sen. There were only a few decisions in life that really mattered and she had certainly blown this one. Now she understood why Sen had always been so courteous and pleasant to her, why he had always smiled so brightly. With him loitering in the café each day, she had actually spent more time with Sen than with her own husband. Sen was always within her sight and often literally within her reach. To make such an arrangement permanent would not be unpleasant. Sen was a kind man who would probably make a good father. Unlike Hoang Long, who seemed strangely indifferent to his own son, Sen often joked around with Cun and gave him sweets. Kim Lan had never felt more lonely in her life. If it hadn't been for the presence of Cun, she would have broken out in sobs.

11 ♦ IS THAT YOU?

After failing to persuade Kim Lan to go with him, Sen drove south, heading for Vinh Chau. He was afraid the highway would be clogged with fleeing refugees, but it wasn't. There was a large crowd at Bac My Thuan and it took him three hours just to get on a ferry. On the dock, vendors were pushing the usual sugarcane cubes, pineapple chunks, mango and Coca-Colas, everything but lottery tickets. Regime change or no, poor people still had to make money that day. The man with the withered legs draped around his neck like a pretzel was also out begging. Sen had to pay a ridiculous price for the ferry, ten times the usual rate. Crossing the river, he noticed that the South Vietnamese flag had already been removed from the pilot boat.

He slept that night in Soc Trang and continued early the next morning. All in all, things were going swimmingly until he reached the last ferry crossing, about forty miles from his destination. The ferry was not there for some reason. There were boats and boatmen willing to take him across, but how would he cover the last forty miles without his car? If only his sisters were waiting on the other side to carry him piggyback, tag-team fashion, the last forty miles, but no, they weren't available just when they were most needed.

He sat in a little shack of a café at the river's edge and pondered his options. With the electric fan broken, the heat was insufferable. On a plywood wall, a dozen long-legged calendar babes, baring belly buttons, surrounded a piglike Buddha. Hungry, he ordered rice with pork chops, but the meat turned out to be so old and dry, he flung it in the direction of a mangy, three-legged dog. Two flies suddenly collided in midair and landed in his fresh-brewed tea. *Were they making love?* he wondered. He had seen pigeons, snakes, monkeys, of course, and crocodiles doing the nasty, but never flies. He watched the flies drown before dumping the tea and pouring himself another cup. He noticed that all of the locals—five idling hoodlums and the hag owner of the café—were staring at him as if he were a man from Mars. He suddenly realized that there was no government left to prevent them from killing him and stealing his car. *Which side were they on during the war anyway? Probably neither. Some of them probably didn't even know there was a war. It was because of stupid hicks like these that I had to escape to Saigon in the first place.*

By sunset, the ferry still hadn't turned up, so there was nothing for Sen to do but climb into his car and try to sleep. Tossing and turning all night in the backseat, he woke up at dawn groggy, thirsty and dreading what the café had on its breakfast menu. There was no ferry and there wouldn't be a ferry. Sen approached a hick and bought a rusty bicycle from him—at a monstrous price. These hicks weren't so stupid after all. Then he asked another hick to take him across the river. Not needing his car anymore, he didn't have to hire anyone to look after it. Sitting on the sampan, he looked back at his black 1965 Citroën le Dandy with annoyance and sadness. He also thought of Kim Lan, of how he had almost managed to snatch her from fate.

The ride home on the pebbly dirt road with multiplying potholes, their stagnant rainwater reflecting clouds and sky, so beautiful, required all the stamina Sen had and he nearly fell off his bike several times. He only reached the outlying fields of Vinh Chau at sunset. Serenaded and mocked by the monotonous heavy metal riffs of a million cicadas, his eyes blurred by rivulets of sweat, his muscles breaking down, it was pitch-dark when he nearly crashed into the gate of his old house. His father's villa boasted the only wrought iron gate in the village. There were cacti outside the high walls, which were topped with colorful shards of glass, and German shepherds inside them. He didn't hear the dogs barking that day for some reason. He draped himself against the gate and thought he would die soon if no one came out to carry him inside immediately. Seeing light shining through the wooden slats of the second-floor windows, Sen shouted for his three sisters. "First sister! Second sister! Third sister!" It took forever, but someone finally came out. At first Sen thought that it was a new servant, but no, too well dressed to be a servant, she was actually the lady of the house. "What do you want?!" she snapped at him in a thick northern accent.

Understanding everything immediately, Sen mumbled, "I'm sorry, ma'am, but I must have the wrong house." He quickly got on his cheap bike and blundered away.

Not everything was lost; there was a second house Sen could go to. He willed his bike another mile to reach his wife's house. Yes, Sen was married. Back in 1948, during the feast to celebrate his birth, that month-long bacchanal of grilled meat and wine, his father's best friend promised his next daughter to Sen when the boy grew up. Flushed with wine and gratitude, Sen's father readily accepted the offer. "We are best friends! So our children should also be best friends when we're gone!" With three wives, the other man had no problems turning out daughters. At seventeen, Sen was married to fulfill his father's pledge. The couple lived together as polite strangers for a year before Sen disappeared to Saigon for good. They tried to have sex a few times and found the experience absurd and humiliating, but the outcome was a son. Now, having come full circle, dumped by destiny in front of his old roost, his rejected wife and forgotten son just on the other side of a broken-down, warped door, Sen shouted, "Open up! It's me!"

"Who is that?"

"It's me!"

"Is that really you?"

"Yes, it's me."

She opened the door a crack and saw that it was really her husband. His face hadn't changed after six years, unlike hers. "What are you doing with that bicycle?"

"I just bought it. Open up so I can come in!"

"It's been so long." Mrs. Sen suddenly started to sob. "How come you never returned from that trip to Saigon?"

"It's a long story. I joined the army. I fought and almost died several times. In any case, there's no more Saigon so let's not talk about it. Let's just forget the past. Open the door so I can come in!"

Over dinner, Sen was told by his wife that the Vietcong had taken over Vinh Chau five days earlier. His family had escaped by boat apparently. During the war, the ARVN controlled little of Vinh Chau beyond the post office—it was more or less VC country.

Sen stayed home for seven days. On his first night, yearning for Kim Lan, he decided to give sex with his wife another try. It was really Kim Lan, beautiful, glorious Kim Lan, who lay under, over and next to him in the dark, the scent of coconut oil and rapid, breathless Chinese emanating from his suddenly excitable wife notwithstanding. Sen had a thing for Vietnamese women. It wasn't because they were any more beautiful than Chinese females, he simply wanted them more because they were off-limits to him. If two women looked exactly the same but one was labeled Vietnamese and one Chinese, he would pick the Vietnamese one. It enraged him to think that such a good-looking, qualified dude as he was could be deterred from having sex with some hot Vietnamese chick by the vigilant alpha, beta and gamma males of Vietnamese society. He was determined to change this unnatural natural law. On the eighth day, he silently exited the house before dawn, got on his bicycle and pedaled away. He would never see Vinh Chau again.

Sen reached the ferry landing in the late afternoon and was astonished to see his car still parked on the other side. The hicks had been too intimidated or honest to mess with it. *This is a great omen,* he thought. Inserting the key into the ignition, Sen became so giddy he actually burst into song. As he drove away, the hicks could clearly hear him singing in English, "I got you, babe!"

Kim Lan was giving Cun a bath at the back of the house when she heard someone rattling her steel gate and calling her name over and over. She knew who it was immediately because she had been thinking about him for over a week. Still she thought, *It cannot be him.* When she opened the steel gate and saw Sen standing there, smiling as usual, she pretended not to be shocked and happy. "What are you doing here, Sen?!"

"I came back because of you."

"I thought you had left by boat."

"How could I leave without you?"

12 ◆ JAR GAMES

From 1975 to 1986, Saigon went through a dark age. Hundreds of thousands of people were sent off to concentration or labor camps. Food shortages became a fact of life. Rice, cooking oil, salt, sugar and MSG were rationed. Yam was served for breakfast, lunch and dinner. Letters sent from overseas were often lost and packages stolen. Wine was made by fermenting the cores of pineapples. Jackfruit pits were boiled, peeled and eaten. Love songs, known as yellow music, were banned under penalty of imprisonment. Trinh Cong Son, Vietnam's greatest songwriter, was sent to mine-strewn fields to plant cassava. Monks and priests disappeared, to be replaced by phony monks and priests. Nearly everyone was hungry nearly all the time. There were blackouts twenty-one days out of the month and water pressure plummeted. Yellow sorghum, a rice substitute, got stuck in everyone's decaying teeth. Toothpaste became scarce and laundry detergent was used as shampoo. Head lice multiplied, leading to shorter haircuts, even among women. Fresh milk disappeared and condensed milk became a luxury item. Anything could be stolen by anyone at any moment. There was nothing to read and nothing to watch on television. Everyone conspired to escape by boat, but only a few succeeded. Among the boat people were former supporters of the National Liberation Front, now contrite and yearning for America.

One needed connections and careful planning to escape by boat. But above all, one needed money. To buy a place on a boat, one had to pay about a thousand bucks, not a small sum in a bankrupt country. Some people tried a dozen times without success. Many made it to international water only to die of thirst, starvation or by drowning. The ones who headed toward Thailand—the land of smiles in tourist brochures—were often robbed and raped by Thai pirates. Neighbors who don't speak the same language rarely make good friends. After arriving in a refugee camp, the boat people had to wait for years to go to a third country. Many were eventually sent back to Vietnam. The ones who persisted, those who had to get out at any cost, were often the best of South Vietnamese society: doctors, lawyers, engineers and intellectuals. Most Chinese merchants were also hounded into leaving. Though less radical than its former protégé, the Khmer Rouge, the Hanoi regime was still systematically destroying an entire society. An enduring legacy of this period is a deep yearning in the Vietnamese psyche to leave Vietnam at the first opportunity. Birds, bees and salmon do it, but the average Vietnamese can only dream of crossing a border.

The only people who did well through this time were the bribe-taking government officials and police. They took bribes for everything, even for allowing a boat full of refugees to set out to sea. People would pay one set of officials to leave the country, only to be captured and thrown into jail by another set of officials.

Kim Lan could not keep her café open because of the government ban on private businesses. She sold all her jewelry and Sen sold his car. They learned how to survive on the black market by selling fish sauce and laundry detergent. Each evening she went to the market to buy the leftover, nearly spoiled chunks of fish to make a very salty fish sauce. There was hardly any fish in her sauce but her customers never complained because they couldn't afford anything better. *Have rice, eat rice, have broth, eat broth,* goes a saying. Starved, even a phoenix will eat chicken shit.

Ignoring the government monopoly on laundry detergent, Sen learned how to make his own and sold it in plastic bags with counterfeit labels. Sen had never worked before, but now he had no choice. Kim Lan marveled at her new husband's industry. She never would have suspected that he could spend at least twelve hours a day making detergent. Before, he only crawled from bed at nine or ten, but now he rose at the break of dawn, as the cocks crowed. (Even now, you can hear cocks crowing in Saigon. Chickens are kept two or three to a cage before they are slaughtered.) Sen's productive years would prove to be an aberration, however. As soon as hard times eased up, he reverted to chess.

So many houses were broken into around this time, Sen had to buy a roll of razor wire and uncoil it on the roof. Ubiquitous during the war, like tanks and sandbags, barbed wire is an American invention. The devil's rope was originally designed to keep cows from roaming, Indians from encroaching, and the cowboys from singing their lonesome ballads. At night, Sen slept with a knife, Kim Lan with a flashlight to shine at the source of any trouble. Through this nightmarish period, they embraced and comforted each other. He proved to be an ideal husband and an excellent father for Cun. Kim Lan kept a photo of Hoang Long on the altar and lit incense sticks in his memory, but she rarely thought about him. He did show up in her dreams a few times. Once, she heard her name called, turned around, and saw Hoang Long standing there, his body maimed and bloody, his face reproachful, and the sight panicked her into screaming. Waking up, her eyes wet, she was grateful to see Sen still next to her. She would look at Sen and think, *I finally have a real husband, someone who is faithful and tender, not a man who ignores his own son, makes love like a brute and takes off his wedding ring to run off with some mistress.*

About the only thing Kim Lan disliked about Sen was his table manners. She had always considered the Chinese a vulgar people who even farted as they ate. The first few times Sen did it, she ignored it, but once she became so enraged she had to scream, "Why don't you go fart on your father's grave?!" Sucker punched by this outburst, Sen spat a mouthful of yam (fart) all over the table (fart). To be fair to Sen, it was well known that yams cause the stomach to boil (fart). Even Kim Lan farted steadily as she ate, chewing with her mouth wide open, but she did it very quietly so no one could hear. With superhuman effort, Sen willed himself to stop farting at the table, but he couldn't stop eating fried fish with his hands, forsaking chopsticks, while spitting little fish bones onto the floor. After each meal, he ran to the back door to hack his copious phlegm into the alley. "It's good for my health," he explained.

During this period, Cun often came home from school dirty, dried mud in his hair, his clothes stained, with scrapes on his arms and knees.

"What happened to you?" Kim Lan would ask, though she already knew.

"I got into a fight. I smacked the other kid pretty good, too. I bloodied his nose."

"How many times have I told you not to fight with other kids?"

"He said, 'Your father sucked American dicks.' I had no choice. I had to fight him."

Cun hadn't bloodied anybody's nose. He was one of those kids other boys practiced their punches and kicks on. They tripped, elbowed and kneed him in the hallways, pushed him down stairs and spilled ink on his notebook. Loving to fight, they needed no pretext. During recess, they divided into gangs to hone their skills at injuring and humiliating each other, to feel the thrill of fist against face. Cun stayed out of these rumbles, but he couldn't dodge the after-school ambushes. There were days when he was too frightened to go to class.

During this period, there was a rash of deaths involving young children. Because of the low hydraulic pressure, people had to buy large jars to store water inside their houses. Kids liked to stand on chairs to look at their reflections inside these jars. They also liked the echoes of their own voices talking or singing that the jars produced. Playing these jar games, many kids ended up falling headfirst into the jars and drowning.

13 ◆ PARIS BY NIGHT

F acing economic disaster, the government allowed people to resume petty capitalism in 1986. Reopening her café, Kim Lan renamed it Paris by Night. That year she also had her second child, a baby girl. Hung Vuong Hospital was much dirtier than before, run-down, its equipment American leftovers from the war, its filthy hallways crowded with relatives of patients. Many people had come from the countryside because rural hospitals were in even worse shape. The nurses and doctors made so little that you had to tip them constantly if you expected them to perform their duties. Even traffic-accident victims were left to die if the medical staff wasn't tipped on time. Sen didn't want to take any chances. He tipped all those involved with his daughter's delivery twice the going rate. To Sen and Kim Lan, this daughter embodied all of their hopes for the future. They named her Hoa, which means both "flower" and "Chinese."

Business at the café was going extremely well, allowing Kim Lan and Sen to hire a servant to take care of the baby. They decided on A-Muoi, a Chinese-Vietnamese woman in her midforties. Sen had insisted on a Chinese babysitter so Hoa could hear and learn Chinese from the beginning. "You and your Chinese Chinese!" Kim Lan jeered at her husband before relenting. As always, she picked the ugliest domestic servant available. She preferred the bucktoothed, cross-eyed and level-chested. That way her man wouldn't be tempted to pounce on them in the middle of the night. That way they wouldn't disappear into a karaoke bar. She would have picked them old, but the old ones didn't work as hard. A-Muoi was as homely as they came. Plump, splayfooted and dragging a pair of pink plastic slippers around, she had a sullen, sweating face with a double-wide mouth filled with way too many teeth, none matching, in at least a dozen improbable colors. As she worked, she mumbled half-swallowed snippets of an ongoing soliloquy of self-pitying complaints. "Work, work, work," she would huff. As long as she never winked at Sen, Kim Lan was happy.

Cun was fifteen by now. He was listless and did badly in school. He hated history class because he didn't want to hear about how his father was a lackey for the bloodthirsty Americans. He cringed at photos of the My Lai massacre, like everybody else, but dismissed the story behind them as Communist propaganda. *They probably killed those people themselves.* He hated literature class because he couldn't stand having to memorize Ho Chi Minh's poems. He hated just sitting in a classroom because Ho's face was always smiling at him from high up on the wall. Above Ho's portrait was the slogan ALWAYS REMEMBER YOUR DEBT TO THE GREAT UNCLE HO.

In literature, they studied a 1979 poem by poet laureate To Huu:

> *A mother showed to her son*
> *A photo of Stalin next to a child*
> *His white shirt among pink clouds*
> *His eyes kind, his mouth smiling*
> *On a vast green field*
> *He stood next to a small child*
> *With a red kerchief around his neck*
> *With a common belief*
> *They looked towards the future*
> *O Stalin!*
> *How lovely it is to hear one's son*
> *Learn how to speak by calling out Stalin!*

Cun's literature teacher was a doe-eyed, slightly stooping woman in her late fifties who wore only black and white. Her thin white blouses were so worn out at the back, you could see her bra strap as she stood at the blackboard scratching her neat letters. Her black pants had become threadbare at the knees. The students joked that one day their teacher would just show up naked.

A spinster living with her ailing mother, she had never strayed beyond the suburbs of Saigon, though she loved to stare at any and all large, colorful maps, mooning over them in her spare moments. Seeing all seven continents at once always gave her a special thrill. It was as if she were perched high on a satellite, cheek by jowl with God, the first and last astronaut, with her arm around him, or even, God forbid, as if she were God himself. Far below, five billion-plus people were enduring their ridiculously petty yet murderous lives, hyperventilating or gnashing their teeth over the tiniest fears and aspirations. At such moments, she could forget her own tiniest fears and aspirations. God had left, she suddenly realized one day. Hungry, she peeled back the aluminum foil from her space dinner: one quarter of a freeze-dried chicken over rice with vegetables on the side. As she ate, she noticed with rancor that God had forgotten, again—how many times had it been?—to close the lid on the space commode, leaving his copious leavings to drift out and form a ghastly nimbus around her head.

She asked the class, "What is poetry that does not save nations or people?" Fifty-five faces stared at her blankly. Hearing not a peep in response, she provided the answer, "Poetry that does not save nations or people is a song of drunkards whose throats will be cut in a moment!" Baring her yellowed dentures, she sliced a crooked finger across her wrinkled neck while making a spine-tingling slurping sound. "And readings for shallow girls!" As an example of poetry that does save nations and people, she had the class read a To Huu poem about Marx:

Before He was born
The earth was wailing
Man was not human
A savage night lasting
Thousands of years
But from the day He stood up
The earth started to laugh
And mankind started to sing
The October song

Cun's history teacher was a young man with solid revolutionary credentials. His father had fought the French; his two brothers, the Americans. One brother was killed by ARVN troops during the last days of the war. Growing up poor in Lai Thieu, he studied by candlelight. Out of candles, he squatted under a flickering street lamp. Once he even tried placing fireflies in a jar, having read about the trick in some pamphlet. He now lived with his wife and four children in a rented room in Thi Nghe. The two youngest, aged one and three, slept with their parents on a bed. The two oldest, aged seven and nine, slept on a straw mat on the floor.

Glaring at Cun, the history teacher began a lecture, "The Saigon puppets loved the Americans, but the Americans hated them. The Saigon puppets worshipped a race that called them Gooks and rained bombs on their heads. The Saigon puppets were like animals the Americans raised to become meaty shields. Absorbing bullets, they spared the GIs from being wiped out even sooner by revolutionary troops. The Saigon puppets denied American atrocities that even the Americans admitted to. The entire world witnessed these monstrous crimes, and became even more aghast at the spectacle of the Saigon puppets abjectly denying everything. The Saigon puppets existed only to receive chump change from their American masters. . . ."

Cun had had only one direct contact with an American. When he was three, an American had come into his mom's café accompanied by a Vietnamese woman in a miniskirt. Well groomed, in civvies, he was twice her age and size. His prominent beak contrasted sharply with her bridgeless nose. Ignoring an iced plastic mug, he drank his beer straight from the can. When not shouting in sentence fragments, they communicated with exaggerated laughs, grins and grimaces. A housefly pinged against his lips, drawn to the hop-sweetened spittle. Beneath the table, their legs dallied awkwardly. Her bare calves clamped his pant leg for a moment, before a mosquito landed on his sockless, white ankle. Thrilled by this rare derma, it drilled its serrated proboscis into a fatty capillary, drank deeply, closed its eyes and sighed as its abdomen swelled to capacity. It needed this rich protein for its egg development. Nectar and fruit juice just wouldn't cut it. The American's blood tasted a bit like vanilla ice cream. As it sucked, the mosquito's spit lubricated the bite mark to lessen his victim's pain. Entering the bloodstream, malarial pathogens inside the saliva quickly reached the man's liver, where they could begin to search and destroy his liver cells. Staring at the couple, Cun tried to mimic their conversation. He said, "Woe me yo fat hotel!" He said, "Yo me boom boom cheap?" He repeated these two phrases around the house for more than a year, but gradually forgot about them as the novelty of speaking English finally wore off.

There was a girl in Cun's class who was rumored to be half American. She had a thin nose on a pink, freckled face that drove all the boys crazy. Her hair was chestnut brown, and she either tied it with a thin, bright ribbon or kept it braided. She dressed simply yet impeccably, betraying a sense of style no one else had. Shunning pastel colors, she preferred darker hues like maroon and indigo, which made her seem very grown-up and elegant. There was a small gap between her two front teeth, but that imperfection only added to her allure. Even the history teacher appeared moonstruck whenever she opened her mouth to speak. He always insisted that she sit in the middle of the front row, apparently so he could better admire her face. Once he even had to cut short one of his anti-American rants because it was clear the girl was about to cry. She used her mother's last name and whenever anyone asked her about her father, she'd only say, "He lives very far away."

"How come you're so pretty?"

"Because my mother is pretty, and my father is pretty, and my grandparents are pretty."

"But who's your father?"

"He lives very far away."

During recess, all the teachers sold snacks to make extra money. The literature teacher offered sugarcane cubes and pineapple chunks in plastic bags. The history teacher pushed pudding. In the evening, he diversified by peddling balloons of cartoon figures, Barney and Mickey Mouse, etc., up and down the street. As an entrepreneur, he was superfriendly toward everyone, even Cun. However phony, the common courtesy encouraged and enforced by capitalism did make life more tolerable. Like all parents, Kim Lan gave Cun money to give to his teachers to bump his grades up. Cun hated them so much, however, he always kept these bribes for himself. In the spring of 1987 he quit school over Kim Lan's weak objection. He decided he was going to spend the rest of his life sitting in his mother's café. From now on he would live life as painlessly as possible. To pass the time, he sipped iced coffee and chewed on one toothpick after another.

14 ✦ POETRY AND USURY

Renaming her café Paris by Night proved to be a stroke of genius for Kim Lan. The glamour it evoked attracted an entirely new class of clients. Aside from neighborhood people, the café became a magnet for poets and intellectuals. On any day, you could find a dozen poets, writers and hacks congregating at the different tables. Kim Lan knew little about this milieu, but she could recite half a dozen of Han Mac Tu's shortest poems by heart. Occasionally, she would join the poets at a table and perform, in a shrill, earnest voice, "Tears" or "Sleepless Night," her eyes shut tight with emotion. The poets dreaded these embarrassments, but they always applauded Kim Lan heartily afterward. Moved by her own voice, she nearly cried several times. The sight of Sen playing chess with some sucker also added to the intellectual atmosphere of Paris by Night. Cun had his own table where he could brood behind a bottle of root beer, talking to no one. With yellow music no longer banned, Kim Lan went out and bought cassettes of Trinh Cong Son's and Pham Duy's music. Khanh Ly's warm voice washed over her café, alternating with Thai Thanh's.

Fortified by Saigon beer, the poets chattered about life, love and literature, or they flirted with each other. One who came often was Nguyen Quoc Chanh. Bearded and a bit scruffy, he always wore the same pair of jeans and a faded indigo T-shirt. Chanh told Kim Lan he had just finished his first collection of poems, *Night of the Rising Sun.* "My mind was racing, sister. I stayed indoors almost continuously. Inside my darkened room, I scrawled pornographic images on the walls with a pencil. I was hopped up."

Another was Bui Chi Vinh, ex-combat soldier, solidly built, tall, in a crew cut, with the air of a gangster. Vinh's racket was the detective novel. "I write two hundred pages a week," he boasted to Kim Lan. "Most guys are lucky to sell five hundred copies of a book but each one of mine sells five thousand copies."

There were also women poets among them. One called herself Lynh Bacardi. Bespectacled with thick, rimless glasses, she was often seen in a red-and-black-plaid turtleneck and plaid skirt. Despite her name, she always drank whatever was available: gin, vodka, whiskey, rum, sake, or snake wine, often in combination, without showing the least sign of drunkenness. "It's a special gift," she said to Kim Lan once, smiling. Though she was half Kim Lan's age, Bacardi always used the pronoun "I" instead of "little sister," as was customary. She used "I" with all her elders, a fact that annoyed Kim Lan considerably. Kim Lan remembered with distaste the time Bacardi kissed Hoa on the eyelids and said, "You'll grow up to be a poet, won't you? We need more girl poets."

Sometimes the poets did get a little rowdy, though Kim Lan could never figure out what they were arguing about. Reading Han Mac Tu, she had assumed that poets were suffering creatures, frail individuals with wild hair, bad breath and worse skin, but she was wrong. The poets in front of her were quite happy, much happier than anyone else she knew, though they seemed to have no reason at all to be happy. They had neither money nor status and most of them couldn't even publish. Photocopying their poems, they distributed them in her café.

"The trick is to square first thought best thought with last word best word."

"Why enjamb if you don't want to sucker punch the reader?"

"You've got to see behind what's behind, man!"

"There's no self to excavate, don't you understand?"

"If you can't turn a poem inside out, then don't write poems!"

"Your problem, you see, is that you always write horizontal poems. You don't know how to go up or down. You should try a vertical poem every once in a while."

Occasionally a wild-haired, feverish-eyed old man came to sit with the poets. He'd speak incoherently in the foulest language, obsessing about how he wanted to fuck the actress Kim Cuong over and over, and how he was going to blow up Ho Chi Minh's mausoleum. Once or twice he came close to taking his clothes off. Each time she saw him, Kim Lan wanted to kick him out immediately, but the poets insisted that the madman was a famous poet, perhaps the most renowned in all of Saigon, that he was even a scholar and a translator of French and German. The poets told her she should feel honored to have someone of Bui Giang's stature in her establishment.

Bui Giang lived one of the more peculiar lives in twentieth-century Vietnam. Born in 1926, he'd grown up the scion of a wealthy family in Quang Nam, an arid province known for its egg-noodle soup and harsh accent. They owned lots of land and the only two-story house in the village. After graduating from high school in 1945, Bui Giang stayed in Quang Nam to marry his sweetheart and to raise goats. He had over a hundred animals, most of whom he knew by name. Already there were alarming and charming signs of his eccentricity. He followed his goats into the hillside each morning, holding a thick French book, according to the peasants who saw him, and was led back into town by his flock each evening. Weaving garlands of wild flowers to drape around the necks of his beloved goats, he never sold or slaughtered any of them, but only squeezed a glass of goat milk each morning to give to his young wife. In 1949, Bui Giang joined the anticolonial resistance. He lived in the jungles for two years and fought the French. In 1956, disaster struck: His wife died at the age of twenty-six after an illness. Bui Giang finally left Quang Nam to move to Saigon. There he

wrote many poems and befriended all the leading Saigon intellectuals of his time. The celebrated and sneaky Trinh Cong Son even
stole a couple of lines from him. Already fluent in French, he taught
himself German, translated Heidegger and wrote a two-volume
study of the existentialist philosopher. He also translated Camus,
André Gide, René Char and Antoine de Saint-Exupéry's *Le Petit
Prince*. He wrote about Sartre, Confucius, Lao-tzu, Gandhi and the
classical poets Nguyen Du and Huyen Thanh Quan. In 1965 his
house burned down, destroying all of his manuscripts. By his own
admission, he started to become "brilliantly mad" in 1969. Though
he never went abroad, he explored all of southern Vietnam with the
curiosity and appetite of a foreign adventurer. He sampled the
whores in each town but never remarried, so as not to desecrate the
memory of his dead wife. He complained of catching the clap in
Cho Lon and bragged that a hotel owner in Long Xuyen gave him
free lodging "with all amenities." After 1975 he slept in a squalid
shack next to a fetid pond. He knew all of Saigon's neighborhoods
intimately and wandered its meandering streets and alleys like the
city's lost soul. He wrote:

> *You who return centuries later*
> *See if the moon still retains its color*

The café was not Kim Lan's only source of income. She also lent
money at 20 percent interest a month, a rather mild, humane rate,
much less than the 50 percent charged by some. It was still a messy
and ugly business. Kim Lan only lent to people she knew well. That
year she bought a motorbike—a Honda Dream, the latest and most
expensive model—and hired another servant. As always, Saigon was
awash with girls from the countryside trying to find work as
domestic servants. Kim Lan didn't have much to do but go food
shopping in the morning then look after the till the rest of the day.
Those two tasks could not be assigned to servants because she didn't

trust them with her money. She also didn't trust them to pick the right groceries at the market. The merchants had so many tricks to fool the unsuspecting shopper. They rubbed blood under fish gills and turmeric on chicken to make them appear freshly killed. They sold cotton pods as black peppers and buffalo meat as beef. Further, a servant could not be expected to fritter away her brief span on this earth by shrewdly, intensely haggling with someone else's money.

In her free moments, Kim Lan played with Hoa. Hoa was everything Cun was not: a beautiful, alert child who radiated intelligence. She was open to the world and easy to feed, unlike Cun, who still refused many foods even as a teenager. Hoa could be amused by the simplest things: a large leaf, the rain, geckos on the wall. She laughed constantly and danced whenever she heard music.

On Hoa's first birthday, Kim Lan placed a pen, a ruler, a set of keys, money, a lump of clay, scissors, a mirror, a ball of sticky rice and a pack of playing cards in a basket for her daughter to choose. If Hoa chose the scissors, for example, she would grow up to be a seamstress; the playing cards, she would be addicted to gambling. Leaning over the basket and nearly falling into it, Hoa took a long time deciding before picking up the lump of clay, meaning she would mature into a mud-smeared peasant. Some parents would have spun this into an indication that their child would own land or become a real estate agent. Unhappy with the peasant prognosis, Kim Lan cheated and allowed her daughter a second dip. This time Hoa plucked the keys from the pile, meaning she would become a businesswoman. *She'll buy and sell and make lots of money*, Kim Lan smiled. *She'll take good care of me in my old age.*

15 ◆ DEAREST WIFE

January 5, 1988

My Dearest Wife,

I miss you and Cun very much. Don't despair! I know how difficult life must be for you now, but you must fight to keep your composure and be patient. Don't worry about me too much. I think about you every second of every day and am only kept alive by the thought that I will be able to hug you and kiss you again one day. If not for this happy dream, I would have already killed myself. Saigon seems like a dream, but I know I will survive this ordeal to one day see it again. They told me the train is running every day now and in fact some of the other prisoners have already received visits from their loved ones. If you can afford it you must come to see me immediately. Buy a third-class ticket, it is not expensive, and please bring me the following items, if you can afford them:

Vitamin pills
Cold medicine
Malaria pills
Toothpaste
Toothbrush
Paper and pens
Soap
Detergent
Underwear—only briefs, not boxer shorts! Briefs will keep my testicles from sagging, as I do hard labor.

Sesame salt

A thick blanket

Sweaters—make sure they're long sleeved. It's very cold here.

A knit cap

A raincoat

Dried fish

Shredded pork

Tea

Coffee—to be drunk only on special occasions.

Cigarettes—the best kind, to bribe the wardens.

Bandages

Nail clippers

Powdered soybean

Sugar

Instant noodles—I can even eat these raw when I'm out in the fields doing hard labor.

Red-grained rice—it's more nutritious than regular rice.

Bread—cut the bread into slices, dry them in the sun, then place them in plastic bags. I can steam the bread later. I'll eat the bread for breakfast. It's easier and quicker to prepare than cooking up a pot of rice.

Ginger—so I can drink it with tea, to keep from getting a cold.

Pork stew

Toilet paper

Sandals

Slippers

Socks—very thick. It's very cold here.

Pajamas

Slacks

Dried banana

Dried onions

Dried garlic—to keep from getting a cold.

Dried chili peppers—to keep warm in winter.

Black peppers

Cookies
Candied fruits
Soy sauce
Fish sauce
Fresh cabbage

Please bring all these things to me as soon as you can. Don't leave any-thing out. I'd not have listed any item if it wasn't absolutely necessary. Please know that I think of you night and day. Soon I will be able to come home and we can start our lives together again. In fact, it will be better than before because I won't have to go off to war. I will be able to stay home with you all the time. Do not lose heart.

Being here has allowed me to reflect on many things. I realize that I haven't always been an ideal husband. I promise I will make it up to you when I return. I love you very much, Kim Lan.

Your husband,

Hoang Long
Ha Nam Ninh Reeducation Camp
Ha Nam Province

16 ♦ UNEXPLAINED PORK STEW

While Kim Lan read Hoang Long's letter, Sen sat at his usual table. He had just sacrificed a rook and a knight to corner his opponent's queen. Focused on this imminent triumph, he never noticed his wife's agonized face. As usual, the poets were arguing and Khanh Ly was singing Trinh Cong Son's lyrics:

Which grain of dust became my flesh
To blossom and rise up someday
O marvelous sand and dust
The sun lights a wandering fate

The very next day, Kim Lan went out to buy all the items on Hoang Long's list. It took her two days to finish shopping. So as not to arouse Sen's suspicion, she kept everything at a neighbor's house. She also went downtown to buy two round-trip train tickets to Hanoi, first class, two sleeping berths to a compartment. Knowing she would have to spend forty-eight hours on the train each way, she didn't want to risk sleeping with strangers in a six-berth compartment, not with all the valuable things she had to bring her husband. The most precious was a tight wad of money stuffed into a plastic pouch, then inserted into a stinking jar of fermented shrimp paste. No warden would stick his fingers into fermented shrimp paste, she reasoned, to search for contraband. She didn't forget to dry the sliced bread and stew a potful of pork, with extra salt so it would keep longer. When everything was ready to go, Kim Lan announced to Sen that she and Cun had to go to Phan Thiet for an aunt's funeral. They would be gone for eight days because she needed to catch up with her relatives in the Phan Thiet area. Sen had seen Kim Lan make that pork stew, which he never got to eat. *Now why would my wife take pork stew to a funeral?*

17 ◆ IF JACK KEROUAC WERE VIETNAMESE

There was little passenger train travel in the North and South during the war. The railways were constantly sabotaged by all sides during that long conflict, with practically all the bridges and tunnels bombed or blown up at one time or another. Kim Lan and Cun hefted their two bags onto the train, then entered a small cubicle that would be their home for the next forty-eight hours. They discovered a tiny oscillating fan bolted onto the ceiling, a table folding neatly into the wall, and a sink inside a cabinet. When Cun turned the tap, water actually came out. The relative luxuries of a first-class compartment made them giddy and took the edge off their mission. Neither one had been on a train before. Feeling strangely relieved, they were only vaguely conscious that this lightness came from having idleness forced upon them. For the next two days they would have to make no decisions.

The train lurched along with a tremendous racket, but the service was fine. Not expecting meals with their tickets, they were pleasantly surprised to be fed three times a day: rice with stewed pork, deep-fried tofu, vegetables, noodle soups and fruit. Each compartment had its own thermos, tea pot and cups. The view out the window was blocked by a screen mesh. The conductor explained that children had been throwing rocks at train windows. The screen mesh also kept thieves from climbing in at the stations. As if to frighten them further, he told them that sometimes thieves rode on top of the train, waiting for an opportunity to snatch a watch or a necklace through an open window. "In short," he scowled, "don't open that screen mesh!"

Feeling dizzy from the train's motions, Cun untwisted a jar of Tiger Balm and rubbed the ointment on his temples and under his nose. Breathing in deeply the scents of cajeput, camphor, mint and menthol, he leaned back and stared through the screen mesh at billboards, rice paddies, buffaloes, peasants, shacks and schoolgirls in *ao dais* riding home on their bicycles. Soon he got tired of it. Climbing to the top bunk to lie down, he noticed a book lying facedown in a corner. His first instinct was to throw it away or burn it, but then he saw a bikinied beauty on its shiny cover. He opened the book, hoping to find more half-nude women. The language was foreign to him, but then all language was foreign to him. Looking over Cun's bony shoulder, we can see that it's a Lonesome Globe *Guide to Vietnam*, first edition, 1987. Let's read a sample page: *Vietnam is a thin, long country, with the railroad serving as its spine. One either goes up or down, with little interior to explore. If Jack Kerouac were Vietnamese, he would have had more or less one road to wander. The lush green mountains are populated by tribes, with the Vietnamese confined mostly to the coast. With such a long, lovely coastline, one would assume that the Vietnamese are a great seafaring people, but the sea has yielded only anchovies and foreign invasions, and there have been no Vietnamese explorers, only a few world-class wanderers like Ho Chi Minh. Fearful of discoveries, timid and sluggish, the Vietnamese dare not scour the earth to spread their ceramics, coins and semen. While other peoples sing of the open road, write picaresque novels and make road movies, Vietnamese sing of going home, although most of them have never left home in the first place. A Vietnamese can feel homesick in the very house he was born in. Just look at the one sitting next to you, for example. He's already homesick, ten minutes into his first train ride. Leaving home is depicted in songs and popular literature as a grave misfortune, a curse that happens only under duress, never an opportunity. But the aftermath of the Vietnam War, and not the war itself, has finally scattered Vietnamese across the globe, forcing a people loath to emigrate into relocating to majestic, pristine Norway or exciting Israel . . . one can even get a decent spring roll nowadays in exotic Vladivostok or sunny Ajaccio. (See our catalog for the most reliable guidebooks to these marvelous destinations.) To Vietnamese overseas, the Fall of Saigon is a black day in their history, marked by a solemn ceremony every year. (Inside the country, some people have also inverted the term* giai phong—*meaning "liberation," as in "the liberation of Saigon"—into* phong giai, *meaning having your crotch burned.) Yet even after living in California for thirty years, for example, Vietnamese still sigh about being homesick, although most of them are so Americanized they would never go back to Vietnam to live. Most of them are so Californian they would never leave California. The country that many Vietnamese long for is a kitsch, mythical Vietnam of smiling peasants, gentle mothers, and flute-playing boys perched on water buffaloes. Perhaps an idealized, Platonic Vietnam, however poorly imagined, is a necessary mental anchor because the country itself is constantly being deformed, reformed and disintegrated. Steered against their will, hijacked, Vietnamese speak often of having lost their country.*

That night, lying on the top bunk, Cun thought about the upcoming meeting with his father, a man he had no visual memories of. From the photos, his old man didn't look that much different from how Cun looked now: the same short arms and legs, the same dark skin, the same smirk. But there was a difference. Whereas Cun always tried to make himself smaller, to shrink into the most compact shape possible, Hoang Long projected his small frame onto life as if he were a giant. Cun thought of his father's cockiness as tragically misplaced. It would have been better to be a coward like Sen, to just sit out the war and play chess. And yet, there was something about his dad's suicidal boldness that was inspiring. Bunching his fists, with his lips peeled back into a frightful rictus, Cun imagined himself charging into combat. He'd scream obscenities and shoot in a wide arc at everything that was in the way—men, plants and animals. He'd mow everything down—he was born to kill! The enemy's frisky bullets merely fanned and tickled him. Suddenly his mom murmured, disrupting his reveries.

Cun leaned over the edge to stare down at his mother's face: She was talking in her sleep. Stray strands of hair fluttered across her troubled forehead. He couldn't remember the last time he had seen his mother, or any woman, for that matter, sleeping. Writhing and cooing, Kim Lan was revisiting her wedding night in her dream. This time, however, her arms and legs would not get in the way. She would yield to him more readily because she knew what to expect now, and he was going to prison right afterward.

"You must take care of yourself," she said between sobs and babyish love sounds.

"Don't worry. I'll use my time in prison to study English so I can translate the US Constitution."

"You're so brilliant!"

"No, you're the brilliant one. You've changed, Kim Lan." His voice became uncharacteristically tender. "You're no longer lying still like a piece of wood."

"I wish you hadn't said that," she grimaced. "But don't worry. I will never lie still like a piece of wood ever again."

Cun could only hear half of the conversation. His mom's chest heaved with each audible breath. He saw nice even teeth like corn kernels between slightly parted lips. She has nice hands, he noticed. He felt intrusive, guilty, as if he had already done something wrong. As his blood surged upward in pulsing waves, he forced himself to avert his gaze but, only seconds later, was compelled to stare down again at her dim, soft form lying under the thin blanket. She lay quiet and motionless now. As the heavy train lunged forward through the deep dark, he clutched himself with a frantic rhythm. As it rumbled past a darkened Hoi An, he finally emptied his first clip.

18 ✦ THE DUMPSTER OF HISTORY

The earth spun rapidly backward as the train rolled forward. It was near midnight when they entered Hanoi, three hours behind schedule. Houses were built so close to the tracks, they could look into windows and see families sprawled on floors, watching TVs. They could make out numbers on calendars, consult astrological charts. They saw an old man bent over a desk, straining to read fading definitions in an out-of-print dictionary. They saw a naked girl or the ghost of a naked girl standing on a dark balcony. Had they wanted to, they could have reached out and slapped someone standing by the tracks, knocking glasses and false teeth into the next province.

To travel from Saigon to Hanoi is to go back in time. The navel of Vietnamese civilization, a place of ancestors, Hanoi is haunted by a thousand heroes, tyrants and poets. It first became the capital in 1010. By contrast, Saigon is only three hundred years old. The main stage for much of Vietnamese history, Hanoi is also its dustbin. So much has happened there only to be ignored, distorted, or forgotten. Entire centuries reduced to hearsay and ashes. Perhaps one should call Hanoi a dumpster. Cun and Kim Lan had come to this dumpster to see what was left of Hoang Long.

As they prepared for their arrival, a man poked his head into their compartment. "Sister, do me a favor. Please give me your used tickets. You won't need them anymore."

"What do you need our tickets for?" Kim Lan asked.

"I'm traveling on government business and bought a third-class ticket, hard berth, very uncomfortable. I slept sitting up for two nights in a row. My neck aches, my back aches, I'm too old for this. But if you help me out, I can get reimbursed for a first-class ticket."

"Why do you need two?"

"I'm traveling with a colleague, sister."

Kim Lan handed him their tickets. Stepping off the train, the first thing they noticed was the extreme cold. Now they knew what Hoang Long was talking about. Even in their thick sweaters, it felt as if they had been dunked into ice water. Outside the station, they looked for shops to buy extra sweaters, but found nothing. They had no choice but to endure the cold and go search for a hotel. You would think there would be hotels near the train station, but, no, there was nothing. They looked for a cyclo, but all had been taken by the other passengers. Lugging their heavy bags, they trudged down the empty street, hoping something would turn up sooner or later. Already Cun was becoming a little angry at his mother for placing him in this ridiculous situation.

After a minute, they paused to take a break at a traffic circle. There were no vehicles in any direction. The exertion had not made them feel any warmer. Penetrating their clothes, the wind swirling through the open space made the temperature drop to antarctic levels. Overhead, sooty leaves shuddered on tinderlike branches, lit by an orange light. A piece of trash skipped down the street. A stray dog, its fur nappy with grime and disease, peeked at them from a blind alley. Nothing else moved. Their skin and lips were chapped, their mouths breathed out cold, they felt exposed, naked. They looked in all directions for signs of a hotel or a restaurant, but saw nothing. It made no sense to walk down any of these streets because as far as the eye could see, there was no place, there was nothing at all, where they could go inside. On the point of panic, Kim Lan and Cun heard a male voice from behind them. "Are you lost?"

A man of about fifty had appeared out of nowhere. Just seconds before, there had been no one on that street.

"We just got off the train, half an hour ago."

"Where do you want to go?"

"A hotel. Any hotel."

"It's past midnight already. You won't find a hotel in this neighborhood."

Not knowing what else to say, Kim Lan and Cun simply stared at the stranger.

"I live right here." The man pointed at the house right behind him. "You're welcome to stay with me tonight if you want."

They gratefully accepted. Inside, the stranger handed them blankets and indicated the bathroom, but said nothing else. They lay on the floor while he slept on the bed, in the same room, behind a plywood partition. All night long they heard him snore.

Just before sunrise, Kim Lan heard him boil water for tea. He even went out and ordered three bowls of *pho*, beef soup, from a street vendor. Never before had Kim Lan or Cun met so kind a stranger. The man obviously lived alone. They noticed dozens of watercolors taped to the walls. He painted all subjects: landscapes and famous buildings copied from postcards, nudes sketched from glamour magazines, everything carefully rendered with an earnest, sweet innocence. There was a Sophia Loren in the buff, next to a gleaming Taj Mahal, next to a solemn Mount Rainier. He did have a funny-looking face, however, sort of like a cock's, complete with a beak and a flaming, palmate crest twice as large as the rest of his head.

Slurping the beef soup, Kim Lan said, "Thanks for allowing us to stay in your house. You saved us!"

"Saved you from what?! It was nothing!"

"We would have died of the cold. We were freezing when you found us."

"What cold? This is not cold! Nineteen sixty-seven was cold!"

"You have an excellent memory, brother. I can't even remember what the weather was like last weekend, whether it was rainy or sunny."

"That's because there's no weather in the South—you're from Ho Chi Minh City, no?—Ho Chi Minh City has no weather."

"Have you been to Saigon?"

"No, but I was up and down the Ho Chi Minh Trail during the war. I know the South: The South has no weather."

"What about the monsoon?"

"What monsoon? I don't remember any monsoon in the South, the South has no weather."

They ate in silence for a minute before the Cock said, "Is this your first visit to Hanoi?"

"Yes, I'm here to visit my husband."

"Is he working up this way?"

"No, he's in prison."

"So he's being reeducated?"

"Yes, he's in prison."

"There's nothing wrong with that, sister. Don't be ashamed. It's good to be reeducated. I can't blame your husband for being duped into serving the American imperialists and betraying his own country. He'll be a good citizen soon. You want to see something?"

"What?"

As Kim Lan and Cun watched, the Cock slowly rolled up his trouser legs. "A mine," he said. "A Bouncing Betty, it's called. Killed the guy right in front of me. Made ground meat out of him while it cut me in half. But what am I doing?! We're eating breakfast, after all! I'm sorry!"

The Cock had walked so naturally, they never suspected he wore prosthetics. "But I have nothing against the ARVN soldiers," he continued. "When your husband is done with being reeducated, bring him here and I'll throw him a party. I really mean it. I'll kill a chicken or two for him. We'll drink some rice wine together. Just knock on my door at any time. Even ten years later! Even twenty years later!"

After his guests had left, the Cock would think often about this visit. He rarely had company. Kim Lan's tense, white face when he showed her his stumps had moved him tremendously. He had never rolled up his trouser legs in front of another person before. Even after two decades, he was still not used to the fact that he had actually lost half of his body. He would ponder how lizards could regenerate their tails. He also knew that salamanders could regrow their limbs and that a worm cut in ten pieces will become ten worms. But he was not a lizard, salamander or worm. A head and a trunk were all you needed, he realized. Anything that stuck out of the head or trunk, such as the nose, ears, arms, or legs, even the lower jaw, was actually expendable.

19 ◆ WAFTS OF DECAY

Ha Nam Ninh Reeducation Camp was about forty-five miles south of Hanoi, in Ha Nam Province. After leaving the Cock's home, Kim Lan and Cun went back to the station to board a train for Phu Ly, the chief town of Ha Nam. The town was not known for much. Most of it had been razed by American bombs during the war. There was a traditional wrestling tournament held there with much pomp and ceremony each January. There was a small Buddhist temple dating back to the twelfth century. In 1985, a student from a local school had won second place in the national penmanship contest.

On the train, Kim Lan overheard a few women speaking with southern accents. Unlike the other passengers, they seemed subdued, cheerless. Only their children looked excitedly out the windows. They all had bulging bags next to them.

"Excuse me, but are you from the South?" Kim Lan asked them in a hushed, conspiratorial voice.

"Yes," they all answered.

"Are you visiting relatives?"

"My husband, he's in the camp."

"Me, too."

"I'm visiting my son."

"I'm visiting my brother."

"Is this your first time?" Kim Lan asked.

"No, I come every year. This is my third time."

"This is my fourth."

"This is my second. How about you?"

"My first time," Kim Lan said, feeling apologetic. "I received a letter from my husband only a few days ago."

"You just found out he's up here?!"

"Yes."

"What's your husband's rank?"

"Captain."

"That doesn't sound right, sister. He should be out by now if he was only a captain."

At Phu Ly station, the prisoners' relatives numbered nearly thirty, with many children among them. Squatting on the floor, they waited three hours before an army truck came to take them away. The ride down a bumpy road took another hour. They could not enter the camp itself, of course, but had to sleep in a small house outside the gate. Their men would be brought to them early the next morning.

There were not enough pallets inside the guesthouse, so many people had to double up that night. Many slept on woven mats on the floor. Without blankets, Cun and Kim Lan had to clutch each other all night to keep from freezing. Kim Lan couldn't sleep anyway. Her mind was filled with tender thoughts for Hoang Long. Sen seemed very far away, nearly unimaginable. Knowing that she would see Hoang Long's face the very next morning made her think back to their happiest moments together. Most of these preceded their wedding. She also thought of the wedding reception, when everything was still perfect, before everything had been ruined.

In the morning, the prisoners' relatives stood outside the guesthouse to await the arrival of the men. Everyone tried to remain stoic as thirteen ragged figures approached from afar, accompanied by nine guards. The prisoners' daily ration was two small bowls of rice with bits of vegetables and a cup of water, less for those who had committed infractions. Scraps of meat were reserved for special occasions such as Uncle Ho's birthday. The prisoners craved protein so much, some of them even swallowed cockroaches, when a cockroach could be found. Bliss was snagging a rare frog or a field rat, which they butchered with the improvised knives everyone had learned how to fashion. Harassed night and day by this vicious hunger, they grew to hate their own stomachs. If only a man could exist without a belly, and experience life with just his eyes, existence would be so much less of an ordeal. Maybe that's what heaven would be like. You lying under that warm blanket—yes, you, my friend—may you get to sample cockroaches and field rats someday. The constant thirst was just as bad as the relentless hunger. Only when it rained did they get extra water to drink and wash. Instead of toilet paper, they used torn-up banana leaves. Smooth and cool, they weren't a bad substitution. They also used whiskers from cornstalks. At night, lying in comfortless rows, sexless, cursing, bantering or singing half-remembered songs, they became food for centipedes and whistling, won't-quit mosquitoes. Whoever died from overwork, beating or suicide was buried at the edge of the forest wrapped in a burlap sack, without his family having been notified. Seeing her son, an old lady suddenly started to wail. "My son! My son! It's your mother!" A little girl then ran toward her father, screaming, "Dad! Dad! Dad! Dad!" Hoang Long was so dark and haggard, half his hair turned white, that Kim Lan only recognized him when he waved and called out her name. By the time they had gone inside to sit down, she and Cun were sobbing convulsively. Hoang Long was not crying at all. None of the prisoners were crying. Hoang Long held his wife's and son's hands across the table and sternly said, "Stop crying. We only have fifteen minutes to talk."

As soon as he opened his mouth, they could see that he had no front teeth left. They had either been knocked out or had rotted off. His remaining teeth were surely rotting because wafts of decay were issuing from his black hole of a mouth, with red sores gashing the corners. His skin was cracked and barklike to the touch. Confronting this, Cun felt pity and sadness initially—the shock of seeing his old man a wretched prisoner was overwhelming—but these emotions were quickly supplanted by fear and resentment. His father's survival status and residual strength, as embodied by his steady gaze and oddly arrogant speech, rebuked and challenged him. There were defiance and admonition even in the old man's bad breath and in the wiry strands of black and white hair jutting from his nostrils. For his part, Hoang Long had been disgusted by Cun's sobbing jag. He noted that his son either listed to one side or slumped forward. All his bones seemed made of rubber. His eyes were unfocused, cloudy, as if recycled from the cheapest plastic, and his thin neck was like a dry stem under a dead sunflower, swaying in the breeze. *Give this kid a rifle and he'd shoot his own foot*, Hoang Long thought. By the age of seventeen, his son's age, Hoang Long was already a soldier. Embarrassed by Cun, Hoang Long felt redeemed, on the other hand, by Kim Lan. His wife had lost none of her beauty, but had only become more elegant with age. Now his captors, the guards, could finally see what sort of a man *he* was. The three of them tried to squeeze fourteen years into fifteen minutes. Kim Lan said that the café had reopened and business was excellent. Cun lied that he was still in school and doing well with his studies.

"Do you know when you might be released?" Kim Lan asked.

"I have no idea."

"I talked to some women on the train. They told me that, as a captain, you should be out already."

"Well, I'm still here, am I not? They can keep you as long as they like."

She had noticed his bare neck, but it took her a moment before she realized what was wrong with it. "Do you still have your amulet?"

"My what?!"

"The Cambodian amulet." She lowered her voice to a conspiratorial whisper. "That cobra's fang I got you to keep you from harm?"

"If it had worked," he raised his voice testily, "I wouldn't be rotting in prison, would I?" He then added under his breath, "It's gone, in any case. They've taken it."

"You should always cooperate with them, dear, so they'll let you out sooner."

He cringed. "What do you mean by cooperate? And since when have you become an expert on the ins and outs of life in prison?!"

"I know you. I know how stubborn you can be. It kills me to see you in prison like this. I just want you to be released soon."

Hoang Long thought it odd that his wife did not say, "I want to see you *home* soon," only, "I just want you to be released soon." He stared hard into her eyes and said, "Have you met someone else?"

"No! No! Of course not!"

Hoang Long turned to Cun. "Is your mom telling the truth?"

"No! I mean yes! Of course she's telling the truth! And I mean no! She hasn't met anyone!"

Hoang Long looked at Kim Lan, his eyes cold. "What's wrong with this kid? Can't he talk?"

"He's telling the truth, and I'm telling the truth. I have no one in this life but you."

As Kim Lan was trying to think of what else to say, a guard announced that the visiting period was over. Hoang Long stood up and leaned awkwardly across the table to give Kim Lan a kiss. It was the first time he had ever kissed her on the lips.

20 ◆ INESCAPABLE ASS KISSING

After his wife and son had left, Hoang Long opened the two bags and found each of the forty-four items he had asked for. Nothing was missing. He put on a sweater and the knit cap, then sniffed the coffee, tea and bar of soap. As he held the jar of pork stew in his hands, his eyes brimmed with tears. He hadn't eaten pork stew, his favorite comfort food, in fourteen years. He also noticed something he hadn't asked for: a jar of fermented shrimp paste. Fermented shrimp paste is used as a dip for boiled pork. Purplish gray, it tastes great—once you get the hang of it—but it smells like garbage. Fermented seafood is inevitable in a tropical country with a long coastline. The ability to eat fermented seafood separates real Vietnamese from fake Vietnamese. In Vietnamese restaurants overseas, fermented seafood is often left off the menu. Vietnamese traveling overseas are routinely warned against bringing fermented seafood aboard an airplane, lest a leaky jar give the whole country a bad name. Hoang Long loved all types of fermented seafood, but he was willing to sacrifice this jar. Without hesitation, he went to the head warden to give it to him as a gift.

"What the hell is this?"

"Fermented shrimp paste from Chau Doc, sir. My wife told me she wants you to try it!"

It pained Hoang Long to have to call this asshole sir, but the guy was in charge of the whole stinking joint and could determine when a prisoner would go home. It had taken Hoang Long forever to learn how to kiss ass in prison. He hated everything about his captors, from their hard, humorless faces to their catchphrases and jargon—their vocabulary, in general—to their heavy northern accent, the way they turned l's into n's, which he had even hated when it came from the mouths of his own soldiers during the war. During his first few years inside, he'd talked back to the wardens, provoking savage beatings and long stints in solitary confinement. He jeered at other prisoners for being submissive and spat on the ground as he walked by them. His contempt was visceral and vindictive and many inmates despised him in return. Others stayed away from the angry man because he was a liability. Their shared hardship, frustration, danger and uncertainty were not alleviated by much comradeship, as in wartime, since in prison they were encouraged daily to turn on each other. As a final condition of release, a prisoner was always asked to snitch on his peers—to finger those he considered not yet reformed. On the cusp of freedom, with home and wife only a train ride away, many inmates had not hesitated to single out Hoang Long. This was one reason he was still a prisoner after all these years, when many ARVN officers of higher rank had already been released.

At first, Hoang Long only understood the cruel irony of being in prison: Your enemies are finally out in the open, but you're not allowed to shoot them. All of the wardens were sadistic assholes, he soon found out; even the cook was an asshole, so he felt justified in having spent so much of his life trying to kill them. *These men exist primarily as dispensers of pain*, he thought. *They may give some meager bits of pleasure to their wives and children, but I seriously doubt it. Each time I killed one of them, I lowered the pain quotient in the world. And if, occasionally, a stray bullet struck a child or a peasant, so what? You can't go through life without breaking a bottle or two, no use crying over spilled soya. The bottom line: For every innocent I killed, I must have improved this earth immeasurably by getting rid of bad guys while also helping to control its runaway population. Who needs five billion people anyway? It's not how many souls there are, stupid, it's the quality of life they enjoy. Just think of all the gasoline consumed and gastrointestinal gas emitted each and every second by each individual asshole, eating away the ozone layer and the quality of life for the rest of us.* But as the wardens continued to beat him senseless, Hoang Long finally began to see prison as a reprieve—an act of mercy bestowed by a deadly enemy.

The objective, then as now, as ever, was not just to survive, but to outlast your enemies *and* your comrades, to witness death, to mourn, even, at least a little, with true feeling, before you yourself went under.

The head warden was a pissy guy with an enormous dried prune for a head. His grinning charges were always bringing him gifts, all sorts of foodstuffs, packs of cigarettes, articles of clothing, even an original poem once or twice, but no one had ever presented him with a jar of fermented shrimp paste. Rotating it in his right hand, the warden remembered the odd gleam in Hoang Long's eyes and thought: *This maggot is fucking with me. He's giving me a stinky jar of fermented shrimp paste as a way of saying, You stink! Well, if I stink this bad, I'll make sure he rots in prison.*

That evening, the warden's wife discovered the money hidden inside the fermented shrimp paste. She smoothed out the creases and counted it twice. From every bill, of every denomination, Uncle Ho's face smiled back at her approvingly. *A nice round sum*, she sighed, her face suddenly angelic. Instead of showing it to her husband, she kept it for herself. There were so many things she needed to buy and he never gave her enough money.

Respecting her husband's job, the warden's wife understood that the puppet troops needed to be reeducated to function in a socialist society, but she still worried about some of the things he did to them. To atone for his sins, she had decided to become a vegetarian, abstaining even from milk and eggs. To make up for these deprivations, however, she bought handbags and clothes compulsively. It is not easy being a warden's wife.

21 ◆ GOING HOME

The head warden called Hoang Long to his office. "I have a surprise for you, Hoang Long. You're released."

Hoang Long stared at the dried prune for signs of a practical joke but saw nothing. The man was apparently serious. Not wanting to risk changing the head warden's mind, he asked no questions, but mumbled in his most humble voice, "I thank you, sir."

"You've made good progress and that's why I'm releasing you. You used to be a real asshole, but you've changed. After you gave me that shrimp paste, I thought, *Is this asshole fucking with me?* Were you fucking with me, Hoang Long?"

"No, sir. I would never dare."

"Of course not. You'd never dare because you've been reeducated. You're a socialist citizen now. I've cured the assholeness out of you. It took a while, but I've cured you."

"I thank you, sir."

"And you should. You're one of the toughest rehab cases I've ever had. I should have just shot you a few years ago, buried you in an unmarked grave, turned you into horseshit. I really should have."

"I'm glad you didn't, sir."

"So am I, actually. You're living proof that even an extreme asshole can be rehabilitated. But enough of this chattering! Here's a train ticket to Saigon. If you hop on the truck waiting by the gate, you can catch the overnight train and be with your wife and son by tomorrow morning."

"Tomorrow morning?!"

"Yes, tomorrow morning. I didn't like that exclamation in your voice just now. Are you being sarcastic with me? I'm putting you on the express train, Hoang Long. After all these years, you still refuse to give this government, and socialism, enough credit," he shook his head, frowning, sending shivers up Hoang Long's spine. The prisoner was ready to kneel down and beg. "Now get out of here before I change my mind."

"I thank you, sir!"

The truck took Hoang Long and a handful of other released inmates to Phu Ly station. There they boarded a local train for Hanoi. By midnight, they were on the express heading toward Saigon. No one complained about having to sit on hard benches in a third-class carriage. Pumped by the shift in their fortunes, they stayed up all night to chatter or simply to stare at their compartment, steal an anguished glance at a dozing female nearby, or gaze out the windows at a darkened landscape enlivened sporadically by dim orange lights. It was as if they were afraid to fall asleep, wake up and find themselves back in prison. Each passing mile brought them closer to home. Once they saw and heard a series of explosions on a hillside, accompanied by tracer bullets and the unmistakable pop-pops of small arms fire. They exchanged confused, excited looks. "Is it us?" someone asked, but no one knew the answer.

Suddenly a sleeping girl opened her eyes and caught Hoang Long staring at her. Instead of becoming angry, she actually smiled at him, her face radiant and serene, seemingly relieved, as if she had mistaken him for a lover or, even more improbably, had just been dreaming about him. Whether intentional or accidental, this intimacy between them lasted but a few seconds, for she lapsed into sleep again, a development that caused Hoang Long to feel a maudlin, abject pain filled with inexplicable regret. Dawn broke as they entered the suburbs of their beloved city. Heating up slowly, the pale sunlight angled in on their brightened faces. All the old buildings looked exactly the same. Nothing had changed. They saw slim girls in white *ao dais* riding their bicycles to school. At numerous sidewalk cafés, men drank coffee and smoked. The train lumbered into the station. They got off, walked outside and saw that the clock tower over Ben Thanh Market had become colossal in the intervening years. They couldn't remember it ever looking that grand. Upon parting, the men promised to get together soon for a proper celebration.

From his cyclo, Hoang Long could see the sign for the Kim Long Café coming into view. The painted golden dragon was as gaudy as ever. The almond tree stood leafy. Everything looked exactly the same. If Kim Lan had remarried, if she had lied to him, then he would find out now. Walking in, he saw her serving a customer, the antiwar idiot, what's-his-name. His wife looked gorgeous, even from behind. He sneaked up and hugged her suddenly, startling her into screaming in a voice at least an octave too low, "What the fuck, Hoang Long! Are you trying to fuck me up the ass again?!"

He opened his eyes to find his arms wrapped around Tung, his hard-on sprung against the other prisoner's back, his new blanket draped against his ankles. All around him, dozens of men lay shivering under burlap sacks. The cold was inhuman.

22 ✦ A CYCLO RIDE

After visiting Hoang Long, Kim Lan and Cun returned to Hanoi. With two more days to go, they were content to be tourists. Hanoi was like another country to them. From the station, they took a cyclo to the center of town and found a cheap hotel. A frowning man greeted them at the reception desk, his morose self framed by a string of dead Christmas lights and two dozen postcards. A room was available on the fourth floor that cost forty thousand a night.

"How about sixty thousand for two nights?" Kim Lan shot back at him.

"Take it or leave it, lady. We have plenty of customers here, classy ones from Australia and Japan. I'm giving you the Vietnamese rate. With foreigners, I charge double."

They discovered the room was fairly clean and the bed plenty wide for two people. Inspecting the yellow ocher blanket and threadbare, grayish sheet with suspicion, Kim Lan wondered if they had been changed since the departure of the previous guests, if ever. Neither had been in a hotel before so they did not know what to expect. They were pleasantly surprised to find a low fridge squatting in a corner, with even a bottle of spring water inside it. *We're inching up to international standards*, they thought simultaneously, grinning with pride. The bathroom did look and smell moldy, with a showerhead aligned almost directly over the toilet, but it was still more luxurious and cleaner than at home.

While his mom freshened up, Cun stood at the window and stared down at the mossy red tiles of Hanoi's old quarters. Labyrinthine, with thirty-six streets with names like Sugar, Hat, Tin, Chicken, Paper, Cotton, Coffin, Leather and Bucket. Originally, each street had featured a single commodity sold by merchants who came from the same village. Granted narrow slots on the sidewalk to display their wares, they built long tube-like houses behind them that were broken up by one or two court-yards. A tube house rarely had a second floor, and never a second-floor window facing the street. It was forbidden to look down at the king's head should he pass by. As many as twenty families lived in each tube house. You could picture them as indoor alleys. Alleys were designed for the human body, not horses or automobiles. So unconsensually intimate, so pungent, they would alarm most contemporary sensibilities.

Wandering the streets around their hotel, Kim Lan and Cun noticed that the people in Hanoi were dressed more carefully—more formally, in a certain respect—than those in Saigon. Most men wore shoes, not sandals or flip-flops. The women's dress looked more *considered* with their scarves and gloves. In spite of all that, Hanoians still seemed provincial, almost quaint, with no real sense of fashion. They only dressed more carefully, Kim Lan concluded, because of the weather.

Some older people in Hanoi still had black, lacquered teeth. Traditionally, white teeth were considered ugly, a sign of poverty and likened to the teeth of dogs. Kim Lan noticed that many men smoked a very strong tobacco called *thuoc lao* from bamboo water pipes. *Thuoc lao* gave you a better high than weed, but the buzz only lasted for about five minutes. There is a poem about *thuoc lao*:

> Thuoc Lao *improves one's general character,*
> *Rids one of diseases, makes one's breath fragrant.*
> *One must lift the pipe like a warrior his sword,*

Suck in deeply like a steam engine moving,
Then blow it out like phoenixes and dragons ascending

Older women chewed betel leaves with lime paste and areca nuts. Turning their mouths and teeth bright red, this mixture also got them high. Everyone drank fresh green tea with every meal.

Hanoi was even dirtier than Saigon, yet more pleasant, thanks to its parks and lakes. The food was uneven but there were also unmatched delicacies. Two dishes from the end of the nineteenth century had come to define Hanoi: *pho* and *cha ca la vong*. The name *pho* derives from the French pot au feu, or pot on the fire. Beef broth made the two dishes similar, but the Vietnamese eliminated the potatoes, carrots, celeries, leeks and parsnips, and added rice noodles, cilantro, slivers of onion, ginger, star anise, fennel seed, cassia, cinnamon and mint leaves. *Pho* had become a fast food, ready to be served for breakfast, lunch or dinner. By contrast, *cha ca la vong* was much fancier. Slivers of fish were marinated with galingale, turmeric, sesame, pepper and fish sauce, then fried in seasoned oil on a clay brazier at the table. The best fish for this dish was found at the confluence of two rivers in the town of Viet Tri. The swirling currents forced the fish to swim vigorously, firming its flesh. A male fish was preferred because it had more flesh. *Cha ca la vong* was served with peanuts, dill, scallions, chopped fennel, shredded lettuce, basil and cilantro, on top of rice vermicelli. The dipping sauce was fermented shrimp paste freshened with lime juice and sharpened by rice wine. True connoisseurs also added two pungent drops—exact, squeezed from an eyedropper—extracted from the gland of a beetle. Sesame rice crackers were also needed to add crunch to the meal. Cun wanted to try *cha ca la vong* but Kim Lan said to him angrily, "Your father is starving in the next town and you want to eat like a gourmet?!" They ended up settling for two simple bowls of *pho* a day.

Kim Lan knew of only one Hanoi landmark: the One-Pillar Pagoda. Single-chambered, it was tiny and perched on a stone pillar in the middle of a lotus pond. An enduring symbol of Hanoi, it was first constructed by King Ly Thai Tong in 1049 and rebuilt many times, the last in 1958 after Catholic Vietnamese troops under French command had it dynamited before the French quit Indochina. Tired of walking around, Kim Lan and Cun decided to take a cyclo to the One-Pillar Pagoda.

Cyclos in Hanoi were wider than the ones in Saigon. This allowed two thin-assed people to sit side by side fairly comfortably, with the smaller of the two leaning his or her head against the upper arm of the other, purring in abject contentment. Hanoi cyclos were also equipped with tinkling bells, like ice cream trucks. The wider cyclo was harder to steer but less prone to flopping on its side. Kim Lan flagged a white-haired, goateed man wearing crazed bifocals. Being so old, he always underquoted the prices to avoid losing customers.

"How much to the One-Pillar Pagoda?" Kim Lan asked him.

"Five thousand, lady."

"What?! Five thousand?! Are you mad? One thousand!"

With a crestfallen look, the old man moaned, "Four thousand, lady, please. I can hardly eat on what I make a day."

The sentimental card, Kim Lan thought with irritation. Though she had no idea how far the One-Pillar Pagoda was, she was sure she was being swindled. *What the hell, I can afford a little charity.*

After Kim Lan and Cun had gotten on, it became clear that the old man had trouble pedaling two people. This was fine with Kim Lan, however, because she didn't want to go too fast. Grunting along slower than walking pace, they labored down a wide boulevard toward a monstrous block of granite silhouetted against the sky. This grim edifice was like nothing else in Hanoi.

"What is that?!" Cun barked at the old man.

"Uncle Ho's Mausoleum!"

"I told you to go to the One-Pillar Pagoda," Kim Lan said.

"It's where I'm taking you. The One-Pillar Pagoda is right behind Uncle's Mausoleum."

"Turn around! Turn around!" Kim Lan commanded. "Please take us right back to our hotel."

The One-Pillar Pagoda complex had included a monastery and a shrine dedicated to illustrious monks from centuries past. Both had been destroyed in 1985 to make room for a Ho Chi Minh Museum, which now stood in the shadow of the Ho Chi Minh Mausoleum.

23 ◆ THE AWAKENING

After Hanoi, Saigon felt very chaotic, insane, terribly exciting. As Kim Lan and Cun entered Paris by Night, Sen emerged from the back of the room to give his wife a big hug, the first time he had ever allowed himself to show such affection in public. "Look at these teenagers in love!" someone shouted, which made everyone laugh.

"How was Phan Thiet?"

"It was fine, but I'm exhausted. I had to talk to so many people."

"Were there a lot of people at the funeral?"

"Nearly a hundred."

"How was Phan Thiet, Cun?"

"The beach was very beautiful."

"Did you swim?"

"No, I did not swim."

"I hear they have the whitest sand in Phan Thiet. Is that true?"

Cun grinned, but did not respond.

"He doesn't know his beaches," Kim Lan interjected. "White sand, black sand, it's all the same to him. Isn't that right, Cun?"

"Well, I'm very happy to see both of you back," Sen said. "I was getting very lonely."

A-Muoi brought Hoa into the room. Seeing her mother, Hoa was so happy she burst into tears. Kim Lan took Hoa from A-Muoi's arms. "So you missed your mother, did you?"

"She cried the whole time you were gone," Sen said with a

touch of reproach. "But look at her now! Look at how happy she is!"

Sen's effusive behavior continued later on that night—in bed. Heretofore their sex life had been OK yet unvaried, with the only weirdness her penchant for sucking his nipples. While enjoying each other's bodily warmth, they had generated no white heat. As soon as the light was out, he started to kiss and undress her. She had never seen him like this before. He went on to make love to her with surprising finesse and shocking ardor. Nudging her breasts upward, he swallowed them whole and playfully sucked on her erect nipples with his tongue. He probed each one of her holes with fingers and nose and drove his engorged *cazzo* into her tight *culo*. He serviced, enslaved and manhandled her. "Stop, stop," she pleaded, "the servants can hear us." But Sen would not stop. To her dismay and ecstasy, he orally pleasured her down below. Turning her inside out, he overcharged and gouged her until her mind short-circuited as the room exploded with a million flashlights. Her eyes swiveling inward, her throaty screams reverberated throughout the house and onto the street. In the next room, Cun heard everything and spilled his seed at about the same time Sen did.

After Sen was done remaking her and she lay beside him serene and happy, it made Kim Lan blush to think that it had taken her forty-two years, two husbands and two childbirths to arrive at this point. Thinking of the man in prison, she felt pity sharpened by shame. She immediately chased the annoying thought away by mounting Sen in his sleep.

24 ◆ AMAZEMENT

On the train Cun had discovered his dick in dramatic fashion. Now he was ready to become a man. Already he could count three dim strands of hair jutting from his upper lip. His calcium-deficient jaw had never achieved its proper width, however, forcing his mouth to trumpet forward into a snout, while his eyes stayed stuck to the sides of his head, like an herbivore, ready to be hunted by a big cat that would devour his entrails and thighs, leaving his neck and feet to the slobbering, glazed-eyed hyenas. In fact, his face couldn't be seen from the front at all, but only in profile, like a knife or an ax. Deprived of all dairy products in early infancy, he had had to be breast-fed an extra-long time, until there were a dozen nubby teeth crowding his puckering blowhole, encouraging it to shoot out even further. Even a well-timed Manny Pacquiao left would not have fixed it. Though his balls never dropped, it didn't matter; Cun was ready to become a man. He started to scan left and right for glimpses of smackable flesh. He studied the servant girl as she squatted on the floor washing the dishes. When she took a shower, he stood outside the door and listened to the splashing, gurgling music. He heard the red plastic ladle being whacked against the nicked rim of the red plastic bucket. He heard her rubber flip-flops plop-plopping on the wet ceramic tiles and strained hard to parse and understand the complicated audio of her cheap panties being washed and wrung. Made in Vietnam, 100 percent polyester, their one advantage was the fact that they could be dried in the sun in no time flat. He sniffled with emotion when he heard her long, languorous sigh. *Why do we deny each other our lovely bodies, my friend?* Cun was amazed that all that separated him from transcendental experience was a thin plastic door, a very artificial thing, almost an abstraction. With the metal latch loosely screwed into rotting wood, it wouldn't take more than a light shove for it to swing open. A strong blow from a fable pig would do it. The bathroom took up one corner of the kitchen, its walls falling well short of the tall ceiling. Cun figured he could stand on a chair and look down without being detected. As he was carrying a chair to the bathroom door one day, his mother walked in. "What are you doing with that chair?"

"It's the lightbulb, Mother. It flickers. Something is wrong with the lightbulb."

Kim Lan gave Cun a look that said, *I have no idea what you're up to, but don't you even think about it. I'm your mother and I have eyes in the back of my head.*

Wandering around the neighborhood, Cun mooned at women's pants hanging from clotheslines as they fluttered and flagged and dripped in the warm wind. Once he snatched a pair of laced panties, still damp, from a laundry line. Only two degrees of separation, he sniffed, shuddering. He had seen the owner and thought her very pretty. He wondered, he always wondered. He despaired, irrationally, that his opportunity would never come. The promise of sex provides meaning, hope, purpose and strength to the male virgin, who's convinced that everything will be all right once he's in there. To maintain this pressurized optimism, it's almost worth being a lifelong celibate. Cun noticed a dozen girls standing in front of the Protestant church each night, dressed in Day-Glo colors and high heels, their faces theatrically, almost clownishly, made-up. They were selling their asses to feed their own mouths. There were also many hostess bars nearby. One day, after drinking a Tiger beer to muster up courage, Cun walked out of Paris by Night determined to finally get it over with.

Too nervous, he skipped the first two bars he walked by. At the third he marched right in and sat down at a table next to a potted reed palm. A girl in a halter top, miniskirt and six-inch platform shoes soon ambled out. She looked about sixteen. The jungle music was loud enough to disorient and the light dim enough to make her really pretty. She smiled benignly at her youthful supplicant. "How are you doing, brother?"

Cun avoided her face and focused on her bare midriff. She had an innocent-looking innie. There was some gummy black dirt in it. "Give me a Tiger beer!"

"I just said, 'How are you doing, brother?'"

"I'm fine!"

"I'll be right back!"

Cun watched the girl's buttocks as she sashayed toward the back. Waiting, he scrutinized the framed posters on the black walls. Two bikinied blondes, each holding a pistol in each hand, were grappling with one another on a tile floor. A pendulous and sand-flecked Brooke Burke smiled coyly behind her stringy hair. Four women flashed their white asses on the back of a red pickup truck. Already he was stiff. When the girl finally came back with his bottle of beer, she sat down right next to him and said, "So, how are you doing?"

"I'm good!" he answered. She grinned and placed a hand high on his thigh. Her bony knee clanked against his under the table. He took a long swig of beer, wiped his mouth with his hand, burped, then said, "How much?"

"Aren't we serious today?!"

"How much?" Cun said again, but in a whisper this time.

Smiling in amusement, the girl suddenly grabbed Cun's crotch, almost offhandedly, and asked, "How much do you have?"

He pulled out a fifty-thousand-*dong* bill.

She glanced at it. "Two of those!"

She led him by the hand into a tiny, windowless room of raw plywood. There was a damp, dismal smell of seeping liquid. If only he had had some Tiger Balm to chase the funk away. She slipped off her panties, then undressed him like a child. Exposed, he gasped. No one had seen him like that before. Placing a threadbare towel on a hard and lumpy bed, she laid him down and slipped a green rubber onto his terrified dick. He panicked as her slim fingers closed in on his leaning member. She spat at his half erection, then sucked on it maybe three times, her moussed hair not losing its shape. It was startling to see a head down there. An ancient part of him was being excavated, a new paradigm introduced. Then she rode him vigorously without even taking her top off. Seeing his eyes glazed and unblinking, she asked, "Did you come?" Hearing no answer, she climbed off, pulled the rubber gently from his dick, threw it under the bed and got dressed in silence. It had taken all of three minutes.

"Come back again!" she yelled as Cun walked away. *Virgins*, she chuckled. Meek and nervous, they were all heads and hands, with no dominion over their lower halves. She'd been one herself just a few months ago. She enjoyed introducing these dorky cadets to the unknown regions of themselves. Some hadn't even gotten around to peeling back their cheesy foreskins yet. Her more experienced clients could be so unpleasant. The worst were frustrated psychos who could never be satisfied.

After he got home, Cun wasn't sure whether what had just happened counted as fucking. He hadn't actually felt anything. He had seen her pussy, though, or at least he'd seen the absence of a penis. She had so little pubic hair that her pussy was like—it wasn't there at all. There was nothing there, really, just smooth skin, so much smooth skin that it had nearly blinded Cun, like staring at the whitest sand on the brightest day. Maybe she was only twelve and not sixteen. Still, it amazed Cun that he'd actually had the privilege of having a pussy bouncing up and down on his dick. It seemed to him miraculous that a man could pay a woman to undress and reveal to him her nonexistent pussy.

It didn't take long before Cun returned to the same bar. The same girl wasn't around so he had to pay for a different one. Each new girl meant a new set of anxieties, or, rather, the same set of anxieties *renewed*, but he had no choice because he needed it so badly. They were all very seasoned, obviously, and could compare his body and (lack of) technique to the ways of a thousand other clients. It wasn't easy being a man. Seeing him sunny-side up and waiting for action, the fifth female he tried—at thirty, a prehistoric specimen in that establishment, perhaps the madam filling in for a sick no-show—even shouted, "You get on top of me! Come on!"

This new habit of his was very expensive. To secure enough money, he started to steal from his mom.

25 ◆ HIGH BLOOD PRESSURE

Kim Lan kept her wealth in jewelry and cash. She displayed most of her jewelry on her person. She kept most of her cash in a locked cabinet. She kept the one key on her person or hid it under her mattress. The first few times she detected a bill or two missing, she assumed she had lost track of how much she had spent. She handled a lot of money each day and could easily have lost track of a bill or two. When money kept disappearing, she immediately suspected one of her two servants. She didn't think it was A-Muoi, Hoa's babysitter, but the other one, a girl from Tra Vinh she'd hired recently. Kim Lan should have known. This girl had quick, darting eyes and was unusually dexterous with knives or anything metal. She had either made a duplicate of Kim Lan's key or knew how to pick locks. Talking to Kim Lan, she always looked down or to the side, a sure sign of dishonesty. She smiled when there was nothing to smile about, another sure sign of dishonesty.

"Pha, where are you? Come here!"

"Yes, ma'am."

"Look me in the eye."

"Yes, ma'am."

"Have you been doing anything against your conscience?"

"I'm still a virgin, ma'am. I don't have a boyfriend."

"I'm not talking about that. Have you been doing anything against me?"

"I don't know what you're talking about, ma'am."

"But I know. I know exactly what I'm talking about. I'm not stupid! I know that you must send money home to your mother regularly. I cannot blame you for that. It's great that you love your mother so much, but I can't have you doing things to me—do you understand?!—right under my nose. I'll give you fifty thousand as severance pay, but you cannot work in this house any longer."

"What did I do, ma'am?" the girl started to sob. "I did not do anything!"

"Stop acting! Do you think I'm blind?!"

Though Pha made a huge scene, sobbing and threatening to commit suicide by jumping into the path of a car, Kim Lan knew she had to be firm. These girls used tricks to play with your emotions. Still, seeing Pha walk out the door carrying a burlap sack containing all her possessions, Kim Lan did feel a twinge of pity. She even thought that maybe Pha had stolen from her out of revenge: *It's true that I yelled at her a lot, but I mean well, I really do—I have a kind heart. I have high blood pressure—from yelling all the time—but I have a kind heart. Don't I have the right to yell once in a while? Haven't I had a hard enough life? In any case, if you don't yell at these servants, they break and ruin everything. I give my servants my old clothes and I let them watch Taiwanese videos in the evening so they can relax. We watch romantic films and cry together. I never let them go out alone lest they come back pregnant. These girls are so naive and horny, they get knocked up within seconds of leaving the house, since they don't know anything about city men or beer or pills or condoms. I warn them against certain neighborhood boys while recommending others. Not too long ago, I even managed to hook one of my girls up with a widower. Ugly as sin, she was pushing thirty and would never have found a taker had I not intervened. They're living happily together down the street, though I hear he beats her occasionally. In general, I tell my servants, Don't be so anxious, calm down, don't be in such a hurry to find a boyfriend, I'll find you a good one when I think you're ready. Your virginity is all you have, I always remind them. Don't give it to a ragpicker.*

Remember the four Confucian feminine virtues: industry, appearance, speech and behavior. You must work hard, look modest, keep quiet and not spread your legs for strangers. That's why they must stay with me twenty-four hours a day, seven days a week. I allow them to go home for Tet or a death in the family—I even pay for the bus tickets—but these girls don't want to go home any more than necessary. Having filial obedience, they do send money back to their mothers, but they'd never want to live in their old villages again. Once you've had a taste of Saigon, you're hooked for life. They also eat much better with me than they ever did at home. Living with me, these girls eat fish, pork and beef regularly. They eat with us, at the same table, and if they're hungry between meals they can even cook up a packet of Miliket instant noodles. Each one of those costs two thousand dong!

Kim Lan finally concluded that, no, she hadn't done anything wrong. *These girls are greedy and dishonest and that's all there is to it. You can't really trust anybody nowadays.*

26 ◆ A SERVANT'S TALE

Pha was twenty-two and had had two jobs in her life. Before becoming a domestic servant in Saigon, she had caught crabs in Tra Vinh. This is her story: *Our house was made of bamboo and palm leaves. It creaked like a swinging hammock. There was no door in the doorway. At night we lay on straw mats on the dirt floor. For privacy we blew out the candle. We grew water spinach in a green pond. Above this pond was a yellow moon. When my father was not drunk, he worked. I stood in mud and caught crabs. We had five chickens and seven ducks. We sold eggs to make money. We rarely ate eggs ourselves. Eggs go well with water spinach. Each day I saved three crabs for us to eat. If I found a shrimp I ate it raw. I love the sensation of mud between my toes. I also like the smell of mud. What I love best is the sight of a water buffalo lying on its back in the mud and the sloshing sounds of pigs eating. If I were tired I'd lie down and sleep like a dead cat by the side of a road. I caught about thirty crabs a day. Sticking my hand into a hole I snatched them, one by one. Sometimes they snapped at me first. A female crab always hurt more. Sometimes a snake slept inside the hole. I also worried about leeches. A leech's sucker looks like the ribbed mouth of a balloon. I would see him but before I could lift my leg he would be stuck to my calf. If you don't pour lime on him he'll be on you for about ten minutes. Some leeches last minutes longer. Say: I am not losing anything, I can spare a little blood, I have plenty of blood left. A leech cannot be destroyed. Chop him into a dozen pieces and you have a dozen leeches. Burn him, scatter his ash, but with the first rainfall, he'll reform himself into a new leech. A girl has to be extra careful around these leeches. If one wiggles into your body's opening you'll give birth to an army of leeches. My legs were purple from leech bites and my hands were puffy from crab bites, but my face was unmarked.*

What exactly is a house made of bamboo and palm leaves? It's called a leaf house. Made of palm leaves woven over a bamboo frame, a leaf house may not be practical in northern Vietnam, which has a cold season, but in the South, it can be the ideal dwelling. First of all, it is cheap: A leaf house can be erected for $150 or less in about three days. You get a room for lounging and sleeping in the front, plus a kitchen in the back. The bathroom is any body of water nearby, or just the ground, with or without a hole in it. Water is stored in three large jars (embossed with dragons) placed just outside the back door. In a leaf house, you don't need to sweep the dirt off the floor because the floor is already made of dirt. A leaf house is much cooler than any other kind of house, so air-conditioning isn't necessary. Many leaf houses now have electricity, so a flickering black-and-white TV can sit next to your laptop on the glass coffee table. You can go high-tech and install a satellite dish on top of your leaf house. One disadvantage of a leaf house is that it will fall apart within five years, meaning you will have to come up with another $150.

Pha didn't mention her town's entertainment center, a sort of nightly country fair on a spread of dirt near the main market. Little lightbulbs were strung between trees; neon tubes illuminated booths. There was a creaking merry-go-round where grim children revolved on rusty horses, cars and helicopters. There was a roller skating rink the size of a New York one-bedroom where teenage boys and girls could grind and bump into each other, pirouette on their haunches, or glide backward to the beeps and thumps of techno music. Pha had never had a boyfriend so she never learned how to skate. At a shooting gallery, one could try to knock Ping-Pong balls from the tops of bottles to win a package of instant noodles, a can of root beer, or soy milk. At another booth, manned by a whistling fairy gone haywire with his made-in-China eyeliner, one could bet the numbers to score laundry detergent or a bag of MSG. Framing all these festivities was a stage at the back on which a forlorn man sat behind his silent drum set.

No clowns, pythons or bearded ladies. A bearded man was rare enough.

27 ✦ A GAGGED AUDIENCE

For the rest of 1989, Kim Lan sent several packages to Hoang Long, but she didn't visit him again. Too many deaths in the family would arouse Sen's suspicions. To fool him, she continued to light incense sticks, close her eyes and pray in front of Hoang Long's framed photo on the altar. She didn't pray for real, of course, but her lips moved with conviction as her mind went blank. Every now and then, she'd let out a long sigh or a sob, even when no one was looking. Another letter arrived from prison with a different list of essentials. Money still rolled in, but money kept disappearing. *So it hadn't been Pha after all.* Though she half suspected A-Muoi, she decided to solve the problem once and for all by purchasing a safe with a combination lock. Fire- and waterproof, it could withstand ten thousand degrees Celsius, the heat of a nuclear bomb—or so claimed its Taiwanese manufacturer.

Deprived of funds, Cun thought of marriage for the first time in his life. It's neither enslavement of woman nor of man but a slo-mo collision of two better halves. He hardly knew any girls who weren't prostitutes, however. The new domestic servant didn't look half bad but, at nineteen years old, she already had a three-year-old born out of wedlock. Cun never thought of applying for a job and making his own money. Aside from an insistent sex drive that was literal, verbatim and monosyllabic, Cun had no volition at all; he was ruled by fear. To him, the world was a frightening riddle, with nearly everyone in it—men and women, young and old, all nationalities—

more powerful and vicious than he was. The world had imprisoned and humiliated his father, a man much more virile and capable than he, so it would no doubt kill him the second he crawled out of his hole. The only ones he was not afraid of were his sister and the domestic servants.

The domestic servants made Cun feel powerful. He felt so potent around them, he literally flexed his muscles in their presence—styling, voguing and doing bits of calisthenics as if he were onstage in a vast yet intimate arena, performing for a gagged audience of just one. He always addressed them with an arrogant, vindictive voice he never dared use with other people. Normally he whinnied and honked, but place a domestic servant in front of him and he could boom like a drill sergeant. He loved to boss them around with abrupt commands: "Get me a glass of water!" or "Buy me a pack of cigarettes!" Because a servant girl could not talk back to him, he felt free to yell at her at any time and to lecture her on the most diverse topics. While she squatted on the floor, doing the laundry or the dishes, he'd try to educate her about politics, Buddhism, the pope, or manned flights to the moon, whatever tidbits of news he'd managed to snatch from the television that day, things he half remembered or simply made up. He would say, for example, that the United States had fifty-two states, all covered in ice. "That's why they have free love over there. It's the weather." If she dared to laugh or roll her eyes at him, he'd smack her on the head. "Do you know that in Japan, men and women take showers together?" he said one day. "Utter strangers taking a shower together. To save water. If you and I were in Japan, we would be taking a shower together every day."

If two people take a shower together, they still use the same amount of water, the servant thought, but said nothing. Standing a few feet away, Cun had just taken his shirt off. Wearing only shorts, he started to do his exercises. Having seen this performance many times, she paid no attention. Sweating a river, he stretched and contorted until his swelling finally went down.

One day, Cun saw a strange girl squatting on the sidewalk in front of Paris by Night. A fishmonger, Phuong had just arrived from Chau Doc. Southwest of Saigon, Chau Doc was right next to Cambodia. Even with its lucrative border traffic in contraband, it was still an unusually poor town. Half the houses were thatch huts. (And we're talking leaning, decrepit thatch huts, with their one item of luxury a constantly glowing black-and-white TV.) Back home, Phuong's mother would just stir-fry some rice with MSG and call it dinner. That's why Phuong had to come to Saigon. Too homely to work in a hostess bar, she didn't want to deal with the nonsense of being a domestic servant either. That's why she sold fish.

Phuong hardly ever talked or smiled. No one had ever seen her laugh. Maybe she had crooked teeth, or no teeth at all, and was afraid to open her thin, bloodless lips. From six in the morning, you'd find her squatting behind a tin basin hopping with climbing perches. Climbing perches are small, bony fish that can live out of water briefly and travel short distances overland. They are delicious marinated with fish sauce, sugar and black peppers, then stewed. Some people prefer them in a soup. A sadistic climbing perch monger, Phuong would take a fish and snip, with scissors, its tail, anal fin, dorsal fin, pelvic fin, ventral fin, pectoral fin, then, finally, head. If she had only reversed this order, the climbing perch would not have thrashed about during the process. Sitting in the café, Cun could observe Phuong methodically mutilating her wiggly, pinkie-sized fish. Her casual cruelty horrified and soothed him. Identifying with both fish and scissors, he found them equally arousing. Touching himself each night, his eyes shut tight, his mouth wide open, he'd conjure up Phuong's nimble fingers glistening with fish blood and slime as she snuffed out yet another climbing perch's life.

At first Phuong pretended not to notice the ugly boy who was always staring at her. Having never been stared at before for any reason whatsoever, she naturally assumed that this was love. Soon she couldn't help but smile a little, maybe just once a day, without looking at Cun, of course, without even lifting up her head.

To Kim Lan, the fishmonger was no more than a fly magnet and a visual blight in front of her establishment. There were so many more flies nowadays, all bigger and bluer than ever, all because of the fishmonger and her stupid face. Standing inside Paris by Night, Kim Lan tried to browbeat the fishmonger away, but Phuong always showed up each morning at exactly the same spot.

A few steps from Phuong there was an old man who sat behind an old scale. You came to him to learn your weight. The chubbiest people in the neighborhood felt a compulsive need to step on his scale several times a day. They kept him high on the hog because he charged by the pound. Though he had no knowledge of medicine, everyone called him "doctor." The day was long and sometimes he fell asleep. As soon as he started snoring, thieves and beggars would step on his scale for free. In his dreams, he often saw these lowlifes gleefully weighing themselves, but he couldn't do anything about it. Waking up, he would console himself by looking over at Phuong and thinking, *At least my fingers aren't slimy and I don't smell like fish.*

28 ◆ PRIMATES

It took two weeks for Cun to approach Phuong. He broke the ice by buying half a kilo of climbing perches. Haggling, he bantered, "You're a tough one, aren't you?" which made both of them blush, his face turning nearly black. Then he said, "What is your name?"

"Yes?"

"I said, what is your name?"

"Just call me 'fishmonger.'"

"You're a funny one, aren't you?"

"My name is Phuong."

"I'm Cun."

Back home, Cun gave the newly bought fish to the servant. She had never seen him buy food before. Perplexed, she glanced at his face and saw that it had changed radically. It was peaceful now, radiating with a Khmer smile and a nimbus. For the first time, he didn't look half ugly. *Is he in love with me?* she wondered. She could see herself as Kim Lan's new daughter-in-law. *It's about time I get to boss a domestic servant around.* Lost in reverie, distracted, she brought a meat cleaver down on her thumb, nearly slicing it off. Cun heard her scream and saw blood on the chopping board. "What the hell did you do?!" he cried out, scowling. "You're always so damn clumsy!"

Cun forced himself to wait a day before buying more climbing perches. Phuong also waited. When she saw him coming at last, she almost smiled.

"Half a kilo," he said.

"Half a kilo," she said.

As she wrapped the fish, he took a deep breath and asked, "Phuong, have you ever been to the zoo?"

"No."

"Would you like to go to the zoo?"

"Where is it?"

"I'll take you there."

"OK."

"How about tomorrow at three o'clock?"

"OK."

Phuong spent hours preparing for her first date ever. She applied makeup for the first time and even dyed her hair a muddy blonde. Then she put on her best blouse, a white polyester number with large red, yellow and blue dots, an idea she got from an imported loaf of bread. With her floral pajama pants and new clogs, she was ready to go.

They looked like any other couple on their Dream motorbike. Sitting behind him, she wrapped her arms tightly around his waist, her breasts pressed against his back. Thrilled by the sensation, he did not know that the softness he felt was the spongy lining to her stuffed bra and not flesh. Aroused and distracted, he nearly ran over a legless beggar trying to cross the street lying prone on a dolly, like a swimmer on a body board. "There ought to be a damn law!" he cursed.

The Saigon Zoo, built by the French, was once world famous. The French were fantastic at building zoos, railroads, villas, post offices and churches, often right on top of razed pagodas. Hanoi and Saigon both boast cathedrals erected over pulverized pagodas. You can't beat their locations, though. But by 1990, after several wars and a revolution, the Saigon Zoo was very run-down. Most of the big cats were gone. The giraffes were gone. The hippopotamuses were gone. Cun and Phuong strolled past cage after cage with nothing in them but a damp, earthy smell. Gone in body but held in smell. How was it possible that a foul smell could linger so long without an animal? Look at that gazelle. Look at how miserable it is. Its bones are showing and there are fecal stains on its hind legs. Look at this Kodiak bear the size of a hedgehog. And this alligator looks like a burned cactus. These animals would be better off dead—wouldn't you say?

Phuong had never been to a zoo before and had seen few photos of animals. Pointing to a panther, she asked, "Is that a bear?" Pointing to a bear, she asked, "Is that a gorilla?" All animals are variations of either a dog or a cat, she concluded. Some have horns on them, some don't. Phuong thought the tiger's stripes were either painted on or computer generated. She suspected the entire zoo was computer generated. They paused in front of a rusty cage housing two aging orangutans. On the wet cement floor was a black-and-white plastic soccer ball. A dead elm poked through the wire roof. The orangutans sat at the front of the cage, looking out. The male had a seasoned, well-traveled and philosophical face. Eating what appeared to be five pounds of lettuce, he kept spitting out the chewed food onto his enormous hand, contemplating it for a few seconds, then stuffing it back into his spittoonlike mouth, grinding crookedly, leisurely, his lips turned inside out. The female observed all this with concern and interest. Her round eyes were rimmed pink, making her very feminine and universally attractive. She kissed the male several times and was rewarded each time with a wad of bolus, passed directly from his mouth to hers. Phuong saw a parable of mature love in the orangutans. Far removed from their swinging days in the Borneo jungle, reduced to squalor and poverty, and living in Vietnam no less, they still had each other. She also noticed with envy and irritation that their living space was three times larger than her own.

They moved to a cage filled with mangy chimpanzees. These monkeys were so skinny that some of them slipped out between the bars. Not finding much to eat outside either, most slipped right back in. You might know this already, but a chimpanzee will go berserk at any sign of affection between a man and a woman. Inter-species jealously. As the chimpanzees watched what Cun and Phuong did just outside their cage, they shrieked and howled until they nearly went mad.

Phuong had never been groped before. No one had ever kissed her on the lips. That night she allowed Cun to make love to her in the little tin shack she called home. Rent was sixteen bucks a month for this converted tool shed. There were a mattress and a kerosene stove on the cement floor, and an oval mirror hung on a wall. Her clothes were stuffed into two plastic bags. She couldn't hang them up because they would stink of kerosene. Her hair already stank of kerosene. It rained hard that night, clattering on the tin roof, so no one could hear her hiss with pleasure. Urging him on, she clawed his narrow back and scrawny behind, leaving bloody scratches all over. They did not sleep at all until morning. Two weeks later, she missed her period.

29 ◆ TRUE LOVE AND CROSS-DRESSING

When Cun told Kim Lan he wanted to marry the fishmonger girl, she thought he had gone mad. "What?! That ridiculous girl outside my door?! I'll find you a decent wife. What's the hurry? You're only eighteen! Wait a couple years and I'll find you a nice girl from a decent family. If you marry that stupid hick girl, the neighbors will all laugh in my face. We have standards in this family. I don't get it. I hate that girl! Of all the girls out there, you go out and pick a stupid fishmonger!"

"But I love her."

"Love?! What the hell are you talking about?! You're eighteen! What do you know about love?! You can't just go out and fall in love with a fishmonger. You must fall in love with the right person!"

"But she's pregnant with my child."

Startled by this fact, Kim Lan paused for a few seconds before saying, "You mean you already slept with her?"

"Yes, many times."

"And she's pregnant with your child?"

"She's three months pregnant with my child."

"Why didn't you tell me sooner?"

"I just found out myself."

Three months was a little late for an abortion, but it could be done. Kim Lan knew the right doctor. "Tell the girl she can get an abortion, and I'll pay for it."

"But she doesn't want an abortion. And neither do I."

Kim Lan sighed and shook her head in disgust. "She's taking advantage of you, don't you understand?! How stupid can you be? She got herself pregnant deliberately so you'll have to marry her. She doesn't love you, she loves my money. She's using that unborn baby to blackmail our family, don't you understand?!"

"But it's my child too," Cun said in a cowed voice, nearly a whisper. Knowing he had neither the mental nor vocal energy to compete with his mom in any argument, Cun stopped talking after that point. For several hours she repeated herself, trailing off, then restarting with renewed vigor, usually after a glass of water or a cup of hot tea, until she finally shut up from sheer exhaustion. Although Cun was deeply ambivalent about becoming a father, he knew Phuong would never consent to an abortion. Made giddy by the prospects of her incipient offspring, she even told Cun she hoped the baby would turn out just like him. Each morning, she showed up with her bulging belly to squat behind her tin basin of climbing perches, often with Cun right beside her, their relationship out in the open for everyone to see. The sight of them squatting outside Paris by Night constituted a kind of protest against Kim Lan. The entire neighborhood laughed at this spectacle. Some were whispering their condemnations of the evil old witch for refusing to become a grandmother and a mother-in-law. Others praised Kim Lan for being firm, for not giving in to blackmail.

In one important respect, at least, Kim Lan felt relieved. At least Cun was not *one of those*. There were four in the neighborhood. One was Binh, a thirty-year-old geography teacher, slight of build, who was often addressed as "girl," as in "Girl, how're you doing?" "Very fine! Thank you!" A kleptomaniac, Binh was almost never allowed to enter anyone's home. He only stole trivial things—an orange, a paper fan, a cigarette lighter—nothing too valuable. If it was small enough, he'd just shove it into his baggy pants. He was best friends with Trinh, the biggest gossip in the neighborhood. Once, Trinh yanked Binh's pants down, or so she claimed, and saw the tiniest penis in her life—"It was all skin and no flesh, like a used condom!" Binh's mother once asked a doctor if drugs or hormones could be injected into her son's body. He told her nothing could be done. Binh's brother used to beat him up for putting on makeup, but now wouldn't even chase his flaming friends away. Binh idolized Michael Jackson and could do the moonwalk like you wouldn't believe.

Then there was Dzung, forty-five years old, stocky and balding. Dzung shared a room in his parents' house with his lover, Tuan, a twenty-three-year-old Adonis so handsome all the girls were in love with him. Dzung owned a video rental business and was obsessed with the Goddess of Mercy. He had several large statues of her in his room.

And then there was Trieu, twenty-four years old, who had come out about a month earlier. Trieu's mother, Mrs. Dzau, sold duck coleslaw and rice gruel from a cart. Trieu's father was a truck driver. Trieu had worked in a candy factory, but now stayed home to help out his mother. He had been in jail once for shooting up heroin. There were at least six junkies in Kim Lan's neighborhood. Mrs. Dzau had confided to Kim Lan, "My son told me three weeks ago he wanted to wear women's clothes."

Eating a plate of coleslaw, Kim Lan glanced over at Trieu. Squatting behind a tub of dirty dishes, he wore a pastel yellow blouse with a Peter Pan collar, but his shorts were light blue and still masculine. For a cross-dresser, Trieu was still half-assed. Reading Kim Lan's mind, Mrs. Dzau said, "He's working right now, so he's not dressed up yet. You should see him at night!"

"How does he dress at night?"

"Well, he puts perfume and makeup on and he wears my panties!"

"Your panties?!"

"My panties!"

"Why don't you buy him his own panties?"

"I did, but he won't wear them. He wants to wear *my* panties. I think my son became gay from using dirty needles. You know, other people's blood got into his blood."

"You mean he's HIV positive?!"

"No, just gay."

Kim Lan finished her coleslaw in silence and did not ask any more questions.

One morning, there was no fishmonger squatting in front of Paris by Night. Kim Lan had softened to the point of allowing Phuong inside the house. Her son wasn't such a great catch either, she finally realized. *Any girl I might find for him would only marry him for money. At least this one knows how to work. The fishmonger is stubborn all right, but at least she doesn't have a smart mouth. Her lips rarely move, she barely seems capable of speech. I can deal with a dumb daughter-in-law. You don't want them too smart or they'll challenge all your decisions.*

30 ◆ COMING HOME

ood tidings come in pairs, they say. The same week that Kim Lan welcomed Phuong into her household, someone else showed up and demanded to be let in. It happened on a Wednesday evening, at about nine o'clock. It was September 12, 1990. The café was crowded and Sen was playing chess as usual. Busy giving change to a customer, Kim Lan did not see Hoang Long until he stood right next to her with a huge smile on his face. "I'm home!" he shouted so everyone could hear. Then he gave Kim Lan the tightest squeeze of a hug ever. He pecked her cheek then buried his face in her hair. He ran his hands up and down her back. With her head turned sideways, she could feel his hot breath and wet lips in her ear. Since most customers knew Sen as Kim Lan's husband, they were astounded by this display. They looked in Sen's direction and saw him standing up, his face fierce, announcing to everyone, "Please finish your drinks. We're closing in five minutes."

"Who is that?" Hoang Long asked Kim Lan, though he already knew.

She answered flatly, "He's my new husband."

After everyone had left, the three of them sat at a table, their chairs equidistant from each other, to try to unravel their situation. No one else was allowed in the room. Sneering, Hoang Long leaned back in his chair while his adversary, all grim concentration, hunched forward. "You must understand, I married Kim Lan in good faith. We all thought you were dead."

A Chinese accent, Hoang Long detected, grinning, sensing an advantage already. If his rival had come from Hanoi, he would have had to start calling him sir. "But I'm far from dead. I thank you for raising my son and keeping my wife company all these years, but now that I'm back, I'd like to live with my family again."

"I had no choice but to marry Sen," Kim Lan said in a consoling voice. "You must think back to 1975. If I didn't claim him as my husband, they would have taken the house. I had to say you had died."

"I'm not trying to blame anyone, but this is still my house, and you are still my wife. Sen, you're welcome to stay here until you can find new arrangements."

"But I've lived with Sen for fifteen years now and we have a daughter. If he leaves, then I'm leaving with him."

Hoang Long really hadn't expected his wife to say this. "You're telling me you're staying with this Chinaman instead of returning to your rightful husband?!"

Sen immediately stood up, knocking his chair backward. He was ready to kick Hoang Long in the face. The just-released prisoner looked terribly fragile. Spraying spittle, Sen raised his voice. "Listen, asshole. This house is under my name now. If you don't believe me, just ask Kim Lan to show you the papers. I understand all the shit you've gone through and I'm not going to be unreasonable. You're welcome to stay here until you can find new arrangements."

In his prime, Hoang Long would have torn into Sen—killed him with his hands, if necessary—but he had no fighting spirit left. Fifteen years of prison had conditioned him to accept any sort of humiliation with resignation. Threatened, he became speechless, his eyes blurred, and he sat still like a scolded child. Kim Lan felt so sorry, she wanted to pull him to her bosom. Seeing no reaction from Hoang Long, Sen lowered his voice. "You can stay here as long as necessary. Up to a month even. There's plenty of room in this house. There's no hurry."

That night Hoang Long slept on a cot downstairs while his hosts slept in their usual bed upstairs. Kim Lan was afraid he would break into their bedroom and kill them in their sleep. All night long she listened for the creaks of the stairs, but heard nothing.

In the morning Hoang Long took Kim Lan aside to say he was leaving. "I can't stay in the house a minute longer under these conditions."

"But where will you go? Stay here and relax, for a month at least. We'll work something out. I'm sorry things have turned out this way."

"Why are you whispering?"

"I'm not whispering."

"Yes, you are." Hoang Long shook his head and chuckled. "I'm staying in my own house as a guest, a house I bought with my own money, and my wife's speaking to me in a whisper because she's terrified of her new husband. She's also terrified the neighbors will find out she's a polygamist. That's why I'm leaving."

Kim Lan did not respond. She only sighed, her face hot. They stared at each other for a minute in silence. Suddenly, she understood what he wanted. "I'll be right back," she said. Then she went to her safe and cleaned it out, all of her savings, a very nice sum, returned and gave it to him. He took the money without saying a word, nodded and walked away.

Hoang Long took a van to Cao Lanh that afternoon. It was freakishly thrilling to see the landscape speeding by. Rice paddies had never appeared greener. Another weird sensation was to have a wad of money in his pants pocket. *I lost my wife and a fifth of my life*, he reflected, *but I'm a free man now. Just two days ago I was without hope.* The town of Cao Lanh had not changed much in the intervening years. Walking through its crowded market, he became reacquainted with many smells, shapes and colors. He paused often to inspect a once-familiar fruit or vegetable. Tempted to buy many things, he bought nothing, since he was still in awe of the small fortune he had in his possession. The sight of a policeman made his heart skip a beat. He stood still until the shopping cop disappeared. Laughing at his own nervousness, he had to shake his head. A young female suddenly brushed against him. Turning, he glimpsed her pretty face disappearing. *Life is good*, he thought. *There's a world of wars, prisons and hospital emergency rooms, and then there's ordinary life, where pretty girls go shopping and bump into you. Sometimes they even do more than bump into you,* he grinned at the dim memories. *Everyone's going about their business and no one cares that I've been in prison. No one cares that I've killed either.* A killer lives on borrowed time. To him, life has a lurking sharpness that those who haven't played destiny could never imagine.

Remembering the streets, Hoang Long had no trouble locating his mistress's house. The coconut tree in the yard seemed aged and diseased, its fronds ragged, its fruits the size of oranges, but everything else looked the same. He rang the bell and waited impatiently outside the gate. *I hope she's neither dead nor married.* Suddenly he panicked and touched his pants pocket. Sure enough, all the money was gone.

31 ✦ CONJUNCTIONS

Sen did not know that Hoang Long had left. To avoid his adversary and to give himself space to think, he had spent the morning at a café down the street. *A month is too long,* he thought. *I must figure out a way to get rid of him much sooner. There's no way I'm going to stare at his ugly mug three times a day, breakfast, lunch and dinner, for an entire month. The longer he stays, the more comfortable he'll get and soon I won't be able to get rid of him at all. He'll also grab my wife when I'm not looking. Hell, they might be doing it right now. . . . The guy's also a combat veteran. He's used to killing people. I'm surprised he didn't fight me last night. He didn't want to go back to prison, I guess. He's still a killer inside, however. The next time I cross him, or look at him cross-eyed, he'll stab me.*

At lunchtime, Sen returned home undecided about what to do with Hoang Long. He sat down at the table dreading the other man's presence. Noticing no extra bowl, he asked Kim Lan, "He's not eating with us?"

"He's gone."

"He's gone?!"

"He left this morning. For good."

Sen couldn't help but grin. He felt so happy, he even farted a couple of times.

"Why are you laughing?"

"I'm not laughing."

"Yes, you are."

"Do you expect me to cry?"

"I don't expect you to do anything, but you shouldn't be laughing. He spent fifteen years in jail. You should at least respect his sacrifice."

"Listen, I don't appreciate your lecturing me about how I should feel, OK? You should just be glad that I'm not angry, OK?"

"You angry?! What are you talking about?!"

"Why don't you calm down for a moment? If I'm not angry at you for deceiving me, then you should just calm down, OK?"

"Deceiving you?!"

"Don't you think I know where you went last year?"

"What are you talking about?!"

"You're so full of it."

"Yeah, I'm so full of it!"

Sen got up and walked away from the table. He had not touched his food.

"Where are you going?"

"I'm going to Phan Thiet."

Outside, greeted by brilliant sunshine, his mood improved immediately. It's all nonsense, he said to himself. He walked briskly down the street, feeling better with each step. He knew exactly where he was going and marched right inside. As soon as he sat down, a girl in a miniskirt ambled up to him and said, "How are you doing?"

A whore ages slower than a dog, but faster than a dentist or a secretary. A two-year-old dog equals an eighteen-year-old whore or a twenty-four-year-old dentist. When Cun met the how-are-you-doing girl a year ago, she had looked about sixteen. Now she looked twenty-two. Pinched and kneaded daily by an endless procession of slobbering boys and men, entertaining them, her flesh had slackened, her face hardened and her soul cracked. A year later, people would think she was twenty-seven. Sliding quickly down the longevity grease pole, she became careless and no longer insisted that her customers use condoms. By nineteen, her real age, she was dead.

Sen enjoyed her services that day and was back at the café an hour later, feeling much better. Cun stood behind the till and A-Muoi was playing with Hoa. A-Muoi had hardly said a word to Sen all these years but suddenly she spoke to him in Chinese. "You should never trust the Vietnamese. They are all dishonest."

Sen stared at A-Muoi's chubby face. "You shut up, all right?"

That night Sen went up to the bedroom and lay down next to Kim Lan. Though she faced away from him, he could tell she was not sleeping yet. Feeling a mixture of guilt and tenderness, he touched her on the shoulder, but she simply said, "No." They slept together that night and many nights after that, but they would never make love again.

In January of 1991, Kim Lan became a grandmother. Phuong's baby boy was solid and handsome, his heft surprising considering his parents' puny sizes. Two months later, Kim Lan gave Phuong money to open a stall at the market to sell pork. Cun got up at five each morning to help his wife pick up meat. Relations between Sen and Kim Lan were lukewarm during the day, chilly at night. She continued to feel an aversion to his touch and he no longer persisted. Whenever he was tired of playing chess, Sen would go to the hostess bar. All the girls liked him there and they even gave him a cute nickname: "Biggie Sen."

Sen always tipped the girls a little extra. Talking to them before and afterward, he'd ask them about their villages, and whether they had boyfriends, husbands or children. He'd ask them about their family lives, about their husbands' job and vices, and listen to their complaints.

"My husband drinks all day, Biggie Sen. That's all he does. That's why he can't hold a job for more than a week."

"How's he in bed?"

"Not half as good as you, Biggie Sen. He's not interested, at least not in me. He gives the money I make to other girls. You're so nice, Biggie Sen. You're really the nicest man who comes in here. I've never seen you drunk, for example. The drunk ones are so grabby. They squeeze your tits like they're made of rubber."

Sen had been waiting for this opportunity to debauch for a long time. But before Kim Lan stopped having sex with him, he had no reason. Playing chess all the time can give one an overgrown head, like the elephant man's, and atrophy the rest of one's body. Sex with Kim Lan, or with anyone else for that matter, was a necessary antidote to chess. Without sex, Sen's penis would have become the tiniest adjunct, an imperceptible mole on his colossal head. Grown complacent with the same-old-same-old with Kim Lan, he needed to have his frayed mind recharged with virgin vistas. *Every human body is touchingly beautiful and soothing to the eye*, he reflected, *from the most malnourished to the most voluptuous, from the most underdeveloped to the most worn-out.* Appreciating the naked human form on an aesthetic level, he considered himself an artist, or at least an anthropologist. He could see through clothes now. All of Saigon became a riot of smooth, jiggling flesh in his feverish mind. Waking, sleeping, his mind was always erect. Wandering around the neighborhood, he undressed everyone: the squatting soup vendors ladling hot broth into bowls; the seamstresses behind sewing machines, their ankles moving rhythmically; and all the students coming home from school, preteens, teenagers, shoving each other and laughing. He found them all equally beautiful.

He loved to have a prostitute on all fours, on her hands and knees, her head down, her hair cascading, hiding her face, her breasts hanging down. Before humping her, he would stand to the side to admire her beautiful form.

After Sen had sampled all the prostitutes in the neighborhood, he wandered farther afield. He even went to Tran Xuan Soan Street to try sex on water. The girls there posed as vendors of *hot vit lon*— a delicacy of duck embryo eaten directly out of an egg. For less than three bucks (including fifteen cents for a condom), Sen got to hop on a sampan, take a brief cruise, then rock the boat beneath one of those houses on stilts bordering the river. On board there was a reed mat, beer in a cooler, and a bucket of water for sanitation purposes.

Sen heard that in the fun-loving coastal city of Vung Tau, you could even try sex in the water. During the day, a girlfriend could be rented by the hour on the beach, inner tube included. This was a rather lame arrangement, Sen figured, since you had to share the water with kids, old people and Jet Skis, a situation which made consummation a little awkward. At night, the whores came out for real on Pineapple Beach, a rocky stretch not far from the main post office. These ladies were known as "fairies," celestial beings who would skinny-dip with your mortal self in the South China Sea for a mere thirty-five bucks. The only prostitutes Sen declined were the rare Chinese ones. It'd be like screwing your sister or your first wife or something. He didn't care for it.

Even after Sen had tried a hundred girls, he still had a special place in his heart for Kim Lan because she was the only Vietnamese woman ever to say yes to him without expecting to be paid immediately. Also, by accepting him as her husband, she granted him real citizenship of the country.

As Sen degenerated into debauchery, Kim Lan had plenty of time to brood over the institution of marriage. Late one evening, sipping an iced beer, a brand-new habit, she mused how every marriage has its poisoned moments and unfixable permanent defects. *Since people are flawed, a marriage must be flawed. Though it beats living alone, a marriage is always a misunderstanding between two dishonest people with selfish intentions*, she thought, shuddering, sipping her beer. *That's why most of them end in divorce, murder suicide, or a suicide pact. Marriage is simply a justification for murder*, she concluded. *A good marriage, relatively speaking, is one that ends prematurely in a fatal traffic accident. All in all, I consider myself very lucky.* Her own imperfect marriages she blamed on history. If history can kill and maim, then of course it can yield flawed husbands. A second here, an inch there, and each of us can be dead a hundred times over, so being badly married isn't the worst thing. Having reached middle age, she also realized that in any male-dominated society, women are forced to marry down, not to their social inferiors, but to their inferiors period. She shuddered thinking about whom Hoa might marry in the future.

Meditating on marriage, Kim Lan liked to comb the newspapers for stories of domestic violence. Feeling comforted and edified by accounts of marital disaster, she reveled in the all-too-rare incidents of wives killing husbands. She often wondered why some women retaliated against their husbands' infidelity by splashing acid on the other woman's face. At the market, she occasionally saw Cam Nhung, a famous singer from the sixties whose face had been destroyed by a jealous wife. Reduced to begging, she wore an old, plastic-wrapped photo of herself around her neck to convince passersby of her identity. Her unrivaled, still-beautiful hands also served as proof. Though Kim Lan always gave Cam Nhung money, she never stood around to hear the poor woman sing.

There was another acid victim in Kim Lan's neighborhood. Kim Lan saw it happen. Mr. Quang was the richest man in the neighborhood. He had started a car rental business with money sent to him by relatives in California. It grew to three cars and four vans. His four sons worked for him as drivers. The oldest had a beautiful wife, Huong, and a daughter. Feeling fortunate to marry into such a prosperous family, Huong watched Mr. Quang's declining health with hope and anticipation. Mr. Quang's wife had died many years before. At seventy-six, as he was cruising steadily toward Hades, as the cypresses and stone angels came clearly into view, he decided to take a lover, a forty-two-year-old woman named Thuy. Everyone was scandalized, but Huong was furious. Failing to persuade her father-in-law to quit his shameful behavior, Huong started to threaten Thuy over the phone. "Whore, you better lay off my father-in-law, else I'll peel the skin off your bleeding cunt!" Thuy refused to be intimidated because she also saw cars and vans in her future. That's when Huong decided to get tough. She secretly followed Mr.

Quang to Thuy's apartment, noted the address, then hired a female goon to send her rival a message. The very next day, the goon scraped against Thuy's motorcycle in traffic, sending her sprawling to the asphalt. As she struggled to get up, bleeding, the goon slapped her across the face, screaming, "Are you blind?!"

That will teach her, Huong thought, thinking she had solved the problem once and for all. A month later, however, as she was squatting at the market to pick out some fish, someone called her from behind. Turning around, she could only catch a brief glimpse of Thuy's face, crazed and angry, before she found herself flopping on the ground, her clothes torn from her burning flesh. They had to splash ice water on her as she screamed and screamed. Her face melted like wax. Globs of flesh streaked down her face, her nose collapsed, her right eye dissolved. If she had opened her mouth at the crucial moment, her tongue would have been gone.

When Mr. Quang died soon after, Huong's husband inherited the family business. They had become rich, as planned. Treatments for Huong were so expensive, however, that all the cars and vans were gone after a couple of years. Her husband never abandoned her. Since she could not leave the house, he bought songbirds to keep her company. The day she came home from the hospital, as she walked through the door, her two-year-old daughter screamed, "That's not my mom! That's a monster!"

Part III

1 ◆ ENLIGHTENMENT

Hoa was doing well at the New York School. She struggled with the past, present and future tenses, using them interchangeably, but her vocabulary was growing rapidly. Her teacher was a gutter punk from Staten Island named Sky. In Vietnam for three years, he had no plans to return to New York. He had gone to Vietnam to explore Buddhism, only to discover that there was no Buddhism in Vietnam. Sky had read in all the guidebooks that 80 percent of Vietnamese were Buddhists, but Vietnamese Buddhists, he soon found out, only went to the temples to pray for a winning lottery ticket. Most monks were entrepreneurs who drank beer with their mistresses in the evening. The monks and priests who tried to perform their primary function, speaking their conscience, had been sent to jail.

There is no religious instruction in Vietnamese Buddhist temples. Most Vietnamese have never heard a sermon in their lives. The religious figurines displayed inside their homes are mostly Taoist, the Gods of the Kitchen, of War and of Wealth. There may not be a Buddha. There is also the all-important altar dedicated to one's ancestors. If a Vietnamese Buddhist owns religious texts, they are most likely pamphlets of the popular kind, sanctioned by no Buddhist organizations. In the Vietnamese universe, Buddhism is merely a thin blanket half hiding an animist demon.

Perhaps no Buddhist doctrine is more abused by the Vietnamese mind than reincarnation. Sky had bought a fifty-two-page pamphlet titled *Karma Through Three Lives*, written by someone called Thich Thien Tam (literally the Zen Heart Monk). The cover featured a drawing of a man being sawed in half by two demons. With the help of a dictionary, Sky tried to wrest an epiphany or two from this enigmatic volume.

The pamphlet had three sections. The first answered all your questions about karma and reincarnation. The second recounted "true stories" of reincarnated lives. The last rehashed the first two sections, but in ballpoint pen illustrations.

Question #2 asked: "Why am I riding on a horse, not sitting in a carriage?"

Answer: "Because you paved roads and built bridges in your previous life."

Question #12: "Why do I have both my parents?"

Answer: "Because you respected lonely people in your previous life."

Question #13: "Why am I missing a parent?"

Answer: "Because you trapped birds in your previous life."

Question #24: "Why do I have a harelip?"

Answer: "Because you blew out the altar lamp in your previous life."

Question #26: "Why am I a hunchback?"

Answer: "Because you laughed at ardent worshippers in your previous life."

Question #28: "Why are my legs shrunken?"

Answer: "Because you were a highway bandit in your previous life."

Question #35: "Why was I poisoned?"

Answer: "Because you killed too many fish in your previous life."

Question #41: "Why does my body stink?"

Answer: "Because you sold fake incense in your previous life."

Section Two began rather testily with "Who said that karma is nonsense? A man and a goat can switch places before you know it."

It had nine stories of reincarnation. Below is Sky's translation into English of the first one:

AN IMPIOUS SON BECOMES A PIG

Hau Nhi, of Kim Don, was disrespectful toward his parents. When he saw his mother give rice to the poor, he became angry, hit her, and kicked her out of the house. His wife and children tried to intervene, but he would not listen. Soon after, his body erupted into boils. He suffered terribly and died soon after.

After he died, Hau Nhi appeared to his son in a dream and said, "Because I was disobedient and impious, I've been turned into a pig. I belong to Mr. Truong Nhi, who lives by the Tuyen Vo Gate in Kinh Su. You must go there to ransom me right away, else it will be too late."

Waking up, his son followed Hau Nhi's instructions and arrived at Truong Nhi's house. True enough, there was a sow that had just given birth to a litter of pigs. Among the piglets, there was one with a human face, with whiskers resembling his father's. The son tearfully explained his reasons for wanting to buy the pig, and offered ten bars of gold for it. Truong Nhi would not agree to a deal, however, and promptly killed the pig.

This happened in the thirty-ninth year of the Sung Dynasty [996 AD].

2 ♦ ERSATZ IZODS

Disillusioned with Vietnamese Buddhism, Sky had lingered in Saigon for the cheap rent, food, beer and other earthly amenities. His one objective in life was to stay away from America and, by extension, the West. It was a real bitch to be born into a continent-sized country, Sky believed. A huge country was like a vast, monolithic prison: You were shut off from the rest of the world and didn't even know it. Sky had also lived in India, after hearing on the BBC about a French guru who ran an ashram in Tamil Nadu and walked around naked all day. Leaving Chennai, he endured several cramped and clamorous bus rides to finally arrive at the ashram's gate. He stayed for two weeks meditating, reading, gardening and cleaning the toilets. He found no peace, just a lot of hard work. Sky left because he didn't want to substitute one system for another. He didn't care for Shiva or Jesus or any other god. Life, he decided, would be one drawn-out improvisation for as long as his stamina held up, like a late Coltrane solo, wild and beautiful and always on the verge of disintegration. Sky was, however, open to the possibility of becoming a buddha and that was why he came to Vietnam. In Saigon, he discovered something akin to pure chaos. In India there had been a confusing jumble of deities to be worshipped, but at least the people knew the names of their gods. The average Vietnamese, on the other hand, had no idea whom he was praying to. Every temple was referred to colloquially as Master's or Mistress's Temple. Sky even saw Vietnamese

Buddhists praying in Hindu temples in downtown Saigon. In Tay Ninh they worshipped a mysterious Black Lady, in Bac Lieu they supplicated rocks. Putting their hands together, they closed their eyes, bowed repeatedly while mumbling to stone statues of tigers and dogs. Everything seemed wide open—doors, windows, mouths, genitals—without making sense. It was anarchy. Sky saw a funeral procession led by a marching band jamming Dixieland—"When the Saints Go Marching In"—complete with a drum *majorette* who kept dropping *his* baton, while a traditional quintet brought up the rear, playing mournful music. Separated only by the ornate hearse, the two strains mixed with the theatrical weeping and the beep-beeping of a thousand irritated motorists. It was anarchy. Yet this was partly an illusion, of course, because a country's strictness and mores are often invisible to an outsider. One's first impression of any society, even the most rigid, is often of freedom.

Sky applied for a job at the New York School and was hired immediately after only a cursory interview. Being much taller than his students, he felt very benevolent toward them. Because of his bad teeth, the students and their teacher had at least one thing in common. Sky was disturbed by their materialism, however, and their lack of social consciousness. He noticed that many of them wore designer clothes and rode expensive motorbikes, while thousands of beggars roamed the streets. All the students talked about was brand names and pop music. They thought of America as a vast shopping mall to be envied and emulated. While he searched for a Stone Age Eden, they were trying to crash the twenty-first century. *They'll never get there*, Sky reflected with more sadness than malice. *Poor innocents, they don't realize that all of humanity is about to reverse gear and roll backward down the oily slope of progress. The twenty-first will come to resemble the seventeenth before they know it. Rushing to become modern, these people have swapped their vegetable patches, carp ponds, pigs and geese for a fake pair of Levi's, but the futuristic future they're fantasizing about will be nothing more than a last puff of smoke discharged from the rusty pipe of an exhausted lemon.*

To his students, however, Sky became an instant mascot for the very progress he had no faith in. Ignoring his nose ring, dreadlocks and body odor, they anointed him a harbinger of the future simply because he was a tall white American. To be American is to be huge in every sense, but Sky was sick of all things colossal. He wanted everything smaller, and more handmade. Sky often had a few beers with some of his students after class. He favored the humble sidewalk cafés over the expat bars. He also preferred Vietnamese pop music, where tune after dreary tune were strung along by pathetic, dispirited singers. Music should always be homegrown, to reflect homegrown emotions, Sky reasoned. A surfer should listen to surfing music, a caveman his cave music. Reggae playing at the South Pole would destroy both reggae and the South Pole. Music, just like food, should always be consumed in situ. Sky hadn't had a single French fry since arriving in Saigon. No Coke or Pepsi either, only soya milk and Saigon beer. Coke should not be allowed outside the city limits of Atlanta. Sitting on a low stool to dispense his wisdom, Sky fancied himself a reverse missionary, there to warn the natives against conversion. It wasn't at all contradictory for an English teacher to steer his students away from Anglo culture, he reasoned. They would never master English, no matter how hard they tried. Agents of bad English, they'd bring down the empire. Thinking they were speaking English, they'd only be parodying and perverting it. They were like a virus running rampant inside the decadent English body. There was no vaccine and it was too late for a quarantine. As soon as they opened their mouths, these annihilators of English infected native speakers with their horrific pronunciations, spellings and grammar. With amusement, Sky often found himself babbling like a retard, just to be understood by his so-called students. Drugged by Hollywood films and armed with electronic dictionaries, these students were no more than assassins of English. As for that rarest of foreigners, countable on one hand, more likely one finger, who was capable of beavering forward in a passable English, all they were doing was injecting weird, foreign ideas into the Anglo mind, making it less Anglo. In sum, the corrosive influence of billions of bad English speakers will make the language unrecognizable and irrelevant.

Take Latin: Even after being dead for fifteen hundred years, Latin-based words continued to be sloshed and gargled by billions of unclean mouths around the world. First thing in the morning, people wake up to defaecatus on what's left of Latin. Instead of cruising up and down the Mediterranean, the Romans should have stayed in Rome to hoard and protect their culture. They should have barricaded themselves inside the Coliseum and built no roads, walls, aqueducts and amphitheaters all over the place. They shouldn't have driven the bodacious Boudicca berserk by birching her. If they hadn't colonized England, France and Spain, etc., Latin would not be buggered daily by the Nigels, Jean-Pierres and Julios of the world. A language can only maintain its integrity by being exclusive, shut to outsiders, such as the Native American Ahtena (eighty speakers), or, better yet, the Argentine Ona (three speakers). By cajoling the rest of the world into learning English, Americans are begging for their own death. Nodding in the direction of the many beggars surrounding them, Sky stated that, yes, the United States also had beggars. "I was practically a beggar when I lived in New York."

"Why didn't you get a job?" Hoa asked him.

"I did have a job, I was a bike messenger. I delivered packages to offices, but I didn't make much money. I slept in a closet in a house I shared with five people."

"A closet?"

"It's a tiny room built into the wall to store clothes." Sky had forgotten that Vietnamese homes don't have closets. He was sitting so low, his knees grew level with his chest. A neon tube strapped to a nearby tamarind tree tinted his face an icy blue. Brown tamarind pods, toothpicks and soiled tissues lay scattered around his leather sandals.

"Why didn't you live with your parents?" another student asked him.

"I was seventeen when I left my parents. Americans do not live with their parents. If you're still living with your parents past your eighteenth birthday, you're considered a big loser!"

The students were astonished by this statement. Many of them, especially the men, would live with their parents for their entire lives—until death.

"I love my parents, sort of, but I don't want to live according to their rules," Sky continued. "If you don't live under the same roof with them, they can't tell you jack shit! Jack shit means 'anything,' by the way. But you need a strategy to survive as a poor person. Always buy the cheapest pasta, for example. It doesn't matter what shape it is: fettuccine, linguine, capellini, it's all semolina in your stomach. And you must cut out the bullshit. You don't need Gucci, Polo, Ralph Lauren or Nike to survive. I stay away from brand names on principle. The only purpose of advertising is to make you hate yourself, so you have to run out of the house to buy a Fila shirt or a bottle of Eau Sauvage to slather all over your face, only to make you slap yourself repeatedly!" Sky noticed a student wearing an ersatz Izod. "That doesn't count. It's fake!

"Live simply," Sky advised. "Besides my nose ring, which I bought for a dollar at the Dollar Store, I own no jewelry. I always buy my jeans at Kmart, the worst store in America." To prove he wasn't kidding, Sky stood up and pointed to the upside-down Vs on his back pockets. "You must remember that Kmart jeans are 50 percent polyester, 50 percent cotton," he added cryptically, losing his train of thought. Unlike dialogue in a well-plotted novel, his conversations flaunted their countless loose ends, which could never be cleaned up by an editor.

As he drank more Saigon beer, Sky talked faster, using slang almost exclusively. "I never pig out on fast food because these joints are owned by corporate pigs who run small farmers out of business.

Thanks to Ronald McDonald, there won't be any Old-McDonald farms left in the US of A. No more forty acres and a mule, bluegrass or square dancing. I shit you not, my friends: These motherfuckers torture cows and chickens just so they can stuff you with their poisoned meat! They make cows eat cows and chicken shit, chickens eat cow shit, and feed the sheep corn syrup and aspartame.

"And the music!" Sky continued after a brief beer pause. "American pop music is just one endless come-on. Just one unending advertisement!"

"What's a come-on?" Hoa asked.

"A come-on is when you bring your face really close to somebody's, like this," Sky brought his mug to within an inch of Hoa's, "so you can screw her later!"

"What's 'screw'?"

"Make love! Have sex! Take advantage of, you know, bang!"

"I still don't understand. The music wants to screw you later?"

"Yes, the music is just an advertisement!"

"But what is it advertising?"

"America!"

If he was really trashed, Sky talked in aphorisms. "I own nothing therefore I own everything. I don't buy art because the Louvre, the Uffizi and the Prado are already mine. I buy no land because I am the lord of every country."

At first, Hoa always stayed after class to hear Sky talk. She thought he was cool and sort of cute. Remembering his face so close to hers, she'd actually get shamelessly aroused and imagine licking the tip of his oddly shaped, obscenely forward nose, even swallowing it. But then she got tired of his ranting. She decided it was just drunken bullshit.

3 ◆ ACRID-SMELLING BLOOD

There is a twelve-hour difference between New York and Saigon. At 9:00 p.m. on September 11, 2001, as Sky was sitting on the sidewalk with a group of students, images of the first tower burning appeared on TV. "Your city!" someone shouted. "Your city is burning!" Joining the others in front of the tube, Sky felt shocked and awed. He noticed among the concerned, outraged faces, plenty that glowed with glee. The most horrible things, he soon realized, are mere spectacle to an outsider. Everything becomes entertainment, unless it's your hide that's burning. The only other times he had seen Vietnamese so excited in front of the TV were during soccer matches. Half expecting a comically violent reaction, everyone looked at Sky with pity and amusement. A student said, "Even your disasters are like Hollywood." Sky remembered watching *The Towering Inferno* as a kid, and how much he had loved it, especially the part when O. J. saved the cat.

Living on Staten Island, Sky had approached the rigidly inspiring World Trade Center with dread each morning—just seeing those white towers meant that he was going to work. Each evening, he turned his back to them with dazed relief. On the ferry home, he would think while passing the Statue of Liberty, *I'm free, free at last!* But to watch the towers go down in two monstrous clouds of dust among the aroused foreign faces in that bright café made him feel that something in him had crumbled forever. Although he could not articulate it at the time, Sky sensed that the American story of righteous dominance, a narrative that he had always railed against, had finally ended. The giant had allowed himself to be castrated, his twin cocks severed by two knives ablaze. Incoherently and with a changed voice, he would have a hard time convincing the world that he was still invincible.

That same day, Hoang Long was at home in Archbold, Ohio. As bin Laden's benign face came on the TV screen, he thought immediately of another thin-whiskered man who had lived in a cave and been a determined enemy of America. Ho Chi Minh was the first bin Laden, and bin Laden was just another Vietcong. As guerrilla leaders, they had benefited from the largesse of the CIA or the Office of Strategic Services (OSS), precursor to the CIA. *If I were President Bush*, Hoang Long thought with genuine anger, *I'd make them pay for this outrage! If you have the best army in the world, you ought to use it. Kill them all, let God sort them out later!* Living in the heart of the empire, Hoang Long felt strangely vulnerable and humiliated. He was grateful to America for having brought him to the promised land and given him an honest living with plenty of growth potential. There was no dignity but in labor. He had risen from janitor to chicken packer to chicken zapper to chicken terminator. Foremanship was next. If he wasn't already old, and his bones didn't ache so much from working overtime, he would gladly repay this debt by fighting in America's next several wars, starting with the War on Terror. Wherever there were terrorists, extremists, turbaned minutemen, deaeners, etc., and lots of hydrocarbon under the sand, by the way, he'd volunteer to kick down doors, overturn mattresses, spray righteousness and squash the (non-Monsanto) seed of terror. Kill 'em all, let the Red Crescent sort 'em out. He finished his can of Budweiser, then immediately popped open another one because he was so upset.

Later that day, while changing into his size six galoshes in the locker room, Hoang Long said to a co-worker, a beefy fellow by the name of Joe Banford, "If I am Bush, I will shot them all!"

"You mean 'shoot them all'?"

"No, shot them all!"

"Shoot?"

"Shot!"

"Shoot?"

"Shot!"

"Oh, I get it. You're one of those guys who will get things done yesterday!"

"Yes, I will shot them all if I am Bush!"

Then he stood in acrid-smelling blood, in a blood-splattered white coat, and killed eighty thousand of them. He hung them by the legs and slit their throats as they squawked their last.

4 ◆ A TIGHT POSSE

By 2003, Hoa had graduated from Kentucky Fried Chicken to the bars downtown. She belonged to a tight posse of cool chicks from class who club-hopped every weekend. They'd ride from bar to bar, each on her own motorbike, chatting in traffic. They learned how to shoot pool and drink iced beer. A few sips were enough to make any of them giddy and garrulous. Hoa could never finish a bottle. Fearing their teeth would be stained brown, none of them smoked. They loved to banter about sex.

"Has a boy ever touched your breasts, Hoa?"

"Yeah, right."

"Has a boy ever stuck his tongue into your mouth?"

"You tell me. What does it feel like?"

"It feels like you have two tongues, Hoa. Have you seen it?"

"Seen what?"

"Have you seen a peeled banana?"

"No, but I've seen a pickled cucumber."

"No, you haven't!"

"Tell me, do bananas grow up or down?"

"Everything grows up, Hoa!"

The girls accused each other of wearing padded bras. One girl, Loan, had the annoying habit of always touching Hoa's breasts while saying, "Are they real?" She made up for it by buying Hoa ice cream and yogurt. Loan was a source of weird facts she culled from God knows where. "Hoa, did you know that Cantonese slang for a woman is tofu?"

"I can see that: tofu is soft, just like a woman."

"And it moves like a woman."

"Tofu doesn't move!"

"If you lick it, it does."

"Who licks tofu?!"

"Many people do, Hoa. Tofu stuffed with ground beef is nice but tofu by itself is also nice. There's nothing better in the world than two pieces of tofu smothered in coconut milk sweetened by brown sugar, then sprinkled with slivers of ginger."

"That sounds really delicious. I've never tried that. I didn't know you were a cook. I usually eat my tofu deep-fried."

"Deep-fried tofu! That's disgusting." Loan leaned closer to Hoa and spoke in a conspiratorial tone. Her peppermint breath was not unpleasant. "Did you know, Hoa, that women in China used to stuff a special mushroom into a penis-shaped pouch, then soak it in warm water? The slimy mushroom would swell, filling the pouch, making it ready to use."

"Ready to use for what?"

"Hoa, do you have to ask?!"

"You don't mean they used it for that!"

"But you don't even know what that is!"

The girls dubbed themselves the Metallicas because they were all into heavy metal. They bought and lent each other pirated CDs of Megadeth, Rhapsody, Liquid Tension Experiment, Pain of Salvation, etc. Hoa loved heavy metal for its rage and energy. It had balls and spine and contrasted sharply with the moaning dirges her mother drowned in at home. When Kim Lan bitched about Hoa's new taste in music, she barked right back, "It's American music, Mama! It's what American kids listen to!" There were a handful of garage bands in Saigon, a city with almost no garages. The most famous was the Yellows. Hoa enjoyed their music well enough, but she found their lyrics ridiculous. They sang of friendship and lost love, not exactly metal material. Though they had adopted a new sound, they were stuck with the old sentiments. More to her taste was a band called Love Like Hate. It wasn't heavy metal, but punk, someone told her. Like many girls, she also found the lead singer, Quang Trung, hot. He had the coolest tattoo she had ever seen: an upside-down map of Vietnam on his right biceps.

Love Like Hate was the house band at World War III, just down the street from Apocalypse Now. Hoa arrived early every Saturday night to claim a stool at the end of the bar, right next to the stage. She would chat to Quang Trung during the sound check and look at him adoringly during the show. Everyone assumed she was his girlfriend even before she became his girlfriend. During a break between sets one night, Quang Trung was at the bar drinking a Jack on the rocks. He stood so close to Hoa, he could smell her perfume and feel her breath on his cheek. He also felt, unmistakably, the pressure of her left thigh leaning against his. Between sips, he turned and saw her eyes glistening. She stared straight into his eyes without blinking. The red light made her face glow like burning coal. Knowing this was the right moment, he kissed her hard on the lips, their tongues touching. "I want to see you naked," he said, before he leaped back onstage.

Kim Lan tolerated Hoa going to the rock-and-roll bars because she assumed those places were hopping with Viet Kieus. *You can't wait for a Viet Kieu to come to your door,* she reasoned, *you must go to them.*

"Have you met a nice Viet Kieu at the bar, Hoa?"

"Yes, I've met many, but I haven't found anyone to my liking."

"Don't be too choosy. Just pick a Viet Kieu about your age. A little older is OK too, even ten years older."

"Don't worry, Mama. There are plenty of Viet Kieus at those places. I'll find one sooner or later."

The truth was that there were hardly any Viet Kieus at those rock-and-roll joints. They were frequented mostly by expats and the children of the nouveau riche. Lonely Viet Kieu men preferred the hostess bars, where they could get laid for the price of two or three shots of Jack Daniel's.

5 ◆ MOTHER VIETNAM

Quang Trung's parents were nouveau riche. His father was a high-ranking customs officer who received kickbacks every which way for all the smuggling flowing in and out of the country. They had an American-style house in Thu Duc, complete with a two-car garage and a swimming pool. Quang Trung used his father's money to buy whatever he wanted and to travel the world—he had been all over Europe and Asia—but he had never paid for a woman. He could get his for free, he reasoned, so why go to a sleazy hostess bar just to get laid? Quang Trung also used his father's money to buy books. He read widely yet randomly. He had enough English to read Hemingway with the help of a dictionary. He watched foreign films and was familiar with Tarkovsky, Fellini and Fassbinder. In Paris, he met Tran Anh Hung. They hit it off and stayed in touch via email.

Living in such an impoverished, degraded country, Quang Trung justified his privileged status by becoming an artist. Buying into this rationalization, he never apologized for his expensive lifestyle. The idea was to spend whatever was necessary to become a better artist. A weekend junket to Hong Kong was warranted because it stimulated and added to his knowledge of Hong Kong. His father earned money crookedly, sure, but this corruption of the father was serving to elevate the son. An artist could not waste money simply because money could not be wasted on an artist. He should be showered with money, as much money as possible, even blood money. From Dostoyevsky, he gleaned the crucial insight that everything and everyone in an artist's life has been granted by providence to serve him, or rather, his art, so long as he remains an artist. This is only fair since an artist gives so much back, to so many more people. It would be foolish, ungrateful and a shirking of responsibility to decline any freebie from above. Even if he turned out to be an artistic failure, Quang Trung reasoned, he had at least provoked and/or annoyed other artists. Bad art highlighted, even defined, good art. Even the most deluded, incompetent artist had his reason to be. His own reason to be, Quang Trung had come to believe, was to peer under what was under, to lift the heavy carpet of civilization, at least the Vietnamese one, grimy as it was with mishaps and murders, and expose many centuries' worth of frass, secrets and lost change. Hoa had never encountered anyone like Quang Trung. She didn't know there were people like Quang Trung in the world.

Quang Trung explained to Hoa that he called his band Love Like Hate because that was how he felt about Vietnam. "I love Vietnam so much I hate her. How can I not hate her when I love her so much? I am like a son who froths at the mouth because he has to watch his mother sell her pussy. She's sold her pussy to the Chinese, French, Russians and Americans, and now she's selling it to the Taiwanese. She'd sell her pussy to anyone because she feels inferior to everyone. She's thrilled to be humiliated because someone is paying attention to her. And when she's too old to sell her own pussy, she sells her daughter's pussy. That's Mother Vietnam for you!"

He then sang sarcastically, "*Mother Vietnam with her brilliant eyes! Hears the echoes of peace nearby! Gentle mother with her glittering eyes! Hears her son is still alive!* It's all bullshit, don't you understand?"

Quang Trung blamed Vietnam's sorry state on its men. "The men have been in charge and they've fucked up everything. They beat their wives, go to the whorehouses and come home drunk at the end of the day. They're vicious yet feeble because they have never had to prove themselves worthy of their women. It's that Confucianism shit and Vietnamese women are so sick of it. That's why they'll marry any foreigner who comes along just to get the fuck out of the country. That's a fate worse than prostitution. A prostitute only sells her body for parts of the day, but if you marry someone just to leave the country, or for money, you're selling your body twenty-four hours a day for the rest of your life!"

"Or until you divorce him!"

Quang Trung cringed and declared in a challenging way, "If you sell your body, that's bad, but if you sell your soul, that's even worse."

"Who doesn't know that already?"

"Many people!"

"I know that!"

When Quang Trung ranted, he reminded Hoa a lot of Sky. She agreed with many of his observations, but hearing him run his mouth still gave her a headache. She preferred to hear him talk about his travels.

"Are European cities dirty, Quang Trung?"

"Only Naples and Brussels, but Naples is very exciting, just like Saigon, and very beautiful too."

"Are there prostitutes?"

"Enough. The whores there like to wear vinyl, leather and fishnet stockings."

"Sounds good to me! I wouldn't mind dressing like that. I bet you I'd look fantastic in orange vinyl. I'd be so smooth and shiny!"

"Stop joking around. In Western Europe, many of the whores are from the old Communist countries. In Amsterdam, the prostitutes were all Russians and Romanians. I could tell they weren't Dutch just by looking at their foreheads."

"What do you mean?"

"You know how Vietnamese heads bulge out in the back?"

"Yeah."

"Well, Dutch heads bulge out in the front. I also saw African and Asian whores in Amsterdam. You see, when you're dirt-poor, that's all you have to sell. I walked into a go-go bar in Munich and both of the girls dancing were Asian. One was Thai, the other Filipino. I went to dozens of go-go bars in Europe, but never saw American or Japanese girls dancing. That's because they're rich!"

"But not all Americans and Japanese are rich!"

"I agree. But at least they're not desperate enough to go overseas to sell their pussies."

"But why did you go to those go-go bars? I thought you hated to see people selling their bodies."

"They weren't selling their bodies, Hoa. They were selling the *appearance* of their bodies."

"But who doesn't?!" Hoa replied, a little annoyed. "But you know what I mean."

"I wanted to see who works in those joints." Quang Trung smiled. "I also wanted to see what the men in there were like."

"And what were they like?"

"They were hungry and miserable and they wanted to be hugged!"

Hoa thought for a moment, then said, "Well, I don't think you should blame poor women for prostituting themselves."

"I'm not blaming the women—I think prostitution should be legalized, as a matter of fact—but I'm condemning any society in which women have little choice but to become prostitutes. The red-light district in Amsterdam is tiny, but all of Saigon is a red-light district."

"You're right. Whenever I sit on a public bench by myself, men ride up on their motorbikes and say, 'You're coming with me, little sister?' They all think I'm a whore! But no one is forced to become a prostitute. A girl can always find work as a domestic servant."

"But a domestic servant is a slave, and who wants to be a slave?"

"I, for one, don't treat my domestic servants as slaves. I rarely yell

194

at them and I give them all my old clothes. We watch TV together and we even eat out together."

Quang Trung was so charmed by this response, he stopped talking. Smiling, he leaned toward Hoa and gave her a big kiss.

Quang Trung had a loft by the river he divided into a practice studio and a bachelor pad. Hoa came there almost every day. She loved to just lie on his bed and listen to Blondie, Grace Jones, Burning Spear or the Butthole Surfers. She liked most of Quang Trung's CDs except the jazz ones. Music without singing was too alien a concept to her. Hoa could easily have imagined moving in and staying forever, maybe without telling her parents. They would panic and wonder where she had gone. I've moved to the dark side of the moon, she thought with pleasure, borrowing an image from Pink Floyd. I'm writing to you from a faraway country. Music took her places, or at least it removed her from Vietnam. Grooving to Shonen Knife or Control Machete, she felt liberated momentarily from her native society. With the AC on full blast, she imagined what it must be like to live in a cold climate, where words like "coziness" and "warmth" must have entirely different meanings. To live in a cold country was to be chilled by the AC even when out-of-doors. Every so often, sometimes twice a day, a blackout would happen, shutting down the AC, lights and music. Plunged into darkness, silence and heat, Hoa was reminded that she was still very much a citizen of the Socialist Republic of Vietnam. *It's a real bitch to be born into a closet-sized country*, she thought. A tiny country is like a tiny prison: One is shut off from the rest of the world and knows it.

When Kim Lan asked her where she had been, Hoa always lied. Her job was to go out and hook a Viet Kieu so she could fly to America, not sleep with some punk rocker with an upside-down tattoo on his arm, even if he was superrich. Hoa could just hear her mom's shrill voice yelling, "His father is a crook and will go to jail before you know it!"

Hoa never gave Quang Trung her address or phone number. She

didn't even dare to call him from home because her mom always lurked in the background whenever Hoa picked up the phone. She did say that her mom owned a café called Paris by Night. Even this spurred him into a tirade. "Paris by Night?! To call a Vietnamese café in Saigon Paris by Night is absurd! That's just typical! Typical! Tell your mom the French left half a century ago!"

"My mom thinks it sounds classy and intellectual."

"Intellectual?!" He shook his head, disgusted.

Hoa had never seen anyone with so many books as Quang Trung. She came from a home with no books, only a few tattered magazines. She hadn't thought a mind could contain more than a dozen books. To buy more than a dozen books was sheer vanity and a criminal waste of money, she thought, like having too many pairs of shoes while children were starving. She stared at the hundreds of books lining Quang Trung's shelves. "Have you read all of these?"

"Most of them."

"Why read so many books?"

"Because I don't want to be an idiot."

"I haven't read any books. Am I an idiot then?"

"No, you're a young woman who hasn't had a chance to read books."

"My mom hasn't read any books either. Is she an idiot?"

"No, she's Mother Vietnam! She already knows everything."

Reading Quang Trung's books at random, Hoa became very fond of Ho Bieu Chanh. She had seen his books before, at street stalls among displays of chewing gum, nuts and candies, and had assumed they were cheap romances because of their lurid covers. But Quang Trung told her that Ho Bieu Chanh was a very serious and prolific writer, someone who had produced sixty-four novels over a five-decade career. He also wrote plays, short stories, essays, memoirs, poems and travel books. Ho Bieu Chanh was one of a handful of extraordinary men from the first half of the twentieth century who tried with superhuman effort to modernize Vietnam through literature. By exposing age-old vices and idiocies, they hoped people would slowly change. Their influences remained subtle. Reading a Ho Bieu Chanh novel from 1935, Hoa noticed that the society he depicted was dominated by lust, greed, deceit and abuse of power, just like it was today, only peopled with characters who walked and talked a little slower. One day Quang Trung saw Hoa reading a slim novel by Pham Thi Hoai.

"Do you like her? She's the best Vietnamese writer on the planet. She lives in Berlin."

"Have you met her?"

"Yeah. I met her and her German husband. The guy speaks excellent Vietnamese."

"Will I get to meet them someday?

"What do you mean?"

"Will you take me to Germany to meet them?"

Quang Trung smiled. "Only if you say yes."

Hoa did not answer, she only blushed, because everything was understood.

6 ◆ LOVING DOLPHINS

One beautiful Saturday morning Hoa and Quang Trung took a hydrofoil to Vung Tau. The stretch of the river connecting Saigon to the sea boasts some of the loveliest landscapes in all of Vietnam. Sampans paddled by feet bobbled in the shadows of mangrove forests. Much of what greets the eye is lush green, unmarred by human habitats, a true rarity in an overflowing country. At the mouth of the ocean, bright sky and shimmering sea merge into a single liquid universe, with the warm wind still blowing in your face.

With 2,143 miles of coastline, Vietnam has many beautiful beaches. Although Nha Trang, Ca Na and Phan Thiet all boast finer beaches, Vung Tau is by far the most popular resort in Vietnam, thanks to its proximity to Saigon. During the war, Saigon residents had two options for a quickie holiday: Da Lat, for its cool weather, pine trees and lakes, and Vung Tau. Although it hosted a huge American installation, the Vietcong never shelled it. The joke was that the VC wanted to keep the city safe for their own vacationing officers.

At one end of the city is a pair of gigantic cement Buddhas, sitting and reclining on a hill. At the other end is a gigantic cement Jesus, arms outspread, standing on another hill. Beneath this rip-off of Rio's *Hey-Zeus* is Back Beach, the main bathing area. In a country where palm trees are ubiquitous, Back Beach actually has none. They've all been cut to make room for the widened road and the hideous-looking guesthouses and restaurants. It doesn't matter:

the sand is reasonably clean, the water warm, and all your earthly needs will be catered to you right on the beach. From the itinerant vendors you can order crab, shrimp, ice cream, lychees, durians, snails, a plate of green papaya with beef jerky, rice with pork chops, or a bowl of crab and tomato soup. You can even have your fortune read by a wandering fortune-teller.

After checking into a minihotel, Hoa and Quang Trung relaxed on two beach chairs, drinking iced beer and eating shrimp cooked in beer. Hoa wore a maroon two-piece with large daisies. The bikini was mostly string, with scarce room for the daisies. Quang Trung wore a blue Aquablade brief. In a country where female bathers sometimes wade into the ocean in pajamas, Hoa was drawing quite a bit of attention with her smooth form and meager thread. Dreading dark skin, most Vietnamese women shun both sun and sea, the only two things their country has plenty of. Exposed to the elements, their pores open, the young couple's nakedness was warmed by the maternal sun and stroked and tickled by the sea breeze.

Noticing Jet Skis weaving among the bobbing heads, Hoa remarked, "They're treating people's heads like cones on an obstacle course!"

Quang Trung shook his head. "Those guys should be arrested."

"They're heroin addicts!" a man selling duck eggs, standing nearby, chimed in. "The law doesn't allow them to come close to shore, but they've paid off the cops. You should never hire them. They always cheat when it's over. They'd give you a twenty-minute ride and say it's an hour!"

"Do they ever bonk anybody on the head?" Hoa asked.

"Rarely. But don't swim underwater because they won't be able to see you. Every now and then they actually save lives. This beach has no lifeguards so they come in handy when something happens." The duck-egg vendor had a hard time focusing on Hoa's face. Just seeing her lips was disturbing, but when he lowered his gaze he became even more rattled. He decided to focus just above her head as he addressed her.

"And what are those guys doing?" Hoa pointed to several men pulling a plowlike contraption across the shallows. "Are they catching crabs?"

"They're trying to find gold!"

"Gold?!"

"Yes, gold. Not gold nuggets, but necklaces, earrings and rings left behind by bathers. These guys used to scoop sand into a strainer until someone came up with a new tool. It's made of a net and a scraper attached to a harness."

"Do they ever find anything?"

"They only need to find a ring a day to make it worthwhile. If they find a nice necklace, they can sell it for what I make in a month." Tired of tilting his head up, he decided to focus on her bare knees as he talked to Hoa. *In her bright bikini, this girl looks a bit like a Jet Ski,* he thought. *In a century or two, when Jet Skis become affordable to someone like me, it will no longer be fashionable to own one. Progress is exhilarating and good, I'm all for it, but it's making me a little dizzy. As a poor man, I can only look at progress, not partake in it.* "I thought about joining them in searching for gold, but selling duck eggs is more steady."

Because Vietnamese had little faith in banks or their currency, gold was considered the safest means to store wealth. That's why just about everyone had gold on them, even as they waded into the water. One was reminded of the boat people, who left with all of their wealth converted into gold and/or dollars, most of which ended up in the hands of Thai pirates or at the bottom of the sea.

The sun had turned fierce. Tired of everyone ogling her, Hoa finally said to Quang Trung, "Let's go into the water!"

Is there a better sensation than embracing a beloved body in the ocean? What is more sacred than conjoining in the primordial stew? Some people interpret this to mean sex with dolphins: Male dolphins have S-shaped prehensile schlongs that can grow to fourteen inches. Aroused, they do not object to being handled by humans.

Female dolphins have genital slits that are swollen pink whenever they need to get laid. As a human, you can bury your hand deep inside the soft, spongy interior and slide it back and forth. Dolphins have up to one hundred teeth, all razor sharp, making them unsuitable for an oral connection.

Water on the body, inside the body, water lapping. The sun on one's upturned face, inside the mouth, inside one's body. Salt on two pairs of lips, coming in and out of the body. Two bodies joined, fastened, balanced on two sturdy legs, planted in the sand, in the sea, a tangible sea that connects one to everything. What Hoa and Quang Trung did that day was not perverse in the least. As two members of the same species, they had every right to give their bodies and souls to each other.

7 ◆ TWO AFTER MIDNIGHT

"Are you sleeping yet, Hoa?

"No."

"What are you thinking about?"

"Nothing."

"It wasn't too hot today. The sea was nice. Do you want to stay here an extra day?"

"No, we should get back in the morning."

"What are you thinking about?"

"That was really fun, in the water."

"Yeah."

"People probably saw us."

"So what?"

"Have you ever done that before?"

"No."

"You've never done that with another girl?"

"No."

"How come you've never told me how many girlfriends you've had?"

"What does it matter?"

"Tell me, how many girls have you slept with?

"What does it matter?"

"More than ten?"

"I don't want to talk about this. Let's change the subject."

"More than twenty?"

"Why are you so curious?"

"What were the others like? Did they do anything weird?"

"What do you mean 'weird'?"

"Did you have sex with them underwater?"

"I already told you. No."

"So what made you think of it?"

"It was instinct. It just happened."

"It was really intense."

"We can try it again tomorrow if you like."

"No, it won't be the same."

"You're right. You can't plan these things."

"Maybe you can write a song about it."

"Maybe."

"You can call it 'Man and Mermaid.'"

"No, that's really corny!"

"Do you love me, Quang Trung?"

"You're always asking me that. Of course."

"Of course what?"

"Of course I love you."

"Say it again."

"I love you, I love you, I love you."

"Now you're making a joke out of it."

"I'm getting sleepy, Hoa."

"I'm not."

"I'm really exhausted, Hoa. Let's just sleep."

"Exhausted from what?"

"I spent myself in the ocean."

"Poor man!"

"Let's just sleep, Hoa."

"I'm not sleepy yet."

"Are you wet?"

"No, I'm just kidding around."

"Let's see."

"No! I'm just kidding."

"Now you got me worked up. Just feel it!"

"You're so sensitive."

"It's always sensitive."

"Does it hurt?"

"No, but it's a little annoying. Stop playing with it."

"Have you ever had sex with an older woman?"

"How old is older?"

"Middle-aged."

"Why do you want to know?"

"Because I'll be a middle-aged woman someday. Sometimes I see my mother's face in the mirror and it scares me."

"You're talking like a middle-aged woman right now."

"See! You're already getting sick of me!"

"Stop being so serious. You want to hear a joke?"

"Not really."

"But you must hear this one. It's funny."

"OK."

"A rich kid takes his girlfriend home to meet his parents."

"Go on."

"He says to his dad, 'Dad, this is my girlfriend. I really love her. I want to marry her.'"

"OK."

"His dad gives him a serious look, pulls him aside and says, 'But you can't marry her. She's your sister!'"

"Huh?!"

"That's exactly what the rich kid says. His dad explains, 'I visited a place called Paris by Night nearly twenty years ago. Met a really nice lady there. Supersexy. That's why your girlfriend's your sister!'"

"That's a terrible joke, Quang Trung!"

"There's more: Pissed off, the rich kid tells his mom why he can't marry his girlfriend. She laughs really hard and says, 'There's no problem whatsoever. Go tell your father your girlfriend's not your sister because you're not his son either.'"

"You're really bad at jokes, Quang Trung."

"You didn't think it was funny at all?"

"No, not at all."

"Sorry."

"Don't tell me another joke ever again."

"Hey, I was only trying to make you laugh."

"Good night, Quang Trung."

"Good night, Hoa."

"Good night, sweetie."

"I love you. I love you. I love you."

"I believe you."

"I really, really, really love you."

"I believe you."

8 • HEAVENLY MESSAGES

Kim Lan wondered whether Hoa had a boyfriend and was lying about it. There were too many signs. Hoa claimed to have gone to Vung Tau with Bich, a neighborhood girl, but only Hoa had a deep tan the day after. Hoa stayed out late nearly every night yet never talked about a Viet Kieu in concrete details. The fibs she made up were transparent and laughable. Deciding to seek divine intervention, Kim Lan announced to Hoa that the two of them would go on a religious pilgrimage, to see the Black Lady in Tay Ninh.

Abutting Cambodia, Tay Ninh is sixty miles northwest of Saigon. Going there by car, you will drive over the Cu Chi tunnel complex, where Vietcong guerrillas lived underground for years like naked mole rats. You will also pass by the town of Trang Bang, famous for a thick white noodle called *banh canh*, and for a photograph of a burning, naked nine-year-old girl running away from a napalm strike. (Her name is Phan Thi Kim Phuc. She became a devout Christian and now lives in Toronto.) Kim Lan bought two tickets on a bus that left at five in the morning. It was air-conditioned, but noisy from a TV showing one comedy after another.

During the two-hour ride, Kim Lan explained to Hoa the legend of the Black Lady, "At the beginning of time, Hoa, there was a genie who fell in love with a fairy. He gave her diamonds and expensive dresses, but she paid no attention to him. After ignoring his pleading for years, the fairy challenged the genie to a mountain-building contest. If he could build a higher mountain than she could, she would marry him. After three days, they went to the top of the genie's mountain and could see the ocean and all the neighboring countries. From the summit of the fairy's mountain, however, they could see the entire world. Letting out a bitchy, victorious laugh, the fairy kicked the genie's pathetic molehill of a mountain to smithereens. Only her creation, Black Lady Mountain, remained. So you see, Hoa, the Black Lady is more powerful than even a male god, which is what a genie is!"

The Black Lady Mountain was just outside Tay Ninh. At twenty-eight hundred feet, it was not much more than a hill. It was striking solely because it was the only elevation for hundreds of miles around. Standing on its peak, you could see the vague outline of Dau Tieng Lake, about five miles away. Near the summit, there was a Buddhist temple with the unlikely name Fairy Rock, built in 1997. Most people referred to it, generically, as Mistress's Temple, the mistress being the Black Lady.

Kim Lan and Hoa got off the bus in a huge, dusty parking lot. After buying forty-five-cent tickets, they joined thousands of other pilgrims in trudging up the steep mountain. Some were carrying bags of rice, boxes of (vegetarian) instant noodles and fruit to donate to the Fairy Rock Temple. Porters could also be hired for the purpose. One could tell by the way most of the pilgrims were dressed—floral pajamas and tennis hats—that they had come from the remotest villages. Along the way to the temple the pilgrims passed an alligator pond, a temple dedicated to Ho Chi Minh, a statue of a female Vietcong fighter and countless refreshment stands. They saw plastic trash cans strapped to the backs of cast-iron penguins and tree-mounted speakers blaring tinny pop music. Peddlers roamed the trail to hawk bundles of incense, lottery tickets, chewing gum and fifteen-cent necklaces. "Take a Buddha back to the little one at home!" a small girl yelled as Kim Lan stumbled sideways down a slippery rock. For those too feeble to hike up the trail on foot, there was a ski lift. "But we must walk," Kim Lan explained to a sweating, panting Hoa. "Otherwise, the Black Lady will not help us." Many pilgrims would sleep overnight on rented straw mats, in tents or cabins. After dark, card games, alcohol and curses contributed to the festive atmosphere.

This entire complex, including the temple, was administered by the government. A Communist capitalist venture, it had the feel of a budget Disneyland minus the rides. In spite of its stance against "superstition," that was the one aspect of religion the government minded the least. The more superstitious the populace, the more they donated to temples dedicated to supernatural deities. The government and the monks divided the loot. In his book *Sai Gon Tap Pin Lu* (*Hodge Podge Saigon*), Vuong Hong Sen mentions the original Black Lady, an ancient foot-long limestone figurine, most likely of Cambodian origin, worshipped inside a deep cave. It is no longer there. No one has seen it in seventy years.

After hiking for an hour and a half, Kim Lan and Hoa finally reached the Fairy Rock Temple. They went inside and looked at all the statues but saw nothing that resembled a Black Lady. Kim Lan walked up to a cigarette-puffing monk and asked meekly, "Where is the Black Lady, teacher?"

He was a muscular one, this monk, an iron pumper, his one bare arm rippling. It took the utmost self-control for him to refrain from sporting a tattoo of the Ksitigarbha Bodhisattva, a personal favorite, on his right biceps. "There is no Black Lady!"

"But isn't this the Black Lady Mountain?"

"Yes!" The monk deepened his voice and stressed each syllable as if he were talking to an idiot. "Only the mountain is called Black Lady. There is no Black Lady!"

"So which statue are we supposed to pray to?"

"Any statue!"

Heeding the monastic's instruction, Kim Lan and Hoa went up to the nearest wooden figure—a scowling male deity with six arms and a long tongue sticking out of his mouth. "Just be honest, Hoa, just ask him for a Viet Kieu husband. Ask him to deliver a Viet Kieu husband to you as soon as possible. Tell him you have no skill, no education, and that you will not make it through life without a Viet Kieu husband." Mimicking her mother, Hoa clasped her hands in front of her forehead, but did not pray at all. As soon as she closed her eyes, she saw Quang Trung smiling at her. The gongs, bells, chanting and wailing in the background sounded to her almost like a punk band tuning up. She could not wait to get back to Saigon so she could be with her boyfriend. Around him, she felt grown-up, like a woman. Around her mother, she felt retarded.

Descending from the Black Lady Mountain, Kim Lan and Hoa went into town to visit the Cao Dai Holy See. With its triple-layered roofs, square towers, octagonal minaret and blue dragons intertwining pink columns, all done in painted cement, it was without doubt the weirdest-looking structure in all of Vietnam, not a small honor, and one of the most impressive. It was described by Graham Greene as a "fantastic Technicolor cathedral" and dismissed by Norman Lewis as "the most outrageously vulgar building ever to have been erected with serious intent." Entering it without mockery, however, one could sense the strong belief and dedication of the Cao Dai followers, people who tried to lead simple, faith-based lives in a very debauched and corrupt country.

Founded in Tay Ninh in 1926, Cao Dai seeks to synthesize the doctrines of the three main religions—Buddhism, Taoism and Confucianism. Based on communication with God and other spirits through séance sessions, it uses techniques such as the Ouija board and *pneumatographie*. Blank slips of paper are sealed in envelopes, then hung above the altar for the spirits to write on. The basket-with-a-beak technique is also used. A pen is attached to a stick radiating from a wicker basket. Two mediums hold the basket while the apparatus quivers to deliver messages from beyond the grave. Since it is transparent and direct, this is Cao Dai's preferred method of spiritual communication. Among Cao Dai's many saints are Victor Hugo, Joan of Arc, Pasteur, Tolstoy, Shakespeare, Li Po, Lenin, Chaplin and Sun Yat-sen. God's handle is "AAA" in séance sessions. Priests are like fax machines. On February 2, 1921, God sent us this poem:

> *Hot chili pepper persists in being hot*
> *Salt is still salty three years later*
> *You only stop by when dead broke*
> *A sponger who refuses to learn*

This free-verse quatrain, with its natural rhythm and use of the colloquial expressions "dead broke" and "sponger," shows that God was very much in tune with the poetics of his time. He was au courant with modernism. Some even suggested that he was alluding to the band Red Hot Chili Peppers, an anachronism only he could pull off. When God writes a poem, it appears simultaneously (in his head) in 6,822 languages. He is also attempting a novel, a multilayered, hypertextual mess that will only end when the world ends.

Since Kim Lan and Hoa were not adherents of Cao Dai, they had to stand to the side as they prayed to an eye on a huge blue globe—Cao Dai's symbol for God. "Just be honest, Hoa. Just tell that huge eye you want a Viet Kieu husband."

Mother and daughter returned to Saigon after midnight, exhausted. Kim Lan could see that Hoa had never believed in their religious mission. Silent and distracted the entire trip, her mouth never moving during a prayer, she had betrayed no urgency in entreating the gods. Kim Lan slept fitfully that night and had many unpleasant dreams. In one she saw Hoa in the grasp of a lecherous monk with six arms. He was French kissing Hoa with a bright red, twenty-six-inch tongue. In another she saw a black lady riding a blue globe, shouting, "Your daughter prays on a mountain yet fucks underwater!" The lady in the dream was black all right, but without African features: She was a Vietnamese black lady. And she didn't

210

resemble the conical mountain of her namesake, but a nebulous swamp, with only an enormous pair of breasts and abysmal genitals to define her as any sort of a lady. This last dream was the most disturbing. In the morning Kim Lan decided to ask Cun to spy on Hoa. "I'm almost certain she has a boyfriend. I want you to find out who it is."

In a country with few private rooms, where people live on top of each other, lies and half-truths become the only forms of privacy. People lie because they assume everyone else is a liar. Those who don't lie must be either saints or idiots, or just plain rude. In this shimmering world of big and small deceits, people often have to snoop and spy to hunt down the illusive truth. There is an instructive story of a poor man who won a lottery. He moved his family into a mansion where each of his thirteen children could have his or her own room at last. For the first time, they could think in silence and examine their firm or flabby flesh in a full-length mirror. They could hear the creak and hum of their own brains, feel the drafts from strange doors being opened. Frightful memories ambushed them sporadically. The oldest boy realized he had a flat chest, a beer belly and no muscles. The oldest girl discovered a condor-shaped birthmark spanning her behind. After a month of daydreaming, reading, masturbating and unbearable loneliness bordering on madness, they all decided to sleep in the same room again.

9 ◆ YOU'RE MY FRECKLES

As Hoa left the house one afternoon, Cun followed her on his motorbike. They wove through the mad Saigon traffic to the docks area, where he saw her enter a warehouse. He parked his bike across the street, ducked into a café and sat behind a potted plant to wait for her to come back out. He ordered one iced tea after another. Finally, after half a dozen iced teas, well past sunset, she reappeared with a weird guy with shoulder-length hair and a bushy mustache. The guy wore shades, a black T-shirt and black leather pants. *A rich guy*, Cun thought. *Maybe he's a drug dealer.* Cun followed the couple as they headed back into town. On Thai Van Lung Street, he saw them enter a club called World War III. Too intimidated to go inside, he went home to report to his mother.

Love Like Hate played an excellent set that night. They began with the demented "Born after the Mother Is Buried," then launched into "A Noise Came to the Door." The drummer and bassist were in rare form. Urging each other on, they wove intricate figures into the band's already complex sound. The guitarist surged and pleaded and Quang Trung sang with vehemence. Their snarling, sneering music subjugated the dancing mob and induced from each sorrowful soul fearful, long-lost emotions best left forgotten. Faces and limbs were drenched in sweat, merging, flailing, and eyes were closed or expectant. Mouths were wide open, fragrant, to sing or drink or receive other mouths. Each body, each self, was cocooned by four or five others, and it was fruitless to try to delimit where one ceased and another began. Drowned in music, Hoa felt that nothing existed outside of that throbbing, sweet room. She felt launched on a drunken joyride into the darkest, deepest night after which no dawn would ever come. But the musicians, exhausted, finally had to stop playing after the trippy "You're My Freckles." When the lights were turned on at last, everyone appeared startled. Grinning and disheveled, they looked at each other with disappointment and embarrassment, as if they had just been suckered into something.

Saigon by night loses its blinding glare, mugginess, sharp edges and elbows. Less overwhelming, it becomes more intimate and forgiving. The entire city turns into a raunchy street party promising diversions, sin and drunkenness. Riding home alone that night, with a warm wind blowing on her face, her mind swimming with melodies, Hoa thought that a life with Quang Trung would be just about perfect. There would be music and conversations and trips overseas. Even if he wasn't rich, she would still desire him, because there would still be the music and the conversations. *It's time to tell Mom about Quang Trung,* Hoa decided. *She'll be superdisappointed that he's not a Viet Kieu, and he's eleven years older than I am, and she'll probably think he looks a bit weird, but once she gets to know him a bit, everything will be fine. He's smart and considerate and rich, which is, to be honest, her main criterion. He's probably richer than most Viet Kieus out there. In any case, I'm not really looking for her approval, I'm telling her just to be nice. It's really an ultimatum. I'll do it first thing in the morning.*

Back at World War III, now empty of revelers, Quang Trung sat at the bar with a Jack to think things over. In the mirror, his face looked worn-out, his eyes bloodshot. All that singing and boozing had taken their toll. He was twenty-eight going on forty. Things between him and Hoa had accelerated in the last two weeks or so. He didn't need Mrs. Cloudy to see what was coming. Lately, Hoa had filled him in on her entire family background. She described her chess-playing father and her cretinous half brother. She declared that her mom liked Han Mac Tu, as if that would impress him. Once, she even said "our family" when talking about her own family. *I'm a little too young to stop freelancing,* Quang Trung thought, *but hell, it has to happen sooner or later. I've had enough fun, I suppose. I've been running around ridiculing other men for being irresponsible, for not being men, so it's time I become one. A man, I mean. In the past, I always had an excuse to dump a girl, usually for lying or cheating, or for demanding that I kowtow to her stupid parents before I unzip her stonewashed jeans, but I'm a rock 'n' roller, man—it's all about unleashing your id, isn't it? I've introduced so many girls to their G-spots and their Thanatos, and I've done the same with Hoa, I suppose, but she's really special, there's no bullshit in her. She understands and trusts me. When I talk about this and that, she understands or tries to understand—there's real depth to her. She's like a cave that's unexplored and uninhabited, no bats or nothing, but there's real depth there. I guess I'll have to meet her parents soon. If only girls came without their parents! As soon as a girl reaches eighteen, her parents should just drop dead, not get run over by a truck or anything, just die peacefully in their bed as the clock strikes midnight on her eighteenth birthday.* He paused in his cogitation to call the bartender. The middle-aged man poured him another glass. They were the only two left in the bar. *Who needs in-laws anyway?* he continued. *They've already fulfilled their primary function, that of delivering Hoa to me, and it's not like they've done such a great job either. I mean, she's great and everything, but whatever good-ness she has is due to her own sweet nature, to her chemistry, so to speak, and not to how they raised her. Her mom sounds like a complete moron. I mean, what the hell is Paris by Night?! But I guess that's what love is. Love means you'll have to deal with her stupid mom and her entire family, and not once or twice but forever. I only want to marry the daughter, not fuck the old lady, but I guess I'll have to sleep with both of them, figuratively speaking, of course. If I love Hoa, that is.* Emptying his shot, Quang Trung wiped his mouth, then shouted, "And I do!"

"Did you call me?"

"I do! I do! I do!"

The bartender shook his head. He was washing the glasses and ashtrays behind the bar. He had a wife and three kids at home, none employed. Each night he had to watch a bunch of fuckups get smashed while he stayed sober. By the time he climbed into bed, his wife would be fast asleep, or pretending to be asleep. Looking at Quang Trung, he wearily said, "I think it's time for you to go home, rock 'n' roller."

10 ◆ A HAIRCUT

Having caught Hoa red-handed, Cun marched into Paris by Night with a satisfied and angry face. Worshipping Hoa, his mother had showered her with attention and money, but the girl had turned out to be nothing but a slut hanging out with drug dealers. Cun hated how his mother always talked to Hoa with one voice, all concern and sweetness, and to him with another. He hated Hoa's slick, dolled-up, American look, her English exercise books lying about the house, her American music on the boom box. Everything about her was foreign to him. It was like having a foreigner living in the house. Seeing Kim Lan, Cun practically shouted. There were many customers present but he didn't care. This was his moment of triumph.

"I saw Hoa's boyfriend all right. The guy was a creep in leather pants and shades. He's probably a pimp or a drug dealer."

"Did you confront the guy?!"

"Of course not. He looked like a pimp. He probably carries a knife or something."

Sen interrupted his chess game. "So where is she?"

"She's in one of those backpackers' bars on Thai Van Lung Street. It has an English name. I wrote it down."

Sen said to Kim Lan, "See what you've done? You encouraged her. Discos and bars! It's unbelievable! What kinds of people do you expect her to find in there?!"

Her head spinning, her face red, Kim Lan did not respond to Sen, but started walking out the door. "Let's go," she said to Cun. "Take me there right now."

"What do you think you're doing?" Sen said. "You can't go there and make a scene in public. Just wait a few hours. She will be back soon enough. Why don't you go upstairs and rest? I'll bring her up to you when she gets home."

Sen felt strangely invigorated. He hadn't been that angry in a while. Or rather, he hadn't acted that angry in a while. Too agitated to play chess, he killed the next several hours by drinking one beer after another. "When a stick is bent," he mumbled to himself, "you must bend it back."

When Hoa returned and entered the café, everything seemed normal until she saw her father's scowling face. Cun was behind the till with an even more pronounced smirk than usual.

"What's happening?" she asked.

"You'll know soon enough," Cun answered.

"Your mom wants to talk to you," Sen said as he grabbed Hoa by the wrist.

"What's wrong?"

Sen responded by tightening his grip and dragging Hoa behind him. He yanked her up the stairs. Seeing Hoa enter the room, Kim Lan walked up to her and, without words or hesitation, smacked her hard across the face. It was a move she had been rehearsing in her head for hours. *Order has to be restored. Pampered for so long, the girl thinks she can do whatever she wants. Enough. I'll have to knock the foolishness out of her.* Hoa was struck with such force that she fell backward and collapsed in a corner. Outraged, her eyes blurry, she looked up at her mom's changed face. It was hard and ugly, like painted concrete, fixed in its fury. Hoa was shocked at the amount of spite and rage contained in it. This new face erased all previous versions. Hoa covered her own face and cried. Her mom had never hit her before. Even Sen was a little shocked, yet all he said was, "You disappointed your mother. You betrayed your mother's trust."

That night Hoa was kept locked in a room without any sharp instrument or even a plastic bag. If she had had anything convenient, she would have used it. She sobbed all night until her eyes were puffed shut and her head pounded. She felt very thirsty, but there was no water. Toward dawn she finally fell asleep. She dreamed that she was on her motorbike returning home, just like the night before, but it was raining hard. She tilted her head up to drink the rain, but somehow all the drops managed to miss her wide-open mouth. Below her, the street was flooding, and cold, dirty water quickly rose to her knees, then her stomach, then her chest. Calmly, she accelerated her motorbike and it surfaced like a Jet Ski, swerving around thousands of bobbing heads about to drown. *They don't call it a wave for nothing*, she thought, pleased by her knowledge of English. Desperate arms reached out to grab her, clutching at her clothes, but she sped right by them. Within sight of home, her motorbike sputtered and sank as it ran out of gas. Unseen hands grabbed at her as she started to swim. As she kicked and struggled, water rushed into her nostrils but not her mouth. Someone punched her hard in the face, the hardest she had ever been hit, the hardest she could imagine anyone being hit. "Mom! Mom!" she screamed. "Help me! Help me!" She opened her eyes in panic and saw with tremendous relief, then horror, that she was already in her mother's house. Staring up at the familiar ceiling, she realized that her mother was the author of her pain, and not her savior.

That morning, a still-angry Kim Lan appeared to announce that Hoa no longer had the key to the motorbike. She was not to leave the house at all, not even to go to the New York School. To make sure his sister would be too ashamed to go outside, Cun barged into the room with a pair of scissors to snip clumps of hair randomly from Hoa's head. He snapped her head back with one hand and clipped with the other as he called her a slut and a whore. Hoa was too exhausted to scream or resist this dangerous man, her brother. Her father was still sleeping and she wasn't sure if he would defend her in any case.

11 ◆ PHOTOGRAPHIC EVIDENCE

For years Sen had left Kim Lan alone to educate Hoa. She knew more about these matters, he reasoned. She had finished high school while he had never gotten past the sixth grade. He also understood Kim Lan's wish to find Hoa a Viet Kieu husband. The only problem was that every other Vietnamese mother also wanted a Viet Kieu son-in-law. Viet Kieu sons-in-law were so desirable that people were actually paying them to marry their daughters. The idea was to use a Viet Kieu son-in-law as a ticket to get a family member to America. Two decades after the Fall of Saigon, the airlift had begun again, with a Viet Kieu son-in-law as the single-passenger jet taking Vietnam's daughters straight to the land of dreams. He was a three-legged bird with bright plumage swooping down from a glittering sun to pluck his teary-eyed maiden from the smoldering ashes. Once in America, the daughter could rake in the bucks and recoup the initial investment a thousand times over. She could also bring other family members over. The going rate for a Viet Kieu son-in-law in 2004 was around twenty-five thousand bucks, half of which usually went to a middle man. It wasn't a foolproof racket because US immigration authorities were becoming expert at sniffing out these fake marriages. To make them less fake, the fake couples often went through the rituals of a normal courtship—a stroll through the Saigon Zoo, sunbathing in Vung Tau, a romantic meal in a restaurant—but telescoped into a few days and treated merely as photo opportunities. A wedding reception had to be staged, complete with fake guests, or guests could be borrowed from a *real* wedding. The fake couple would crash someone else's reception at a busy restaurant, snap a few quick photos, then disappear before anyone knew what was happening. They also had to stand in front of the altar, clasping incense sticks in front of their foreheads, to ask for blessings from their ancestors. The idea was to have convincing photographic evidence to trick US immigration.

When is your husband's birthday?
What is the color of his underwear?
What is your mother-in-law's name?
What does your husband like to eat?
Does he smoke or drink alcohol?
Are you a Communist or a terrorist?
Have you ever been paid for sex?

Sometimes these fake couples even fucked for real because the Viet Kieu sons-in-law—who held the trump card, after all—were simply too horny not to. To these dudes, the wrongness of it all was no deterrent, but only a bonus thrill, belated bangers and mash and payback for all those nights of kneeling in front of the computer in some ice-packed, deep-frozen city of North America, mooning at digitized pussies. Sometimes the girl got pregnant, resulting in a quick abortion, or not. A pregnancy was actually welcomed by some families, since it provided a more definitive proof of the staged marriage's authenticity. In any case, the poor had to borrow astronomical sums if they wanted to play this game. Sen thought that this Viet Kieu business was too risky a gamble. After dinner one night, while picking at his relatively new dentures and spitting discolored flecks of imperfectly masticated animal tissue onto the floor, Sen decided that a much safer bet was to find a Taiwanese son-in-law. He already had one in mind.

12 ✦ A CEO

y 2004, the Taiwanese had become the ugly foreigners in Vietnam. They were rich, they swaggered and the prostitutes loved them. Some had come to do business but most were there only to shop for a woman. A few had picked out their brides on the internet, and were in Saigon to pick up the goods. Unlike many Viet Kieus, the Taiwanese didn't charge, but paid relatively good money to marry a Vietnamese woman. Most of these bachelors were old, ugly, diseased or handicapped. The Vietnamese press loved to ridicule this phenomenon. One article began:

A surprising thing about the groom, T.D.C. (a Taiwanese), was that, although he was not famous, he was always accompanied by two "bodyguards." They were always by his side to assist him . . . take each step. That's because he was ninety years old! No one will dare toast "a hundred years of happiness" to the newlyweds. The bride, N.T.L. (from Bac Lieu), was only thirty.

The goal of the brides was to live in a nice Taiwanese house and to send money back to their parents regularly. These fantasies were darkened somewhat by rumors of women who went to Taiwan only to be sold to whorehouses, and of women being forced to sleep with a father-in-law or brother-in-law. To play it safe, some women would defraud their suitors by disappearing after a sumptuous wedding.

"An immigrant is an unenlightened ignoramus who thinks one country better than another." So wrote an unenlightened Ambrose

Bierce. But how does one compare two countries? By income, the average Taiwanese made $13,320 in 2003, thirty times more than the average Vietnamese. The life expectancies for Taiwanese were age seventy-four for men, eighty for women; for Vietnamese, sixty-eight and seventy-three. Suicide rates were not available for either country. Further, it has often been noted that the average Taiwanese tends to laugh louder and longer than the average Vietnamese, slap his thigh with more gusto, and become much more boisterous when drunk.

An optical scanner for measuring the gleam in the eye was invented by Dr. Hideo Suzuki of Kobe University. The more gleam, the more happiness. Scanning eyes from across the globe, Dr. Suzuki was able to determine that adolescents anticipating their first sexual experience had the most gleam, and Vietnamese of whatever age, in any situation whatsoever, the least. (Those who doubt Dr. Suzuki's findings should rewind to the opening ceremonies of the 2004 Athens Olympics, when the Vietnamese delegation entered the stadium absolutely stone-faced, without any gleam in their eyes whatsoever, their deadened demeanor a bizarre contrast to the joyful exuberance displayed by the crowd as well as the athletes and officials from the other 201 nations.)

Sen's choice for a future son-in-law was A-Chen, a man of thirty-four, only twice the age of Hoa. He was actually a good-looking guy, with refined manners. He was a bit fat, but in a country of rail-thin men, his corpulence was a distinction. His only defect was a missing hand, the result of a childhood accident. Most important, A-Chen was the CEO of the Great Wall Toothpick Company. Great Wall toothpicks were simply the best. Whether round or flat, each was sculpted by hand by a master craftsman. Made exclusively from birch, each toothpick was veneered, flavored with mint and sterilized, before it was hygienically wrapped—also by hand—in biodegradable paper. To sculpt and wrap toothpicks by hand was too expensive a proposition in Taiwan, prompting A-Chen to set up shop in Vietnam. A-Chen's right hand had been milled by a farm machine when he was only five years old. That's why he hated all machines and wanted all of his toothpicks to be made entirely by hand.

A-Chen had had another misfortune in childhood. At eleven, he stared at a solar eclipse for about three seconds. Since the retina has no pain receptors, he unwittingly destroyed his eyes forever. A few days later, his eyes became bloodshot and his vision blurred. Thereafter, he had to wear a thick pair of glasses, giving him an intellectual air that was entirely unearned and unwarranted.

When A-Chen first arrived, he lived in the Dien Bien Phu Mansion on Ly Tu Trong Street. For a furnished one-bedroom, he paid twenty-three hundred bucks a month. He didn't mind it because it was designed according to the highest standards of luxury, comfort and taste. After work, he could relax with a body-toning session or chill in the outdoor kidney-shaped pool, with a perfect vodkatini in his hand. He could also lift weights in the fully equipped gym, sweat in the steam bath or sing in the karaoke room. Only later, after A-Chen had grown more comfortable with being in Vietnam and had learned to speak some of the language, did he move into a house near his toothpick factory—just down the street from Paris by Night.

As a businessman in Vietnam, A-Chen had a close-up look at the country's economic mess. He had never known there could be so much capitalist exploitation in a supposedly socialist society. It amazed him that many Vietnamese had to work for a dollar a day to make $140 sneakers to be lusted after, and sometimes even bought, by other Vietnamese. If a worker wanted to buy a pair of Nikes he had just sewn, he would have to wait for half a year and not eat at all during that time. No such problem existed at the Great Wall Toothpick Company. A-Chen treated his workers fairly and gave them free toothpicks to take home for the holidays.

When A-Chen first arrived, he ate only in expensive restaurants. It wasn't for the quality of the food, but because he didn't want to be molested by vendors and beggars. Once he ventured into a regular noodle joint and was immediately surrounded by several desperate people trying to sell him lottery tickets, newspapers, or a shoe shine. Unbidden, a young woman started to massage his shoulders. He waved these people away, but saw a girl in rags still standing there. About eight years old, she was holding a naked two-year-old boy on her hip. Both of their faces were darkened with grime, their hair disheveled and burned brown by the sun. Transparent mucus cleared a short, pink path down the baby's face, from his nose to his upper lip. Buzzing flies orbited around their heads. He gave them several bills, only to be immediately surrounded by a dozen more beggars, coming from God knows where. He patiently gave money to each beggar in turn, but finally decided enough was enough, he would now try to enjoy his bowl of noodles. But as he ate, he noticed a leg stump pointing at the side of his face. He looked up and saw a middle-aged man, a vet or simply someone who had lost his limb in a traffic accident. One hand was upturned in supplication, the other bracing a dirty, nicked-up, duct-taped crutch. A finger or two was missing from each hand. The one-legged man said nothing, but would not steer his leg stump from A-Chen's face. It was more or less a holdup. Quickly losing his appetite, A-Chen ate only the sweet pork, the battered shrimp and the wontons, leaving most of the noodles untouched. When he shoved the bowl aside to drink his iced coffee, the one-legged man quickly grabbed it to gulp down the leftovers, slurping the excellent broth with relish. As A-Chen got up to leave, the one-legged man finished the watery remains of his iced coffee.

Another time A-Chen was sitting in the back of a dark café, trying to sip a beer, when a tiny ragged boy approached. Before the boy could open his mouth, A-Chen gave him ten thousand *dong*. The boy refused the money and walked away, looking hurt and angry. It turned out he was a shoe-shine boy and not a beggar. Other beggars tugged at A-Chen on the streets, and cursed at him in Vietnamese, Chinese or English if he ignored them. A-Chen could not give money to every beggar in Vietnam. He could not save millions of people, he figured, but he might be able to save one.

Everywhere A-Chen went in Saigon he saw either socialist bill-boards boasting of heroic, exuberant workers, soldiers and peasants, or capitalist billboards seducing the masses with images of the affluent hitting golf balls or sipping martinis. As with all billboards, the people on them had nothing to do with the working stiffs milling on the streets, but the contrast between the superrace shown on Vietnamese billboards and the dazed and wasted specimens sprawled on the dirty sidewalks just below them was so startling as to be comical. An appropriate image on all Vietnamese billboards would have been a Hieronymus Bosch painting.

There were few beggars in Thanh Da, A-Chen's new neighbor-hood, because there were few foreigners. A-Chen also found a few restaurants with second floors, where beggars don't venture. Stop-ping in Paris by Night for a beer one day, he was delighted to meet Sen, who could speak Cantonese, and the two became fast friends. A-Chen wasn't much of a chess player, but he enjoyed playing with Sen. Though he always lost, he didn't mind. "I'm paying you for chess lessons. I'm slowly getting better, no?"

Experience had taught A-Chen that the more money you gave a Vietnamese, the friendlier he became, the brighter his smile, his demeanor improving with each dime given. Losing to Sen was A-Chen's way of softening him up, because he had been eyeing the man's daughter for some time. Hoa was the best-looking girl A-Chen had seen in Saigon and she wasn't even that tacky. Each time Hoa was in the room, A-Chen's face softened, his eyes lit up and he would even forget whose turn it was.

"Is it my turn, Sen?"

"It's always your turn, A-Chen."

A-Chen was stumped by Sen's curious statement. Then he chuckled and said, "You always move fast, Sen. And you have a quick eye too!"

A-Chen dreamed of rescuing Hoa from her miserable country and taking her to Taiwan, where she could be properly educated and live like a lady and sleep on his big brass bed. To achieve all this, he would gladly have given her parents a nice chunk up front, in a discreet white envelope, of course. After that, they would get a monthly stipend until they dropped dead, sooner rather than later, hopefully, to be supplemented with an annual gift of an electronic gadget. For Hoa, on her birthday, A-Chen would always surprise her with something hard, shiny and moderately precious.

Sen was only waiting for Hoa's hair to grow back so he could introduce her to A-Chen. *Everything comes full circle*, Sen thought. *My father came from China, and now my daughter will go to Taiwan, which is really a part of China, although they do have a separate (and much inferior) Olympics team. China netted over sixty medals in Athens; Taiwan just five. I have it written down somewhere. Am I glad I never invited A-Chen to a whorehouse. It would be a little unbecoming for a father and a son-in-law to have this memory in common.* Hoa was in her room twenty-four hours a day, watching TV and not doing much else. It would take at least a month before she became presentable again.

13 ◆ A DRUNK BIDDY

When Hoa kissed Quang Trung good-bye that night, she said she would see him the next day. When a couple of days went by and she didn't show up, Quang Trung thought that maybe she had been in a traffic accident. Everyone in Saigon, without exception, had been knocked off his bike or motorbike at least once. There were dozens of accidents each day. In Saigon, there was no such thing as a one-way or a two-way street; every street was ten-way—traffic came at you from all directions. A vehicle would suddenly turn left from the right lane, and right from the left lane. The variety of things moving made the situation even more chaotic. There were taxis, cyclos, beggars on dollies, peddlers pushing food carts, eighteen-wheelers, three-wheeled delivery trucks, American jeeps left over from the war and top-heavy, overladen buses, not to mention dogs, chickens and blind men jaywalking. This swarming madness engulfed every neighborhood from five in the morning till ten at night. Encountering this mess, foreigners often remarked on the energy of the Saigonese. What they didn't realize was that many of the folks rushing about were unemployed. If they had had jobs, they wouldn't crisscross town for a bowl of soup or a cup of coffee.

Quang Trung's drummer had been in an accident the year before. Swerving to dodge a bicycle going the wrong way, he had slammed his motorbike into a passenger van, sending him tumbling across the asphalt. Skin was scraped off his face and forearms, showing the muscles and fat underneath. He lost all his front teeth. While still in pain, recovering, he memorized chunks of Ecclesiastes and contemplated the priesthood. Weeping, he apologized to God for being a punk rocker.

Quang Trung could not imagine Hoa without her front teeth. *Would I still love her if she were disfigured or brain damaged? Hmm. Not bad for a song title. I would like to think I would, but who knows, maybe I'm just kidding myself. I don't know about disfigurement, but I must have loved plenty of girls who were perhaps brain damaged. Hmm. Does a pierced labia count as disfigurement?* He stopped ruminating and picked up the phone. Calling around, he soon found out that the Paris by Night café was in Thanh Da, north of downtown, by a leafy stretch of the Saigon River. Anxious to see Hoa, with or without her front teeth, he got on his motorbike and headed there immediately.

Thanh Da is known for restaurants serving duck-rice gruel or dog meat. Dog meat is really a northern Vietnamese thing—most Saigonese won't eat it—but if you crave dog meat in Saigon, Thanh Da is the place to go. It has a rich, complicated, aromatic taste, as testified by a proverb: "A piece of dog meat stuck between the teeth is still fragrant three days later." Vu Bang, a Hanoi writer, wrote in 1950: "If you take a lovelorn, suicidal person to a dog-meat restaurant and tell him he can kill himself afterwards, I'm sure he will change his mind after the meal." Thanh Da is also known for pitch-dark cafés where young couples can go to grope each other to soft music. Thinking that Paris by Night was one of these love joints, Quang Trung was surprised to discover that it was completely nondescript—large and bright with only beer posters for decorations: white women with silicone breasts hugging giant beer bottles tilted at an angle. Only the sign was distinctive: It featured not just the Eiffel Tower and the Arc de Triomphe but even the Georges Pompidou Centre. The lady behind the counter, a cranky, overly made-up biddy, most likely drunk, gave him a testy look before he even said, "I'm looking for Hoa."

"There's no Hoa here."

"But this *is* the Paris by Night café?"

"Yes, but there's no Hoa here."

"I'm pretty sure she lives here. Are you Hoa's mother?"

"Listen, I told you there's no Hoa here. Do you want me to call the cops?"

"Call the cops for what?! I'm looking for Hoa!"

Quang Trung noticed that two guys had appeared—a middle-aged man balling his fists and a young, scrawny guy clutching a long stick. Absolutely pathetic, he thought, yet menacing enough. He could kick these guys' asses, sure, but they would leave a few bruises on him too. The scrawny guy was so nervous, his stick was trembling. Quang Trung looked around and saw that many customers had stood up, ready to join the fray. At a corner table, behind a chessboard and a just-poured glass of beer, a Taiwanese guy sat grinning. Sensing excitement, neighborhood children crowded the entrance, tittering, their eyes gleaming. Unseen, a toy dog started to bark hysterically, its vocals mixing with Donna Summer on the stereo. It was so ridiculous, Quang Trung had to laugh. Shaking his head in disgust, he walked out of Paris by Night, got on his motorbike, then rode away. *It was like a bad chop-socky scene*, he thought, *not that there's ever a good one. Well, maybe Jackie Chan. I don't need to put up with such trash. I've got a mission in life. Maybe I'll write a song about this episode. Nothing is ever wasted on an artist.*

14 ✦ VIA THE TIN ROOFS

The house had a front and a back door. Hoa could not leave by the front because she would have had to walk through the café, past Kim Lan, Cun and/or Sen, and she could not sneak out the back because she did not have the key to the steel gate. The only escape was to jump from her window onto a neighbor's tin roof—a drop of about five feet. Once on this roof, she would have to walk across six more to reach a leaning coconut tree, where she could slide down to street level. The older of these sloping, corrugated tin roofs were rusty and tetanus inducing. Leaking, they were patched with brittle plastic or even nylon sheets. TV antennas and live wires further complicated Hoa's escape. Though she had never climbed up or down a tree before, she was game. Imprisoned for two weeks, she could wait no longer. The best time was nine in the morning, when her mother was at the market. Hiding her hideous hair under a baseball cap, she climbed onto the windowsill, hesitated for a few seconds, then let herself go. Landing awkwardly, she pitched forward, rolled and got up in one motion. It sounded like a car crashing into a series of trash cans. Nothing was broken, so she started walking. Adrenaline made her deaf to the commotion of neighbors spilling onto the street to see who the thief was. She didn't dare run, fearing the roofs would collapse. Before she knew it, she was on the coconut tree, hugging it, but the ride down was far from smooth. The notches scraped her hands bloody, tore at her jeans and jacket, and she nearly landed on a woman selling iced gelatin at the base of the tree. As the woman cursed at her, she ran to a street corner, hopped on the back of a motorbike and instructed the driver to go downtown. On every Saigon street corner, there are men waiting on motorbikes to take you anywhere for a modest fee.

Two weeks before, Hoa had made the same trip going in the opposite direction, feeling elated about a future she would share with Quang Trung. So much had changed. What she had gone through had toughened her and taught her a good lesson. She now knew, once and for all, that her family was pure shit and that she would never want to live under the same roof with them again. Their behavior was the catalyst she needed to break free. They had betrayed her. Realizing what she had lost, her selfish and brutal mom would cry, cry, cry, but it would be way too late. *She'll never see my face again. How dare she lay her hand on me?* Even a female alligator would not use her sharp teeth on her babies, Hoa remembered from an adequately dubbed American TV show, although a panda bear would raise only one twin cub and abandon the other one, let it starve to death. Now her mom only had one left, *only had that poor excuse for a man, for a boy, for I don't know what.* Heading downtown, Hoa actually felt more elated and optimistic than ever. It felt so right, this decision, this moment, it felt preordained. Quang Trung had even predicted it in a Love Like Hate song:

> *The fork runs away with the spoon*
> *The spoon runs away with the fork*
> *And everything is gravy ever after!*
> *The fork belongs to the spoon*
> *The spoon belongs to the fork*
> *Because fork and spoon belong together!*

Seeing Quang Trung's building, Hoa felt so happy she could barely refrain from laughing out loud. There was so much life coursing through her lithe body, she thought her chest would explode. Looking up at the second-floor window, she rang his doorbell and waited with a huge smile on her face. She had not seen him in two weeks, an eternity in their brief relationship. Yelling his name, she rang the doorbell again and again. Finally a head stuck out. It was female, someone her age—this girl even looked like her.

"Is Quang Trung home?"

The girl glared at Hoa. "My boyfriend is not home!"

15 ◆ HAPPY BIRTHDAY

There was only one Western-style bar in Quang Trung's neighborhood and it was called Whatever. The interior was velvet and chrome and the music techno. Sitting at the bar, Hoa ordered round after round of Jameson. She didn't care that she didn't have enough money, she just wanted to get drunk and stay drunk. It was not yet noon, but there were a dozen customers in the place, including a middle-aged white guy who was also downing Jameson. Seeing the beautiful girl in the baseball cap, he finally ambled over and said, "May I?"

"Fuck you!"

"Ah, your English is good!"

She scrutinized his face: It was round and smooth like an egg, interrupted suddenly by a prominent nose, thin lips and pointy ears. He sat down beside her. "You are drinking too fast, I notice. You have an attitude toward me because you think I'm American, but I'm not American. I'm French."

She finished her drink and stared at him blankly. He continued, "Everywhere I go in Saigon, I see signs of nostalgia for French culture. I see people eating croissants and baguettes. I see nightclubs called Brodard and Givral. The other day I even saw a pathetic little café called Paris by Night—it's very depressing. But the truth is I hate French culture, I see no future at all for French culture. May I buy you the next Jameson?"

Hearing no answer, he ordered two more and continued, "There is something touchingly pathetic about Vietnam. The people here are so poor, yet everyone seems happy. That's because they haven't lost touch with their bodies. They squat on the ground and piss on the street and everyone fucks happily outside of marriage. That's why everyone here smiles all the time."

"Have you seen Vietnamese dance?"

He paused and grinned. He wasn't sure if the question was a trick or a proposal. He tried to tease a clue from her eyes, but saw nothing. "Of course. I was at Apocalypse Now just last night. There were many Vietnamese dancing on the floor."

"If you've seen Vietnamese dance, then you cannot say that they are in touch with their bodies."

"Ah," he laughed. "You are an observant one, aren't you? And a bit difficult too. But I really don't know what you're talking about because I thought they danced very well."

Seeing her empty glass, he downed his, ordered two more, then continued, "In France, the only sex that's available anymore is masturbation. I masturbated compulsively when I lived in Paris. I masturbated at home, in public, at the park and in the Métro. I masturbated underground, above ground and in the air. Once I even masturbated at the zoo. In the nocturama, I did it. You know what that is? It's where they keep these shy, nighttime animals with huge eyes. But I can't imagine a Vietnamese masturbating at all. There's no need to masturbate here. There's always a whorehouse within walking distance and it costs next to nothing to get laid."

He paused to order two more, then continued, "Most Westerners only get to fuck a machine or a gadget nowadays. You don't know how humiliating it is to screw a vibrating donut. I've tried everything from glow-in-the-dark vaginal facsimiles to lifelike, full-length Lolitas. Western cunts prefer clit stimulators and vibrators to a real prick on a real man like myself. A clit stimulator has five speeds— vibrate, pulsate, surge, escalate and armageddon—whereas a real man only has two: desperate and dire. Westerners prefer sex toys so they can avoid playing mind games with each other. Conditioned by capitalism, they cannot share anything. They must hoard everything from their sins to their thoughts to their genitals. The sexual situation in the West is sorrowful nowadays, and that's why a country like Vietnam is the answer."

He paused to order two more, then continued, "Another thing I like about Vietnam is the absence of mosques. Since Bush started his war, I no longer feel safe traveling, but I feel perfectly safe in Vietnam. I see no veiled women on the streets and there are no Hameds to blow me up as I sit in a bar having a quiet drink. Muslims like to drink too, by the way. I was just in Bangkok and saw a million of them getting trashed and going to the whorehouses. There's nothing wrong with that. Getting trashed is a sacred right and should be recognized as such. If Muslims drank more, they wouldn't be so hostile to the rest of us. Actually, they do drink more, they just don't want to admit it. Anyway, when the entire world is finally destroyed, Vietnam will be the only country left standing. That's because there are no Muslims here."

He paused to order two more, then continued, "That's why I've come to Vietnam to do business. I develop resorts—sun, sand and sex, that sort of thing. For a country with no industries, that doesn't know how to make anything, peddling sex is a great start-up racket, but one must aspire to selling sex on a massive scale, not in these dinky little cafés with the dim lights and the half-dressed hostesses."

After a certain point, she could no longer hear this guy talking. She could barely make out his face. The whiskey burned her stomach and her head was pounding. She felt like throwing up and maybe she did throw up. She wasn't sure what happened next.

Waking up in the middle of the night, she found herself lying under a comforter with him next to her. The room was cold and they were naked. She vaguely remembered peeing on the toilet, his hands on her, her hands on him, and then a taxi ride. She felt extremely thirsty, but was too weak to go find herself a glass of water. She assumed they had had sex, but she didn't care. All she cared about was getting over a massive hangover—the worst she had ever experienced.

She spent all of that day in bed while the guy was away. She had to go to the bathroom repeatedly to throw up. She found grapefruit juice in the fridge and drank gallons of it. Toward evening he came back. Seeing that she was sick, he slept next to her that night, but didn't touch her. The truth was, he was just waiting for her to get well so he could get rid of her. There were so many girls on the streets, he didn't need a sick one.

The next morning she felt a little better. She stayed with him three days altogether and never got dressed the entire time she was there. She lived like an animal. Walking around naked, she even wandered out into the hallway. On the last night they fucked for several hours. On his third revival, unprecedented, inspired, he risked death and procreation and forwent a condom. In the morning they had breakfast naked on a balcony suspended twenty-eight floors above street level.

Saigon had never seemed so beautiful. Standing high above the city, she no longer felt a part of its filth and depravity. The Saigon River, scummy and black up close, shined a silver blue from that height in the morning sunlight. Leafy, majestic trees sprung up from the sidewalks. The streets straightened themselves out, the mad traffic flowed in a more orderly way. Nothing smelled from up there. Leaning against the concrete edge, she felt so weightless, a breeze could have tipped her over.

As they ate croissants and drank café au lait, she said, "Too bad I'm not a virgin, huh?"

"Ah, but you were good, my dear. You have just the right combination of experience and innocence."

"I'm only eighteen!"

"That means you're legal!"

"What do you mean, 'legal'?"

236

"It means I won't go to jail."

"Go to jail for what?"

"Go to jail for being myself, you know, go to jail for fucking!" The guy laughed at his own witticism. "How many men have you had?"

"Two."

"I don't believe it."

She noticed that his dick stiffened as soon as he said, "Fucking!" He had huge balls but a modest member. She had always assumed that white people had blond pubic hair and was surprised to see this guy's black thicket.

"Actually I'm only seventeen," she continued. "I don't turn eighteen until tomorrow. Tomorrow is my birthday."

"So you want me to buy you a birthday cake, is that it? Don't worry, don't worry, I'll buy you one." *This is the second time a Vietnamese whore has claimed her birthday is coming up*, the guy thought with amusement. *They're all the same.*

As if reading his mind, she said, "Did you think I was a whore when you saw me at the bar?"

"No, of course not, I thought you were an intellectual. That's why I expounded to you my philosophy of life."

"I think you're an asshole."

"Say that again! I love how you say that!"

After breakfast, he escorted her to the elevator. As they kissed good-bye, he handed her a wad of money. *It's only fair compensation for what he did to me*, Hoa reflected on the way down. As she walked defiantly down the street, cleaving the crowd and bumping people out of the way, Hoa thought, *I'm a fuckwad with a wad of money. Don't fuck with me if you don't want to fuck me!*

Hoa's hair was totally punk; she didn't even have her baseball cap on. She felt exposed yet not vulnerable, she felt free. Maybe relieved was a better word.

They had spent three days together without even knowing each other's names. It didn't matter to Hoa. All she cared to remember from the experience was one magnificent view from a balcony high up in the sky. From there she could see the future. She was the future. Now that she had money, she could check into a hotel on Pham Ngu Lao Street. That very night she went out to make more money. The next day Hoa turned eighteen.

THE END

A recipient of the Pew Fellowship, the David T. Wong Fellowship, and the Asian American Literary Award, LINH DINH is the author of two collections of stories, *Fake House* and *Blood and Soap*; and five books of poems, *All Around What Empties Out, American Tatts, Borderless Bodies, Jam Alerts* and *Some Kind of Cheese Orgy*. He is editor of the anthologies *Night, Again* and *Three Vietnamese Poets. Love Like Hate* is his first novel.